Julia's voice trailed off

Alex was giving her that look again, a look that burned through fog and layers of pretensions with equal intensity. It made her feel naked—not bare skin, but bare soul—and she didn't like it one bit. In desperation, she marched toward the porch.

Alex fell into step beside her.

Under the soft yellow light, Julia delivered a brisk good-night and a tepid handshake. As soon as he released her hand, she fumbled in her purse for her keys. She was almost home free. But not quite. She felt his nearness before she looked up.

Alex had placed his palms flat against the door, one on either side of her, holding her close, yet not touching her. Her breath caught and held. Julia watched him advance, her gaze locked to his. Every fantasy she'd ever had flashed before her eyes, and they had his name on them....

ABOUT THE AUTHOR

As the only child of a military family,
Connie Rinehold began writing while traveling
from one home to another—on an ocean liner to
Rio de Janeiro, Brazil; by air to Japan; and in the
back seat of her parents' cherry-red fifty-one Ford
sedan to all points in the U.S.A.

After her marriage to her husband of twenty-six
years, Connie pursued careers in dressmaking,
fashion design and retail management. When the
oldest of her three children graduated from high
school, Connie decided it was time to stop
waffling and returned to her writing. Her first
novel, *Silken Threads*, was published by
Harlequin Superromance in October 1989.
Connie and her husband live in Colorado.

Books by Connie Rinehold
HARLEQUIN SUPERROMANCE
374–SILKEN THREADS

CONNIE RINEHOLD

VEIL OF TEARS

Harlequin Books

TORONTO • NEW YORK • LONDON
AMSTERDAM • PARIS • SYDNEY • HAMBURG
STOCKHOLM • ATHENS • TOKYO • MILAN

To my mother and stepfather, Glenna and Mick English—thank you for never placing conditions on your love, for never expecting more than my best and feeling pride in my efforts, and for helping me to see rainbows in the dark. I love you.

To Erica Winkler, a friend to treasure.

And to Tahti Carter for believing. Thank you.

Published February 1991

ISBN 0-373-16380-0

VEIL OF TEARS

Legend

In a time of darkness when superstition cast shadows over Truth and Reality became embellished Myth, there was born a girl child to one of the kings of Albion.

As she grew to womanhood, tales were told of her gentle nature and sweetness of spirit. Minstrels throughout the kingdoms sang of how her smile made the air shimmer in all the colors of the rainbow.

Upon her birth, her father bade his armorer fashion a headdress for her to wear on the day of her marriage. The armorer possessed a skill so great, he was called brother to Hephaestus, god of metalworkers. By day, he made chain mail, armor and weapons. At night, by the light cast by torches set into the wall, he crafted a veil of gold circlets joined together in a delicate weblike design and bordered with mother-of-pearl medallions inscribed with the history of his race. When finished, it would fit over the princess's head like a wimple, covering her shoulders and trailing midway down her back—a fitting adornment for the future queen.

On her wedding day, war swept the land as a tide of avaricious raiders from her fiancé's land attacked the kingdom. From the ramparts of her castle, she watched as her father was slain. All was lost; her family, her beloved, her home.

Stricken with grief and betrayal, she retired to her walled garden to await her fate at the hands of the conquerors. As she sat among her flowers, she removed the veil and dropped it into her lap. Tears fell from her eyes, one for each of her people enslaved or slain by the enemy and then more tears for the words of love and devotion she had believed were genuine. Words which had masked greed and treachery.

Her tears fell all the afternoon onto the shining links of gold, hardening into pearls the color of her favorite ivory rose tinted by the pink of dawn. And when there were no more tears, her spirit fled to the sanctuary of Lyonnesse to await the coming of a better time to live and love.

Seeking the princess, the victorious raiders battered their way into the garden. Remarkably fine in detail, a maiden carved from stone sat amid a bright profusion of summer blooms. Raised to the heavens, the eyes bespoke profound sadness. Carved tendrils of hair flowed around her as if lifted by a caressing breeze. A single drop of dew trailed down the delicate face. The maiden's hands were in her lap, intertwined with a veil of gold studded by lustrous pearls.

A veil of tears.

As the sun melted into the horizon, the flowers wilted and dried into dust carried away by the North Wind.

Prologue

Fog crept in from San Francisco Bay as stealthily as a thief returning to the scene of the crime. Julia Devlin stood at the window, willing her thoughts to become as gray and blank as the world outside, as gray and blank as prison walls, enclosing emotions in a dark and lifeless place.

There were no stars tonight. Faery lights, her beloved ''Da''' had called them as his eyes twinkled with his own magic charm. On just such a night, Julia had watched the police lock him into the caged back of a patrol car. That night, she had discovered that leprechauns were merely thieves, like Patrick Devlin, magic was nothing but lies and illusions, and shamrocks were only four-leaf clovers, nothing but a form of ground cover. Nothing special. Like childhood, they withered and died when torn from their roots.

On that night fifteen years ago, Julia had been thirteen. She'd had her first real taste of anger then—for the policemen who hadn't been able to look her in the eye as they wrenched her from her home of love and laughter to deliver her to the glitzy, too fast world of her Aunt Chloe. Anger because they had exposed her father, shown her that he was far less than she wanted him to be.

All she had left was the torment of inexplicable guilt, and emptiness where faith had been. Why hadn't her father been content to earn an honest wage? He'd taken such pride in the garden he'd designed and tended for Nicholas Alexander. Why couldn't his home and daughter have been riches enough for him? Had she been so lacking? The questions had followed her relentlessly, trampling her youth, leaving muddy footprints over happier memories.

Why hadn't her father notified her of his release from prison? Would she have known if he hadn't collapsed from a heart attack as he was signing out? Those questions hurt her most of all.

Willing herself not to think, Julia poured a cup of coffee from the urn sitting on a table in a corner of the waiting room.

"Ms. Devlin?"

Julia stiffened. She'd been waiting for two hours to hear that voice, dreading what it would say. Turning, she faced the cardiologist, her expression as emotionless as her tone. "Yes." Julia resented the way he was studying her, as if he were conducting an autopsy on her emotions to determine cause of death.

His scrutiny was too discerning, making her aware of what he saw: Julia Devlin, with a face more interesting than attractive; a woman who was alone by choice, free from being victimized by human deception.

Adept at creating new images or resurfacing old ones for the rich, famous or merely hopeful, Julia's masterpiece was the one she'd sculpted for herself, a polished surface of elegant sophistication and dedicated professionalism no one had succeeded in penetrating. No one.

The cardiologist cleared his throat. "Your father is resting comfortably..." His sentence stopped abruptly, severed by the blade of an unspoken "but."

"How long?" she asked in a voice stronger than she was. It was the same question she'd asked after her father's sentencing.

Dr. Benson sighed. "I can't give you a time limit. His condition is stable now, but that could change anywhere from a few minutes to a few months."

Hot coffee flew upward and splashed over her hand as Julia's grip tightened around her cup. She didn't notice when the doctor wiped her hand with a towel and checked for burns.

A few months. Each word was like the blow of a chisel, chipping away bits of her hard exterior, exposing wounds that were still waiting to heal. A few months. Not enough time after fifteen years of learning to live without the dancing light that was her Da'. Learning to live without wasn't the same as knowing the light was gone forever.

Julia turned away and swallowed hard. How many times was she expected to lose her father? She couldn't go through it again. Somehow, she'd have to keep her distance, protect herself from caring for a man who hadn't loved her as much as he'd loved another man's wealth. *Somehow,* Julia knew that she did care and she'd hoped Patrick's homecoming would mean another chance to know him, another chance to convince him that her love was more valuable than things.

Dr. Benson's hand closed around her elbow, guiding her to the Cardiac Care Unit. With a gentle tug, she removed her arm from his hold, knowing she had to make this walk alone. Nothing had changed. She would never have anyone's strength to lean on but her own.

Arriving at her father's cubicle, Julia forced the air out of her lungs, as if she'd been holding her breath for fifteen years.

Patrick's gaze was trained on the door, waiting, hoping. His smile was weak. Tears slid from the corners of his shamrock-green eyes onto the pillow under his head. His breath expelled in a shuddering sigh as if he, too, had been holding it for years.

Something stirred beneath her numb emotions, gently, like the awakening of a child. Julia looked away, afraid that, once again, she would begin to believe in magic and faeries and dreams.

"Julie darlin'," Patrick whispered. "You're still brighter than the end of the rainbow." His voice faded as weakness urged him into a peaceful sleep.

Backing away, Julia groped blindly for the door, shaking her head, denying her need to believe him. No! It was all a lie. If it were true, he wouldn't have left her to be uprooted and tossed about until her emotions had dried and scattered in the wind.

QUICK AS BREATH, the moment would come and go, taking with it another day, never to be lived again. Alex stood on the beach, enjoying the play of waves over his feet, becoming the little boy he had never been, dreaming, seeing magic in the dance of the sea and listening to the music of nature. Sand, fine as gold dust, ringed his island of jewel-toned flora and the setting sun trailed a chain of light across the water to end at his feet.

Sandcastle. A name only Alex knew.

What, he wondered, would people think if they knew he spent his vacations digging his toes into the sand while he waxed poetic about the sunset? Would they believe he shed his persona along with his Savile Row suits or would they continue to see what they wanted to see, unable to comprehend a cynic with a dreamer's soul?

Sandcastle. The only place on earth where Alex recognized the man he saw in the mirror.

As the dispossessed black sheep of the Sinclair family, he had entered society with a modest trust fund, the finesse acquired from a privileged upbringing and an uncanny knack for wrapping Dame Fortune around his little finger.

The King of Diamonds. A fitting name for the young renegade who had made a fortune gambling in the private salons of the world. But, the Ace of Hearts? He wasn't sure he had a heart. He'd left a number of bedrooms over the years, feeling no regret, harboring no lingering memories. He wasn't a misogynist. He liked women. He just hadn't found one he could love.

Because he'd never known love, he dreamed of having it, feeling it, as he dreamed of possessing a priceless treasure that was unique, rare, impossible to reproduce.

St. Ives—galleries in London, Paris and New York— dealer to the most elite art connoisseurs. In all his thirty-six years, art and Sandcastle were the only things Alex had found to love.

Alex headed back toward his house, a sense of fatalism dimming his pleasure in the Southern Cross suspended in the evening sky.

A boat had docked a few minutes ago, bearing a stranger—an invasion Alex wouldn't have allowed but for his mother's unprecedented request. Odd, how he'd suddenly thought of her as a human being rather than a carefully fashioned clone of Philadelphia Main Line society. True emotion had broken through her cultured voice: sadness, defeat, unexplored dreams, a resignation that old debts must be paid. Alex had no doubt that his mother's hunger to repay her debt would be satisfied at his expense. He'd recognized early that Lorna considered him a penance rather than a blessing.

He paused at the steps leading up to the veranda that embraced his home. Painted the color of sun-washed sand and trimmed in rich tropical green, the house blended with the island as if they had both risen from the sea at the same moment of creation.

Alex grimaced and shook off his whimsical thought. His natural elegance undiminished by his cutoff jeans and floral cotton shirt, he joined his guest in the study. Alex sat behind his desk, his expression was vacant, showing neither curiosity nor impatience. An evening sigh of cooling air drifted through the window at his back, a sigh, as if a long wait was about to end.

Gregori Petrov sat with military bearing, calmly watching Alex as if he had done it many times before. He pulled a sheaf of papers out of his briefcase, breaking the silence with the rolled tones and lyrical inflections of someone foreign born. "I have come on behalf of the late Nicholas Alexander..."

Foreboding breathed hotly down Alex's neck. Just as it was meant to do, the name had caught his attention. He had a strong feeling that Dame Fortune was in a cheeky mood.

"Before he died," Petrov continued, "Nicholas—my friend and employer—gave me explicit instructions concerning you."

"I fail to see why he concerned himself with me at all."

"Nicholas was your father," Petrov stated abruptly.

Alex accepted the statement with cold fatalism. Jeffrey Sinclair's last words came to him as if he'd just heard them yesterday. *My son does not exist.*

At gut level, he'd always known. There had been too many clues: Jeffrey's distaste for him; the way Lorna's gaze always skipped over her son as if looking at him too long would turn her to salt; the mirrors that showed Alex his lack of resemblance to the Sinclair family; the gossip of the household staff.

"You are much like Nikki—a renegade, yet more polished and stronger than he was," Petrov observed as he slid a photograph across the desk. "Nikki's realities were in his dreams and his passions. Your childhood gave you a toughness and pragmatism that he could have used..."

"What could you know of my childhood?" Alex asked.

"You did not have one. Nikki and I watched it all from street corners and park benches—I wishing to steal you away and Nikki dreaming and planning for the day he would be rich enough to win back your mother." Petrov cleared his throat. "You became a man and still we observed from a distance. Still Nikki dreamed. When you left for Oxford, we were there to wave goodbye as if you knew us and would wave back."

Listening, Alex felt detached from it all, as if he were putting together the elements of a movie plot. He'd been the result of Lorna's "slumming spree," a last fling before merging the St. Ives name and corporations with those of Jeffrey Sinclair. His disconnection from the family and the adoption of his mother's maiden name had been more prophetic than he'd realized.

He couldn't empathize with the longing Petrov described. Nicholas's life was spent. Alex's had passed the point of no return. It was too late.

Sensing Alex's withdrawal, Petrov channeled the conversation into directions he knew Alex would respond to—business and art. To the photo on the desk, he added a will, deeds, and an inventory of a private art collection, complete with photographs.

Alex glanced at them without interest. The estate outside San Francisco, the millions in liquid assets, the collection—all failed to tempt him. He tossed the papers across the desk. "I'm not interested, Mr. Petrov."

"It is your birthright," Petrov held out a group of photographs. "This, in particular, should interest you."

Alex's gaze narrowed on the top photo of what appeared to be the first of a series. Controlling the excited shaking of his hands, he fanned the photos out in front of him. A quick fumble in a drawer produced a photographer's loupe, which would magnify the details of the images.

As he bent over the loupe, his voice sounded distracted, as if he were thinking aloud. "This can't be real. It's a legend inspired by an ancient statue and perpetuated by an obscure scribe." Hoping he was wrong, Alex raised his head and rubbed his eyes.

"I assure you it is quite real and everything the legends say it is. The workmanship and composition are far ahead of their time."

"And the pearls? They haven't disintegrated?" Alex asked suspiciously. Unlike diamonds, pearls were not forever.

Petrov shook his head. "No. They are intact." He held up his hand to stall anything Alex might say. "The Veil is genuine, Alex. Nikki took a link and a pearl to a friend at the university. Its age has been confirmed."

Alex absorbed the information as he stared at the photographs. It was impossible, yet just last week he had read about another pearl of the same age being found, intact, in what was once Mesopotamia. "How did Nicholas Alexander come by it?" he asked.

"That story you will find in the diaries Nikki left for you. I will not turn them over unless you claim the entire estate."

"Mr. Petrov, I have no desire to claim the estate."

"Nevertheless..." Petrov spread his hands, his meaning dangling in the silence. Although he had fully expected Alex to refuse the inheritance, he had counted exclusively on Alex being snared by this one object. He would let Alex find out for himself that the piece had been missing for the past fifteen years, stolen by Nikki's gardener, Patrick Devlin.

Alex couldn't resist the lure. Glancing once more at the photos, he spoke in a neutral tone perfected at high-stakes games of chance. "I'll be honest with you, Petrov. Nicholas Alexander can never be more to me than an image in a photograph." He indicated the portrait of a man whose features mirrored his. "But the Veil of Tears...for this alone, I will claim the estate."

Nodding, Petrov stood and shook Alex's hand. "I shall await your arrival in San Francisco."

With a distracted air, Alex stood and accepted the handshake, his arm still outstretched after Petrov's departure. The clock showed little more than thirty minutes had passed since he'd walked the beach at sunset. Thirty minutes to acquire a father, more wealth and an art treasure, unique, priceless, its past full of a thousand stories and countless lives, its continued existence a miracle...his desire for it a dream, an obsession.

Chapter One

It had all been a lie.

Alex strolled through the rooms of his new estate, his expression calm, his eyes a cool, reflective blue. His smooth voice held no hint of the fury tearing through him. Cutting his tour short, he veered into the study where Nicholas had obviously spent most of his time. "Well, Petrov, what was in the photographs? A contrivance to dupe me into coming here?"

A drafting table occupied an alcove formed by a spacious bay window. The leather sofa and chairs were soft and creased from long use, the desk immense and functional. A spiral staircase led to a loft filled with one of the best collections of books he had ever seen. Idly, Alex picked up a small free-form crystal statue and stroked its flowing curves with his thumb.

"The piece is genuine, Alex," Petrov stated quietly.

"Your credibility lacks substance, Petrov. Our deal was all or nothing. I've claimed all this for one thing only. Either you produce it or I will renounce the estate."

"Alex, it's your—"

"Birthright?" Alex asked in a tone as cool as the crystal in his hand. "No, Petrov. My birthright is in Nicholas's grave. The things he left me are just another form of conscience money."

Years of sadness and regret were reflected in Petrov's eyes. "You are right. Nikki's conscience weighed on him more heavily with each passing year. He wasn't ill—not in body. I believe he died when his guilt became more than his spirit could bear. In the diaries you will see—''

"What will I see?" Alex's body became more relaxed as he mentally shook off the anger he thought he'd left behind long ago. "The truth about the Veil of Tears?" he asked more softly still.

"It was stolen fifteen years ago."

"I see." With extreme care, Alex set the crystal back on its stand. "Congratulations, Petrov. You've managed to outbluff me, though I fail to see what you've won. I, on the other hand, am losing what is left of a much-needed vacation."

"I have kept my word to Nikki. I knew the only chance to get you here was to use the Veil of Tears."

"Petrov, every time it has surfaced in legends, its fate has been left unknown. Whoever has it now—"

Petrov lifted his gaze to Alex. "You may still retrieve it."

"I am never a fool twice."

"You will only be a fool if you leave."

Turning in the doorway, Alex leaned nonchalantly against the frame, sensing that Petrov was telling the truth. An intriguing truth. Much as he wanted to, he couldn't walk away. Yet.

Nor could he walk away from the rest of Nicholas's world. Not easily. The place captured his imagination; it seemed to be an extension of the legend of the Veil. Had Nicholas—an architect—created his own fantasy world within a world? The house was like a modern castle with clean lines blending circular towers, out-of-the-way nooks and huge expanses of both clear glass and stained glass. The grounds were extensive and ended at a bluff overlooking the ocean.

Alex caught Petrov's look of fond indulgence—not the first since their initial meeting. If Petrov thought he could win him over with affection, he was wasting his time. Alex might have a sentimental nature and a soft spot or two, but he chose when to display that side of himself. Folding his arms across his chest, he glanced at his watch. "You have five minutes to convince me I haven't been set up."

"Ah, but you have been set up," Petrov laughed. "I can, however, supply you with enough information to pick up the trail. It should not be difficult for a man who enjoys a challenge."

Cocking his head and saying nothing, Alex stared at Petrov. He might be treed, but he wasn't about to make it easy for Petrov to shake him loose.

Petrov nodded as if he understood. "Since you are technically my host, I will allow you to offer me lunch."

A deep chuckle rumbled in Alex's chest as he called the housekeeper over the intercom. He couldn't help but like Petrov.

They sat down at a glass-topped table on the patio to a meal of cold meats, cheeses, assorted freshly baked breads and a light wine of excellent vintage.

The flagstone patio overlooked a swimming pool designed to look like a natural cove surrounded by rocks, greenery and trees. Its irregular shape branched into several intimate pockets of water shielded by foliage. Beyond was a garden, woodland and the sea. The whole place seemed enchanted, making one forget that pollution and traffic and chemical waste existed.

Alex drank a silent toast to whomever had designed and executed the landscaping—no ordinary gardener, surely, but a genius with a whimsical nature. Feeling Petrov's stare, he allowed his curiosity to lead the conversation. "Tell me how all this came about."

"Nikki was an educated man and a brilliant architect," Petrov began as he put down his fork. "He appreciated art on a less conventional scale—structures compatible with nature as well as those that had vision and grace, objects that mingled angles, curves and light. The objets d'art in the vault were too tame for him. He acquired them for your mother and kept them as investment property. Beyond that, he ignored them."

Pausing to sip his wine, Petrov seemed to be staring into the past. "Nikki and I served in the Russian Army during

World War II. Near the end of the war, we came upon one of Hitler's hidden caches of art. We had often dreamed of escaping to America. A valuable objet d'art would set us up nicely.'' Petrov's voice trailed off as he sensed Alex's impatience. He shook himself and continued. ''We took the most portable pieces and began a long, dangerous journey to freedom. Looking back, it seems our escape was absurdly easy, but fearing for our lives and looking over our shoulders became a habit it took years to break.

''We met Lorna in New York the day we arrived. Nikki was wild and handsome, a true romantic.'' Averting his gaze, Petrov blinked his eyes and sniffed. ''Poor Nikki. He had freedom of every kind, but that of the heart.''

''And the Veil of Tears?'' Alex whispered, careful not to jerk Petrov too harshly out of his memories.

''Nikki refused to sell it after meeting Lorna. He meant it to be a wedding gift when she finally came to him. But, your mother was not strong enough to defy her family and the customs of a lifetime. Unfortunately, I believe she really loved him.''

Alex removed his hand from his wineglass, fearing the stem might snap from his hold. He didn't want to hear about Nicholas's dreams being lost as surely as the Veil had been lost. He wasn't ready to accept the notion that his mother might be capable of feeling and expressing love. Certainly, he'd never seen evidence of it. ''Petrov...the Veil,'' he said with a hard edge to his voice.

Petrov sighed. ''As I told you, the Veil was stolen fifteen years ago. Our gardener and general handyman had been systematically removing pieces from the vault. Because of Nikki's indifference to its contents, we would not have noticed so soon if Devlin hadn't added some of Nikki's best wines from the cellar to his cache.''

''Was anything recovered?''

''All but the Veil. We were aware of its origin and value, but it would have been ludicrous to claim the loss of something we had stolen ourselves. We hadn't risked having it insured because of the talk it would have provoked. If word of it had circulated, Devlin would not have been the only thief on our doorstep.''

''Devlin? You believe the Veil is still in his possession.'' Excitement surged through Alex. He had a name. In his business, he often had less than that to go on when searching out a valuable objet d'art. Serious collectors were a secretive lot, their network more efficient and discreet than any government intelligence agency.

''Undoubtedly. He could not have fenced such an item on the streets without inspiring a babble of underground gossip. He didn't have the contacts or the time to arrange a private sale. I have been listening to the grapevine very carefully and it still has not surfaced, though Devlin has been out of prison for over ten days.''

''Where is he?''

''Here in San Francisco, living with his daughter...''

Alex raised his eyebrows in silent demand.

''Patrick Devlin has had a heart attack. I have heard he is dying. If he doesn't have the time to properly convert the Veil to cash, he might be willing to negotiate for its return. If not, he will most certainly leave it to his daughter.''

''Tell me about the girl.''

''Hardly a girl, Alex. Julia Devlin is twenty-eight, a dedicated businesswoman—apparently to the exclusion of all else. In another century, she would have been called a spinster. Rumor has it that charm bounces off her like a rubber ball off concrete.'' Petrov refilled both their glasses. ''Considering the precarious state of his health, she is perhaps the best way to get to him.''

''Wonderful,'' Alex said without enthusiasm. A spinster as hard as granite and a dying man. ''To what kind of business is she so dedicated?'' he asked, resigned. He couldn't barge in on Devlin and jeopardize the man's health. He was tough, not ruthless.

''It's called Image Design. She fashions new images and polishes the tarnish off old ones. I'm told her client list has become quite impressive with the aid of her aunt's referrals.''

"Her aunt?" Alex's eyes narrowed at Petrov's undisguised glee. Obviously, Petrov had another surprise in store for him. For a moment, Alex wondered if it was worth it. But only for a moment. The Veil of Tears was worth almost anything, including having to deal with dedicated, hardcase spinsters and wily, old thieves.

Alex's hand itched at having his dream within reach. He could almost feel the Veil—the textures it had taken a lifetime to create, enduring for countless centuries, the stuff of ancient legend. The attraction wasn't wealth, but beauty, the devotion it symbolized, its timelessness, a myth becoming truth. Alex returned from his musings as he distantly heard Petrov's answer. "What did you say?"

"I said, Julia's aunt—Patrick's sister—is a friend of yours. Chloe Bartholomew."

The reflection of fond memories danced in Alex's eyes, a wide grin spreading across his face. "Intriguing," he mused aloud. "With an aunt like Chloe, there must be some softness within the heart of the stone maiden."

"Did you not mention earlier that you wished to expand the American side of your business, Alex?"

Alex toasted Petrov and drained his glass. "Yes. Now is as good a time as any and San Francisco seems a good place for the next St. Ives Gallery. I'll need a good public relations expert. While I'm at it, I'll try to strike an honest deal with a thief."

IN THE DAYS THAT FOLLOWED Julia's first visit to the hospital, she drove herself harder than necessary preparing her more than capable staff to handle the business without her constant presence. It didn't occur to her to question her spontaneous decision to drastically cut her work load in order to tend her father, particularly since he didn't really need tending. At least she pretended it hadn't occurred to her.

But now, as she drove him home from the hospital, the question became more persistent, the answer more obvious.

"You kept the house."

Julia turned into the driveway and switched off the ignition.

Even after two weeks, she didn't recognize his voice. It had always sounded loud, hearty, booming from high places.

"What choice did you leave me? You put it into Aunt Chloe's name and made her promise not to sell."

"I wanted to make sure you always had a home, Julie."

Julia's mouth tightened as she stared up at the house. A home? Home was people, not a place. Home was sharing, laughter, warmth, love. Home was family. She had no home.

"You didn't have to live here," Patrick said, watching her.

"Why should I pay rent or a mortgage when this house was debt free?" Stepping out of her silver BMW, Julia cut off any further conversation. Getting-to-know-you conversations were pointless and unwelcome.

He's my Da'...sick...dying. She shook her head, denying the yearning she felt. She'd take care of him, make him comfortable and keep him at a distance with no attachments to cause pain when they were broken. *How?*

The passenger door slammed shut. Looking at her father over the top of the car, Julia winced at his pallor. She remembered him as being healthy and robust, burnished by the sun. The muscles he'd developed from years of physical labor sagged as if they were melting off his body. Time and confinement had faded him like an old portrait.

Only his eyes were the same, twinkling green with their own magic charm. It hadn't diminished, though he'd smiled little since that first night at the hospital. Just as well, she told herself. His smile was contagious, infecting everyone with his mischief, filling them with warmth. She didn't want his warmth. The cold was a part of her now, a fifteen-year freeze of emotion. If the ice melted, she feared she would be lost in the flood.

Patrick stared up at the Victorian house he'd bought for his wife and daughter. "You painted it," he remarked a bit too casually. "Is this what your life is like, Julie?"

Jerking his suitcase out of the trunk, Julia ignored the question and walked toward the white-trimmed gray house. Gray and white—drab and sterile—exactly like her life. "I redecorated," she stated flatly. It was part of her image, carefully maintained so that she would never overshadow the flamboyance or style she designed for her clients.

"All of it?" Patrick's voice was sharp, alarmed.

"Everything but your room." Unlocking the front door, she stood aside for him to enter first.

He stopped in the living room, a look of horror on his face. "Good heavens, girl. Do you live here or do you just conduct guided tours once a week?"

Setting down the suitcase, Julia straightened, wondering what he found so objectionable. The carpet was a thick plush, shadowed in tones of palest blue-gray, a perfect background for the curved sectional of slate with a delicate oriental print in navy, coral and creamy white. Tables, shelf units and dining suite had the rich glow of fine wood and the soft lines of the country French style.

Everything was lovely...perfect: the wallpaper of pale slate moiré; the embroidered cream sheers; the navy chairs arranged near a corner grouping of bookshelves with glass doors; the navy, cream and coral striped upholstery on the dining-room chairs...perfect. All the accessories balanced one another, just so. There wasn't a speck of dust or a finger smudge to be found...perfect.

Patrick turned to her, his eyes sad, his voice gentle. "What happened to my Julie whose laughter made the air shine?" His hand shook as he held it out, indicating her tailored gray suit of classic simplicity and elegance. "Where is the girl who dressed to match the flowers in my garden?"

She died of loneliness and shame when magic became lies and leprechauns became thieves. Though she didn't voice her thoughts, Patrick looked as if he'd heard them. Picking up his suitcase, she carried it into his first-floor bedroom. She hadn't expected to feel hurt by his criticism and disappointment. Her Da' had always understood her, knowing, without being told, what she felt and why. For years now, however, she'd thought of him as someone she'd never really known, but his appraisal of her made her feel like the stranger.

She entered his room and lifted the case onto his bed. Everything had been left undisturbed, waiting, as if he'd simply gone to the store for some pipe tobacco. The old family Bible occupied the nightstand. A framed portrait of her mother was on the dresser and an antique music box, the size of a small trunk, sat on the floor. A breeze carried in the potpourri scent of his garden, still thriving, waiting. All of his treasured things . . . waiting.

Her throat closed. She hadn't been waiting. Trailing in her Aunt Chloe's impulsive wake, she'd attended exclusive schools and spent holidays with her aunt either in five-star hotels or in one of the houses Chloe owned in various parts of the world. Julia had come to the conclusion that the only way to avoid painful endings to relationships was not to begin them in the first place.

Chloe had given her the world for a classroom, an endless variety of people to learn from and no place for roots to grow and flourish. After burying her third husband, Chloe had commented that she was always a widow, never a divorcée, and wondered which was easier. If those were the only choices, then Julia wanted no part of love. It was just another word for heartbreak.

At eighteen, Julia returned to San Francisco, most of her dreams wiped out by a jet-setting society that slowed down only for death, divorce or dalliance.

"Julie, where did you put my . . . ah, there they are." Patrick spotted his pipe rack. "I was afraid you'd thrown them out."

"You shouldn't be smoking." Disconcerted to find she'd unpacked his clothes and had put them away without realizing it, Julia shoved the empty suitcase under the bed.

"I don't think it can do any harm at this point," he said as he stared out the window.

Julia's eyes burned at the casual reference to his mortality.

"You kept up my garden?"

"No. I wasn't here, remember? Aunt Chloe hired some-one to—"

Patrick tensed. "Chloe had strangers poking around?"

"It was Mrs. Penny from next door." Julia's forehead wrinkled. Twice now, her father had been agitated because of the house.

"Ah, Mrs. Penny." His shoulders relaxed. "She always did have a green thumb. I'll have to thank her."

"She moved two years ago." Turning abruptly, Julia left him before he could ask who had done the gardening since then. She didn't want to tell him that she—

"Thank you, Julie darlin'," Patrick whispered after her, his smile as bright as his eyes.

Chapter Two

The door to her private entrance swung back on its hinges and rebounded off the doorstop with a thud. Julia shifted from foot to foot, discarding her sodden shoes as she hopped across her office to answer the intercom. Water ran down her raincoat and she shuddered at the squishy feel of wet carpet under her feet. Leaning across her desk, she pushed the intercom button and stretched out her leg to kick the door shut. "Yes, Dina."

"Mr. Alexander St. Ives is here to see you."

Already? Frowning, Julia glanced over her schedule, calculating how long she could give him before her next appointment. He wasn't booked for today, but he might as well be. Aunt Chloe had called to make sure Julia would see him and it was impossible to deny her aunt anything. Chloe never stopped talking long enough.

"All right, Dina. Give me three minutes." Running into the small bathroom adjoining her office, Julia struggled out of her raincoat with one hand while pulling off the matching hat with the other. She grimaced in distaste at the arrogance of the man, wondering if he would agree to see new clients without an appointment.

A quick look in the mirror assured her that her makeup was fine although her hair was flattened and dark from the moisture. Tossing her coat into the shower stall, she grabbed a towel. Only a minute left and there was still the wet spot on the carpet.

On her hands and knees, Julia fished one shoe out from under the desk and gave it a careless swipe with the towel. With one hand blotting up excess moisture from the carpet and the other groping for the missing shoe, she recalled what Aunt Chloe had said about the inconsiderate Mr. St. Ives.

"Alex is magnificent, love...an old friend." Naturally. All of Chloe's men were magnificent. And, most of Chloe's male friends were recycled lovers. "He's *rich,* Julie...self-made even though he comes from old money. A renegade...gambled his way into a fortune and turned it into a respectable business. You'll adore him."

Julia doubted it. Aunt Chloe had said more, all of which had left Julia unimpressed. He couldn't have much going for him if her imaginative aunt had had to resort to clichés to describe him.

"Ms. Devlin...oops!" Dina's voice came from the doorway.

Julia glanced at her watch in resignation. She'd always appreciated her assistant's punctuality in the past. With as much dignity as she could scrape together, Julia rose to her feet—an awkward process when wearing a straight skirt. She didn't want to think about which part of her anatomy had been facing the door. Concentrating on straightening her spine and squaring her shoulders, she turned, smiling politely. "Thank you, Di—"

He took her breath away. Her nerve endings vibrated. Her heart leaped into her throat and she had to remember to breathe. Feeling as if she'd been in a hot tub for too long, Julia tried to collect her wits and her strength.

Magnificent was an understatement. Thick and wavy, his hair was a deep burnished gold. His eyes were the elusive silver-blue of moonstones, clear one moment, smoky the next as he regarded her steadily. Heat shot through her body. Julia snapped her mouth shut and blinked.

Alex matched her stare-for-stare, piling up first impressions in his mind. Her hair was simply brown. The elegant suit she wore was in the style he labeled "unimaginative chic." Her slim, well put together figure was neither spectacular nor displeasing. High cheekbones and forehead, a square chin with a slight cleft and large, widely spaced eyes had too much strength and pride to be called fragile, yet her features were refined, definitely feminine. Julia Devlin wasn't beautiful or pretty or cute. On first glance, she was plain.

On second glance, she was stunning. Her mouth alone was a work of art. Alex felt as if he would miss something special if he looked away, such as the dimples on either side of those beautifully shaped lips or the vulnerability peeking at him like a shy child hiding behind a door.

Julia blinked again. He was still there, still devastating, as he leaned casually against the door frame as if it were the most comfortable place in the world, custom-made for him. His nose was perfectly straight. His well-formed mouth invited. The strong line of his jaw and chin fascinated. His tall, broad-shouldered body disturbed. Aunt Chloe was right. Alexander St. Ives was a cliché—Prince Charming in a three-piece suit, perfect as a daydream.

Impossible.

She had to stop gaping at him. Noting that Dina had tactfully retreated, Julia forced another smile and stepped forward. "Mr.—" She sounded like an anemic frog. Clearing her throat, she swallowed and tried again. "Mr. St. Ives, I'm Julia Devlin. Aunt Chloe told me to expect a call from you." There. She'd done that rather well. Everything would be fine now.

A shock passed through her as he accepted her handshake. His fingers wrapped around hers, firm, yet gentle, perfectly proper. Her reaction was not. Her nerves felt like that wonderful first stretch after being confined for a long time.

"Ms. Devlin." Inclining his aristocratic head, he cupped her elbow and led her to the desk, seating her as if they were at a formal dinner.

Oh, mercy, she was barefoot.

Alex lingered behind her for a moment, taking a slow, measured breath. She smelled like rain and spice, clean, fresh, saucy. He focused on her hair, as neat and no-nonsense as the rest of her. His eyebrows arched in surprise, his fancy captured by the combs securing the sides of her hair. He looked at them more closely and bit back a burst of delighted laughter.

The cloisonné combs were brightly painted with lotus-eating dragons that had butterflies perched on their noses. Alex's assessment of Julia did a double take. This lady whose "power" suit was obviously chosen to intimidate the aggressive and discourage the friendly had a streak of whimsy in her nature that she couldn't quite suppress. His mouth quirked as she tried to squirm unobtrusively, her foot moving around under her desk in search of a shoe. Bending over, he picked up a black pump from between the desk and the wastebasket and held it out to her.

Julia accepted it with a trembling hand and bone-deep mortification. "Thank you." At least her voice was holding up. "Would you like some coffee or tea?"

"Did I see hot cocoa on your secretary's desk?" Alex flicked open the button of his jacket and sat in the chair opposite Julia. Her large eyes were dark green flecked with gold, as deep and full of secrets as a sun-dappled forest.

"Oh. Probably. Dina is addicted to it and technically it's her lunch hour." *Don't babble, Julia.*

"Ghirardelli Cocoa? With marshmallows?" he asked hopefully.

At last, something to do with her hands. Julia picked up the phone and punched the intercom line.

Alex leaned back, unable to take his eyes off her. There was definitely something about her...

But what?

"Dina assures me we have plenty of marshmallows, Mr. St. Ives." His stare made her want to don both a suit of armor and a chastity belt.

"Call me Alex, please."

His smile clutched the inside of Julia's chest. Even his teeth were straight. There had to be something wrong with him...

But what?

"Chloe is positive that you can help me, Ms. Devlin."

"I don't see how," Julia blurted out. She couldn't imagine that he had ever needed anyone's help. This time, his smile was lazy, with his eyelids slightly lowered. Now she knew what the term "bedroom eyes" meant. It meant danger.

Dina silently entered carrying a tray with two cups and an extra bowl of miniature marshmallows.

"Thank you, Dina." Julia glared meaningfully at the bowl. Dina never brought *her* extra marshmallows and the short, plump secretary was the closest thing to a friend Julia had. She poured cocoa from the china pot and watched Alex's long elegant fingers add marshmallows to his cup. He took another and rolled it between his fingers before popping it into his mouth. It was all she could do not to hunch within her suit jacket. "How can I . . . Image Design help you?" she asked.

His fingers moved over the striated raw silk that upholstered the chair, absorbing rather than merely feeling the texture. "I plan to open a gallery here in San Francisco and need a consultant familiar with the city and its art community to help me in all phases of development. I want the new gallery to be compatible with the city's unique personality."

Julia dragged her gaze from the lazy movement of his hands and automatically shifted into 'professional mode.' "We work with people, not buildings," she said firmly, relieved that she couldn't help him after all. His mere presence had coaxed a long-undisturbed part of her out of hiding, his smile an invitation to come out and play woman to his man, his movements promising exciting possibilities to the game. During a brief lapse of sanity, she wished she was the type of woman who could do the same to him, a woman who knew as many of the rules as he did and could make up a few of her own.

But she wasn't up to the game. A look in her mirror would tell her that. A longer look into her past would confirm it. She had tried the game and had learned that the only time she was allowed to play was when something was wanted of her. Something besides herself.

"Why not buildings?" Adjusting a trouser leg, Alex crossed his right ankle over his left knee. "Wouldn't you agree that the location and style of a business should be alluring to the public?"

"Well, yes," Julia answered warily.

"I'm impressed with your choice," he continued. "A Victorian house on a side street of a high-rent district—" He scanned the office, assessing the elegant simplicity of her furnishings, the warm colors of the decor. "It represents elegance, discretion, stability. The atmosphere of casual intimacy you've achieved encourages one to relax and be honest more effectively than an office in a high rise." Plopping two more marshmallows into his cup, he stirred until they were half-melted, then sipped his cocoa.

How did he do that? she wondered. Anyone else would have white foam adorning his upper lip. Involuntarily, her tongue swept over her upper lip as she watched him sip and roll the cocoa in his mouth as if it were vintage wine. "Mr. St. Ives—"

"Alex. I'm a family friend, remember?"

She'd rather forget. The idea that Alex might have been one of Chloe's men unsettled her. But then, she couldn't imagine him being anyone's man but his own. Somehow, she just couldn't see this man in the role of lover to her aunt. "I'm sorry. I don't think Image Design has what you need. I'll recommend a realtor and a decorator." Julia wrote names and telephone numbers on a memo pad.

"You have exactly what I need, Julia." He drew her name out on a husky whisper, full of suggestions and intimate promises, not deliberate, but natural to a man whose sensuality was as much a part of him as toenails and hair and everything in between.

Taking the paper she held out to him, Alex crumpled it in his hand and threw it in the wastebasket. "My galleries carry my name. Their image is mine and vice versa. I am quite cautious about trusting either to another person." With undisguised greed, he peered into her untouched cup. "Are you going to drink that?"

"No. Be my guest," she answered, distracted by what he had proposed. The challenge of working with man and business as a total picture intrigued her as much as he himself did. Of course it was his business proposition that really fascinated her.

Of course it was.

"Don't you think you can do it?" The question stabbed her pride. Alex could see it in the flash of indignation she quickly disguised with cool professionalism.

"The question doesn't arise. I'd have to devote a great deal of time to such a project, finding a suitable location, supervising leasehold improvements—"

"Introducing me to the community?"

"Yes," she agreed coolly. "*If* I were to accept you as a client." If she were reckless enough, brave enough, foolish enough. He projected a magnetism and power that she had never before experienced. She wanted to keep it that way.

"Several openings and social gatherings are scheduled in the next few weeks." Alex reached into the inside pocket of his jacket and produced an envelope. "Here is a list of the ones I would like to attend, as well as a check to cover your retainer and expenses for the next three months. Also, I know any number of people who will use your services if I recommend them."

Arrogant so-and-so, she thought bitterly. Did he think that a charming smile and soft voice disguised the threat behind his words? A threat to force her into seeing the error of her ways and accepting his largesse.

"Don't bully me, Mr. St. Ives." Julia said, refusing to give him an inch of the mile he wanted. Seeing his flash of anger, she realized that he wasn't civilized at all. He was merely contained.

Alex was furious with himself as he sensed rather than saw the change in Julia; immovable barriers going up between them, bouncing the less-than-irresistible force of his charm back in his face. Pompous idiot, Alex berated himself, annoyed that he would stoop to such tactics. Since when did he submit to committing acts of desperation? Of course, he knew the answer. He'd been feeling stirrings of panic since he'd first laid eyes on her. Lust at first sight he could handle, but interest at first sight was a new element in his life.

A dedicated, hardcase spinster. *Wonderful.*

"All right. No bullying," he said, his expression sober and reflective. "Shall we try honesty instead?"

Surprised, Julia had to work at being politely indifferent. "All right." She inclined her head in a slight nod. "Image Design is not an ad agency, realty company, interior decorator or escort service. San Francisco has an abundance of all four. If you don't wish to consider my recommendations, then I suggest you let your fingers do the walking."

"Give me one good reason why you're against my proposal," he said, unperturbed by her attempt to dismiss him.

Julia opened her mouth and closed it again. *I don't want to* struck her as being a little too childish for the occasion. She counterattacked instead. "Give me one good reason why you're so determined to pursue it." She kept her gaze level as he settled more deeply into the cushions, seeming to flow over the chair, loose-limbed, elegant, profoundly masculine.

Alex sighed. "It's quite simple. I have neither the time nor the patience to deal with several separate agencies." He smiled. "And, I'm spoiled. According to Chloe and the majority of your clients, you are the best in your field. And nothing but the best will do."

"It will have to, Mr. St. Ives."

How many men had she stoned to death with that cold, hard stare? Alex wondered. He couldn't remember the last time he'd botched anything so badly. The only thing he hadn't tried was an apology and, after his high-handedness, he definitely owed her one.

"You'll have to forgive me, Ms. Devlin. It's been years since I've had to actively seek out anyone's services. The success and fame of my galleries attracts unsolicited offers for everything from plumbing to commercial endorsements."

Have to forgive...? She didn't have to do any such thing. "Someone should teach you how to make a proper apology, Mr. St. Ives." Julia rose and walked across the office. "Since you have so many offers, I'm sure you'll have no trouble finding another agency." Pulling the door open, she watched as he automatically stood. "I'm sorry I can't accept the generosity of your patronage."

"Your sincerity touches me, Julia." Holding his ground, Alex gazed at her with brooding eyes.

"I'm perfectly sincere."

"Good. Then there is no reason for you to refuse me." Alex leaned against her desk and crossed his arms over his chest.

Julia thought of several million as she stood there feeling foolish, her mouth all but dragging on the floor. None of them were acceptable to her. Any one of them would justify his conceit. Sliding her gaze from him to the open door, she pointedly looked at her watch. "If you'll excuse me, I have another appointment."

Alex propped his leg on the desk and plucked a nonexistent piece of lint from his trouser leg. "Then I suggest we set the terms for our association."

Her hand tightened on the doorknob as she cast about for a reply that wouldn't contain a combination of explicit four-letter words. The way she saw it, she could either stand there, open-mouthed at his audacity or she could give in gracefully. Obviously, he had no intention of giving in. In fact, his calmness and relaxed posture indicated she would be under siege until she capitulated. At the moment, she'd do just about anything to remove him from the range of her senses, including give in.

Julia closed the door more gently than she wanted to. "I won't offer you a contract, Mr. St. Ives. I will agree to a trial period of three months at the end of which either of us may terminate without further argument." Her tone clearly said "take it or leave it." She wanted him to leave it. She hoped he would take it. Either way, she had the feeling she would have regrets.

"A gentleman's agreement?" he asked solemnly. He had won, yet on Julia, defeat looked like victory.

"If you like."

"It will do...for now." Alex held out the envelope to her.

Frowning, Julia read the information on the envelope, and felt as if an ice cube were dripping down her back. "But, this is the Alexander estate."

Reality slammed into him like a baseball bat in the stomach. She really did have a remarkable effect on him. He wouldn't have thought anything could make him forget Nicholas or the Veil of Tears, but she had done just that. "Yes. I recently moved in." Carefully observing her reaction, he spoke softly. "Are you familiar with it?"

"I met the previous owner once or twice." Closing her eyes, she remembered Nicholas, a kind and gentle man who had allowed her father to take her with him to work on occasion, to swim in the pool and play in the woods. She'd only seen him a few times, but Nicholas had always sent gifts home to her for Christmas and birthdays. She'd always associated him with images of Santa Claus and magic places.

The moment lasted only a heartbeat, but Alex saw sadness cross her features like a shadow. She actually grieved for the man her father had robbed—grieved as Alex wished he could grieve. On a level Alex didn't understand, he envied her. "You knew him?"

"Not really—" Julia drew in a shaky breath, reminding herself that Alex was a virtual stranger. She shared nothing with strangers, neither her memories nor her present. "Nothing," she said firmly, extending her hand. "I'll contact you in a few days."

Alex returned her handshake, the coldness of her skin and the tension in her muscles giving him sudden insight into what had drawn him to her in the first place. The stress lines in her forehead were faint, yet ever-present as if she never relaxed, as if they were carved there, as if she constantly had to fight people from without and unseen enemies from within.

Alex didn't want to release Julia's hand, the urge strong to pull her into his arms, offer comfort, protect. He hadn't the faintest idea why, but he sensed her need for both. Odd, he'd never indulged in white-knight fantasies before. Unable to help himself, Alex withdrew slowly, trailing his fingers over the back of her hand as he slid his palm intimately over hers, prolonging the contact until a sliver of air separated their fingertips.

Caught by the intensity of his gaze, Julia remained still as she responded from within, his presence stroking her to life. She had a compelling urge to do something embarrassing and totally out of character...such as purr. She saw his smile, tried to interpret the dream that drifted across his face like a wistful sigh. The moment passed, shoved aside by the sound of his voice.

"Relax, Julia. You take life much too seriously," he said with a wink as he sauntered out of her office.

"And you don't take it seriously enough." Julia muttered under her breath, but the words carried and Dina looked up from handing Alex his coat, startled that her very proper employer would make such an improper statement to a potential client.

Watching him wink at Dina and saunter out the door, Julia wondered what it would be like to—just once—sit back, relax and let life happen.

Caught in dark clouds of thought, Alex left the building and stepped off the broad porch as Petrov pulled up to the curb in Nicholas's classic Rolls-Royce. Distracted by the impact Julia had had on him, Alex settled into the car without saying a word.

"Well?" Petrov asked with unconcealed curiosity.

With an effort, Alex brought himself back to the here and now. "Well, indeed."

"What happened?"

Alex gave a short laugh. "In a supreme fit of arrogance, I approached her believing she couldn't refuse my exalted patronage."

"And?" Tilting his leonine head, Petrov glanced at Alex with a questioning arch of his bushy gray eyebrows.

"She called my bluff and put me on a three-month probation." Alex smiled, amused in spite of himself.

Tactfully suppressing his laughter, Petrov concentrated on his driving. "Did you speak to her about the Veil?"

"Mmm..." Alex sobered. "No, I didn't."

"I see."

Alex suspected that Petrov saw entirely too much.

"Could it be, Alex, that you have found yet another objet d'art to pursue."

Could it? Perplexed by his reaction to Julia, Alex maintained his silence and stared out the window. Rain washed down the glass in sheets, blurring the details of the city. He barely noticed. All his attention was focused on Julia Devlin, the sense of... imminence he'd experienced upon meeting her. Julia wasn't the glossy cardboard cutout he'd expected. In her, he'd seen three dimensions, color, texture—facets throwing out glimpses of infinite possibilities.

The Veil of Tears might represent the ultimate possession, and its reclamation, the ultimate gamble, but involvement with Julia Devlin could easily become the ultimate challenge.

He was an expert at meeting challenges and exploring possibilities.

THE MINUTE ALEX DISAPPEARED through the outer door, Dina rushed into Julia's office and stared out the window overlooking the street. "If I were ten years younger and thirty pounds lighter, I'd go after him with a good strong net. Heck, I might do it anyway. He'd look great hanging above my fireplace." She gave a wistful sigh. "I didn't know men like him really existed."

Julia shook herself. "They don't."

"What do you mean, they don't?" Dina glared at Julia. "He talked to me. I answered him. His coat was warm when I hung it up." She peered into the cups on Julia's desk. "He drank my cocoa," she crowed as if that settled the matter.

"He's as shallow as the images we create." Feeling unaccountably let down by the thought, Julia wondered why it should even make a difference to her.

"That man is about as shallow as the Mariana Trench, Julie. It would take several lifetimes to explore him."

"Exploring is a dangerous occupation."

"And exciting. Think of the thrill of victory."

"And the agony of defeat. No thanks, Dina."

"Speaking of images—what was he doing here?"

You have exactly what I need, Julia. Alex's words fluttered through her memory, raising goose bumps on her skin. She tingled in the most intimate places. *Get your act together, Julia.* "He's opening a gallery here, and wants a local consultant to help him choose the proper location, decorate it to fit San Francisco's style, introduce him to the community and do the usual PR."

Dina sank into a chair. "Oh. Well that shouldn't take more than several hundred hours. Piece of cake." She watched Julia go into the bathroom and fuss with her hair. "So, why didn't I type up an agreement?"

"I set a three-month trial period. I should have put it in writing. He's too good at getting his own way."

"Contingent on what?" Dina eyed her suspiciously.

"The job might be more than I can handle. I don't want to be bound by a contract."

"Uh-uh," Dina muttered. "You can handle the job. You're running scared from the man."

Dina looked entirely too pleased with herself to suit Julia. "I don't run to, from or in between men, Dina. They're not worth the effort."

"I think you'd better put on your running shoes, Julie. The minute you saw him, you had the shivering fits. How you made it to twenty-eight without falling in love, I'll never know."

"I didn't." Julia winced. She hadn't meant to say that. Her personal life was private. Even Dina didn't have access to the details.

Dina frowned at the lack of inflection in Julia's voice, a flatness that described more graphically than words the emotions and pain too strong to be expressed aloud. "Julie, you're the most intensely private person I've ever known. I've tried to respect that—" she shrugged, "—but

I have this mother hen complex. The last few weeks . . . well I know something is wrong. You're only working half-days and that's unusual for you. You look tired and you constantly have worry lines on your forehead. I won't even mention that your agreement with St. Ives is totally unprofessional.''

"Gee thanks, Dina, for not mentioning it," Julia said dryly as she ducked into the bathroom and surreptitiously examined her face in the mirror. Yes, the lines were there, mute testimony to the strain of her father's presence and the knowledge that he would soon be gone again—this time permanently. "Don't you have some press releases to do?" Conversations such as this one unsettled her. It would be so easy to dump her pain, her confusion, her fears on to Dina's shoulder.

"They're done." Dina narrowed her eyes on Julia's profile. "You know, your image could use some jazzing up. Wide-brimmed hats and flamboyant clothes would look terrific on you."

"My image is exactly what I want it to be."

"Mmm. Neutral. You ought to have your hair styled too, and highlighted."

Julia shut the bathroom door.

"You're not a stainless steel robot, you know," Dina yelled. "You need love and friendship just like anyone else."

Julia wondered what it would take to make Dina act more the part of an employee instead of someone whose mission in life was to grant Julia three wishes. Pulling the door open, Julia tried to look intimidating. "Why don't you go home and nag your offspring?"

"They don't need it as much as you do."

"Dina . . . don't worry."

"Julie, you can't live your life untouched by human hearts. It isn't natural." Biting her lower lip, Dina looked at Julia uncertainly. "Honey, you're intelligent, attractive and generous to a fault with everyone but yourself—"

"Arf."

"Uh-uh, Julie. Puppies are warm and cuddly and frisky and they soak up love like a carpet soaks up their accidents. You've taken on being cold and hard and indifferent as a personal crusade. Why, Julie? Why do you insist on being so alone?''

Julia flinched at the anguish in Dina's voice. Anguish for her. She felt a need to ease Dina's worry, return her unconditional caring. But that required honesty, a baring of her inner self and she'd worked too hard to bury it where no one could reach or hurt or destroy. She gently squeezed Dina's hand. ''Thank you for caring.''

Dina smiled sadly as she headed back to her own desk. ''Boss, you have a very nice way of saying shut up.''

If only her own thoughts would shut up. All Julia could do after Dina had returned to her own desk was glare at the clock and tap her pen on the sheaf of papers stacked in front of her. Her client was late. She couldn't concentrate and she'd bitten the nail on her little finger to the nub. Rain pounded against the windows like a drumroll announcing some great event. If she made one more trip to the bathroom to stare at herself in the mirror, she would wear a trench into the carpet.

Julia knew she was changing, yet could find no evidence of it on the surface. Inside, she hungered for all the things she'd learned to live without. Everything she'd worked to become was crumbling, her exterior falling away in chunks with every word and gesture from those she cared about.

And now, the model for every woman's erotic fantasies had made her feel far too warm, all too soft and every inch a woman.

She'd just have to keep reminding herself that fantasies and dreams had less value in the real world than works of art, gemstones and pieces of gold. Stunting the growth of her emotions was a small price to pay for protection against the ravages of trusting too much. Trust was such a fragile thing, so easily misplaced, too often broken and discarded as if it were nothing more than cheap glass. The only way to protect it was to keep it on a shelf so high that no one could reach it.

''Earth calling Julie.'' Dina stood in front of the desk, holding a file folder out to Julia.

"Oh. Sorry, Dina. I was lost in thought." Julia smiled vaguely, feeling lost in every sense of the word.

"Of course you were. What else would any sane woman be doing after spending an hour with tall, golden and gorgeous?"

"What is it, Dina?"

"The 'Commercial King' just canceled his appointment. He's afraid the rain will dissolve the mousse in his hair," she said as she slapped the folder down onto the desk and left Julia to her thoughts.

Julia remembered how unconcerned Alex had been about the damp tendrils of hair curling over his ears.

Alex again. Everywhere her mind turned, he was there, waiting, seductive, reminding her that she was a woman. A normal, healthy woman whose hormones had suddenly become hyperactive.

Glancing down, Julia read the name typed neatly on the tab of the file folder. Alexander St. Ives. She dropped her pen and began shoving papers into her briefcase. For a moment her hand hovered over the folder before she picked it up and slapped it on top.

Three months seemed like a very long time.

Chapter Three

Laden with packages, Julia dashed from her car to the house, nearly slipping on the rain-slicked grass. What had begun as a stop at the tobacconist had escalated into an endless shopping spree. She hated to shop and wasn't even sure what exactly she'd bought. The three hours she'd spent going from shop to boutique to department store had been escape, pure and simple.

Her reactions to Alex were definitely not pure. As for the feelings she had for her father, they were complicated, disturbing. She couldn't decide who unsettled her more.

After insisting that Patrick not smoke in the house, she'd bought him tobacco and not one, but two ashtrays—one for his bedroom and one for the living room.

Before leaving her office, she'd decided to back out of her deal with Alex; then, reversing her decision, she'd contacted a realtor to inquire about available commercial property suitable for Alex's needs. She'd even stopped at a successful gallery to scout out the competition.

And after spending years dressing and living in neutral mode, she had spent money on some very splashy items which would, coincidentally, jazz up her existing wardrobe. It hadn't been a conscious effort, but everything she'd bought had seemed to have her name on it.

Silence greeted her as she stumbled into the foyer. She set her bags down and kicked off her shoes. Her rain gear was still in an untidy heap at her office. Another black mark against the two men creating such havoc in her life. She was never untidy.

Frowning, she sniffed the air for the aroma of dinner, which Patrick always had ready when she arrived home. Granted, she was earlier than usual, but she was used to hearing him puttering around, singing one of the ballads he was so fond of.

The silence unnerved her. Had something happened? Was he ill? Fear drove her down the hall to his room. Disbelief brought her up short in the threshold.

The bed had been moved and Patrick was on his hands and knees pressing his fingers to various sections of the floor.

"What on earth are you doing?" she demanded, relief at finding him well giving an added edge to her voice. He started so violently, she feared for his heart.

Recovering quickly, Patrick looked at her over his shoulder with a smile that was two parts saint and three parts mischief. "Why Julie darlin', I have it on good authority that the Little People buried treasure here."

Barriers shifted and crumbled inside her, exposing the child who had dug in the garden for leprechaun gold while her Da' made tales of magic come alive for her. Her eyes burned and her throat tightened. She felt unutterably weary of fighting herself. Julie of the bright colors and even brighter smiles was still alive in spite of all Julia's efforts to pretend otherwise.

Taking in Julia's wet clothes and the droop of her shoulders, Patrick's smile faded as he rose to his feet. The pop of his arthritic joints sounded unnaturally loud, proclaiming his mortality. "Go take a long, hot bath, girl. I'll have dinner ready by the time you're through."

"No. I—"

"Go." Patrick gave her a gentle but uncompromising shove toward the stairs. "Julie, I just spent fifteen years in cooking school. Do you want me to waste all that education?" His tone was deliberately aggrieved, his expression an exaggerated glower.

In spite of herself, Julia's mouth twitched. When he wanted to, Patrick could talk the devil into becoming a fireman.

"Be careful, Julie. It would never do for you to smile."

You take life much too seriously. Julie mentally snarled as she climbed the stairs.

Too tired to do more than put on her nightgown and robe after her bath, Julia walked into the kitchen where hot roast beef sandwiches and fresh salad awaited her.

With barely a glance at her, Patrick set glasses of wine on the table. "You should be spending your Friday nights with a beau, instead of staying at home to watch my hair grow."

"I don't have one," she said around a bite of lettuce.

"No? Why not?"

"Why should I?" she countered.

Patrick took several bites before he answered. "Are you content to live through your clients and the images you dream up for them?"

The question hit her like an unexpected blow. Through her clients—because she only went through the motions of living? Dream up—because she was afraid to dream for herself? It sounded so wasteful. She felt like a naughty child who'd been sent to sit in the corner. In that moment, she felt very, very small.

"Ah, Julie. What are you waiting for? The ideal man to go with your ideal career and your ideal house?"

Julia thought of Alex. He couldn't possibly be ideal, though he gave that impression—as long as he had his way in things. If he were ideal, he'd be boring. The sudden insight startled her.

Sighing, Patrick took a sip of wine. "You're like a ghost passing through life and leaving nary a footprint, Julie. How can you know if you're alive unless you let yourself feel?"

Julia dropped her fork with a clatter and balled her fists. The past, its anger and bitterness, regret and pain threatened to choke her. "Believe me, I know. I *felt* plenty when you were arrested. And I *felt* shame when my friends were forbidden to associate with me—the criminal's daughter—for fear I'd steal their pencils and lunch money." Her voice thickened with the fermented rage of fifteen years. "When Aunt Chloe took me away, I made new friends who didn't know about you, but we never stayed in one place long enough for me to say more than hello and goodbye in the appropriate language."

As she stared at the knife on her plate, anguish ripped into her like a dull blade, tearing her apart instead of cutting cleanly. "I *felt* guilty, as if what you did was somehow my fault. I couldn't understand why you chose being a thief over being my father. I still don't." Her indrawn breath became a whimper. "I knew I was alive all right and it *felt* like hell."

Blinking his eyes, Patrick abruptly stood and carried his plate to the counter. "I've always been a fool, acting on impulse and taking chances, looking for the pot of gold. My shortcoming, Julie, not yours." His voice cracked in a dozen places.

"The rest of the world didn't see it that way." Julia avoided looking at him. His regret and guilt should have pleased her, but it didn't. She wanted to end this confrontation and couldn't. She was crumbling too fast now, the words pouring out before she knew what they were. Emotions ran out of her in a flood before she could seal the cracks and regain her control. "My prison was as brutal as yours. There were no walls to keep others out, just bars, and people kept poking sticks at me as if I were some kind of freak."

"The bars on your cell are made of fear and a false sense of piety. I paid for my crime in this world and I'll answer for my sins in the next. None of that will change because you're wearing a hair shirt." He took her plate and slammed it onto the counter. "You're a bigger fool than I am, Julie, throwing your life away for nothing. And you're a coward."

Julia pinned him with a blank stare. "Oh yes, Father, I was a fool. But not anymore. Now, I'm simply a coward."

"Is that why you don't go out?" Patrick hesitated, then went on. "Chloe told me that you'd had a couple of bad experiences. But, Julie, everyone gets hurt by love at one time or another."

"Of course they do," Julia said flatly. "That's why I took another chance and fell in love with Scott Richmond. I was very careful not to make the same mistakes with him as I had made with the others. Scott was too rich to care about Aunt Chloe's money. I made sure that he wasn't carrying any torches for ex-wives, girlfriends or mistresses." Her voice lowered to a choked whisper. "So careful."

Patrick held on to the edge of the table. "What happened?"

Julia's smile was as bright as gold leaf. "He courted me—flowers, candy, rowboats on the lake, dinner and dancing, flattery and nonsense." Julia's body trembled with the memories of the sweetness followed by bitter rejection, delivered in an oh-so-civilized manner. Scott Richmond had been a very refined bigot.

Her voice lowered even more, "He found out about you, or rather, his family did. They'd had me investigated to make sure I was suitable. Needless to say—I wasn't. They were absolutely convinced that criminal tendencies were carried in the blood like a disease." Her hands curled around bunches in the tablecloth. "That's when I stopped being a fool and started being a coward."

Patrick's voice was hoarse, agonized, filled with outraged wrath. "Damn him—"

"No, Father. Scott was a product of his environment and upbringing and I am a product of mine. He was a prejudiced snob and you were a three-time loser. That made me a three-time loser, too."

Patrick pried her fingers from the tablecloth. "Julie—" His face had paled. His expression was stricken, twisted with the effort to hold emotion at bay.

"Stop it," Julia shouted. Her chair skidded back and toppled as she pushed herself up from the table. She was breaking from the inside out—not because of painful memories, but because of what she'd just done to her father. He'd paid. So had she. Why had she felt the need to punish him further? What had she become?

Backing out of the kitchen, Julia shook her head and whispered, "I'm sorry, Da'. I'm so...sorry."

She ran up to her room and curled into the window seat. Clouds shut out the stars and moon. The only light was artificial, turned on and off with the flip of a switch, like her. She couldn't hide or turn herself off of life anymore. No more. It was wrong. It had always been wrong. And, it didn't work.

She thought of Aunt Chloe—sincerely loving in her own haphazard way—and Dina—concerned and aching for her employer and friend. She listened to the small sounds of her father clearing the table, small as if he were being very careful not to break any more than had already been broken in their lives. The only pain Julia felt was for her actions. After all the years of hiding from them, she'd finally faced her demons, talked about them, seen them for what they were.

But, at what cost?

The wind scattered darkness and blew the curtains aside. Light pooled around her, as unbroken, brilliant and beckoning as hope and forgiveness. For the first time in years, she wanted to touch and be touched, hold and be held. She wanted to dream again.

Leaving the window seat, Julia ran to her closet and rummaged through the bags she'd piled on the floor. She found what she wanted and returned to the kitchen.

Patrick was wiping the counters vigorously as if he were trying to wipe out more than food stains. Pausing, he stared at the image reflected in the window above the sink. The dishrag fell from his hand and his shoulders squared. He turned toward the doorway to face Julia, then lowered his head as if he was ashamed.

"Please don't, Da'." Julia held out the items she'd dug out of the shopping bags, a small gesture, inadequate compared with the ruthlessness of her actions. How easy to regret damage already done. How difficult to keep from doing it in the first place. How impossible to wipe out the suffering it had caused. And all for nothing. The past couldn't be changed no matter who bore the guilt. Everything that had happened before this minute would remain static, frozen in time. Frozen as she'd been. Too frozen for anything to grow inside her. She had to walk away from it, leave it behind and take the first step into the present.

She'd known it that first night at the hospital. It had been early spring then, the season of awakening, renewal, a gradual budding of a multitude of potentials. She'd been too much of a coward to admit it.

Walking into the kitchen, Julia set down her meager offerings on the table. "I brought you some tobacco and ashtrays. I've...missed the smell of your pipe."

Patrick picked up each item, turning it over in his hands, touching it as if it were the greatest treasure in the world. His body shook and his tears fell onto the tops of his shoes.

JULIA COULD HAVE SWORN she wasn't dreaming, yet she heard it again, a voice from her memory, a voice that had awakened her to new days and bright expectations. How long since she'd felt that warm, calloused hand against her cheek nudging her from sleep? How long since she'd smelled hot, fragrant tea and fresh pastry at her bedside? How nice it would be to greet the morning chatting about plans for the day....

Her eyes opened and she felt as if she were a little girl again. Sunlight flowed into the room, golden and bright as a second chance. Tea and croissants beckoned from her nightstand. Patrick sat on the edge of her bed, his favorite pipe clamped between his teeth.

"You must have gone a long way to sleep so hard, Julie." His voice was hushed as if he were afraid their peace was too frail to withstand more than a whisper. "Was it a bad place?"

Her heart lurched at the familiar question. He'd always asked her that when night terrors struck. "I was chasing rainbows."

He nodded in understanding. "The rainbows you can see in the dark are the best kind."

"Yes—" Noticing his clothing, she stopped in midstretch. "You're wearing green tights...and a green jerkin...and a green three-cornered hat." Her eyes narrowed on his green shoes with bells attached to the curled up pointed toes. "Aren't you?"

Standing, Patrick struck a comical pose. His eyes twinkling in pure mischief, he spoke in a lilting brogue. "Faith and don't I make a sight? Men at the fair will be chasing me to steal my gold and women will be wanting me body."

"What fair?" she asked suspiciously.

"The Renaissance Festival. Mugsy's Bar has the beer concession and I'm going to help him out." He held up his hand as Julia started to protest. "Now don't you go trying to spoil my fun. I've been looking forward to this all week."

"But, your heart—"

"My heart will give out when it's time no matter what I'm doing, Julie. I'm not going to stop living till then."

The phone rang before she could argue and Patrick smiled as if he'd personally arranged for the interruption. Frowning, Julia picked up the receiver. "Who on earth could be calling at eight-thirty on a Saturday morning?"

"Julia? Hello." A voice the texture of raw silk came through the line. Her breath solidified in her throat. Holding her hand over the mouthpiece, she coughed to clear away the obstruction. Her other hand jerked the covers up to her chin, yet she felt every part of her body warming in a rush of sensation. Julia averted her gaze from her father, who smiled whimsically at her reaction.

"Julia, are you there?"

"Yes. Who's calling please?" she croaked. She wasn't about to let him know she recognized his voice.

"Alex St. Ives," he answered with a dry amusement that told her he knew that she had already recognized his voice. "I apologize for calling so early, but I wanted to give you enough time—"

"Time for what?"

"There is a party tonight I wish to attend. Since I won't know anyone but the hostess, I'll need you to accompany me."

"Tonight?" Julia's mouth tightened. "It's not on the list you gave me Mr. St. Ives."

"Even so..." he responded smoothly. "It will be tedious if I have to attend alone."

"Then don't attend. Or better yet, have your hostess introduce you. I am not on twenty-four hour call," Julia said just as smoothly, though her nerves felt like sandpaper.

"We have an agreement, Julia. Are you reneging already?"

"That's a distinct possibility, Mr.—"

"Alex," he reminded her dryly.

"Our agreement did not include my asking 'how high' every time you tell me to jump, Alex." Hearing him sigh, her ear tingled as if his breath had touched it.

"I wasn't sure that I had told you to do anything, Julia. I've merely requested your companionship for a social evening."

"You could have fooled me."

"I didn't ask, did I?"

"No."

"Shall we hang up and begin again?"

A tiny smile tugged insistently at the corners of her mouth, "I'll save you the trouble. I can't go with you. I'm spending the day with my father."

Standing at the window with his back to her, Patrick stiffened.

"That shouldn't be a problem, Julia. We aren't expected until nine this evening. I'll pick you up at eight-thirty."

"No. I'll meet you there." Too late. She bit her tongue, exasperated. Panicking at the thought of him picking her up as if it was a date rather than a business arrangement, she'd agreed with her mouth wide open and her wits locked away. He'd done it again—darn him—and if his chuckle was anything to go by, he was feeling diabolically self-satisfied. How did he live with all that arrogance?

"I wouldn't think of it, Julia. I always escort a lady to and from her door."

Julia felt as if she'd just lowered the drawbridge and invited him in to plunder at will. She had no doubt that he was enough of a rogue to do a very thorough job of it, too. "Has anyone ever said no to you and made it stick?'' she asked irritably.

"Once or twice," he answered lightly after a short silence.

There was something in his voice that sent frissons of recognition through her, subtle, more subliminal than obvious. Something like vulnerability and anger, disillusionment and...yearning. Rubbing the bridge of her nose, Julia closed her eyes.

"Julia..." His voice startled her out of her thoughts. She shivered at the way he made her name sound like an endearment suitable for bedroom use only. Her hand tightened around the blankets she still held up to her chin. Her toes curled. His voice alone affected her composure like boiling water stirred into instant oatmeal.

"Julia," he repeated. "I'll see you this evening."

"Yes. All right."

"Enjoy your day, then : . . and Julia? I do apologize for being presumptuous."

The phone clicked in her ear before she could add highhanded and inconsiderate and irritating to the list. Dropping the receiver into its cradle, she acknowledged to herself that she was in big trouble.

Patrick turned to her with an insincere look of contrition. "I, ah, forgot to tell you that Alexander St. Ives called last night while you were taking a bath."

Without comment, Julia drank her tea.

"He seemed like a nice young man."

Nice? Alex? Only in his mother's dreams. And young? The look in his eyes came from experience, not youth. Straight-faced, Julia gazed at Patrick. "Forget it, Father. Alex St. Ives is not suitable 'beau' material." *Remember that, Julia.*

Averting his eyes, Patrick walked toward the door.

"Father...? Can I go to the festival without a costume?"

Patrick remained still as if he'd heard the anger he'd expected, then relaxed when he realized it wasn't anger he heard. "We'll get you rigged out there, Julie. One of the shopkeepers sells just the thing." Turning, he saw a smile on her face that made the air shine.

Chapter Four

It was appalling...infuriating...humiliating...

Alex paced the length of the wraparound porch, trying to appear calm, at ease, as if it was perfectly natural for him to park his car in a strange neighborhood for the sole purpose of taking the air on someone else's doorstep. Across the street, a woman kept peeking at him from behind her curtains as if she expected him to pillage the neighborhood and then burn it down. For the fifth or sixth time, a group of boys rode by on their bicycles to cast sidelong glances at his Rolls. "What's the matter, mister—you been stood up?"

Definitely humiliating.

As casually as he could, he sank onto an old-fashioned glider and slid over to a corner obscured by twilight shadows. If any other woman had done this to him, he knew he wouldn't have felt a tenth of his present irritation over the situation. Of course he was only speculating. He'd never been stood up before.

How long, he wondered, did one wait before accepting such an ignominious fate? He should simply write the whole thing off like a bad debt and go on to the next order of business. But, he couldn't bring himself to get into his car and drive away. Julia had affected him too strongly, touched him in a way unfamiliar to him. He needed to know why...and how.

Would he be as fascinated by her if she hadn't responded to him as if he were just another bully who needed to be shown the error of his ways? Was it arrogance compelling him to pursue her so vigorously and show her the error of *her* ways?

No, he decided, he wasn't that arrogant. But, he was a treasure hunter, specializing in the unique, the rare and the priceless. Once in a while, he would find something that literally hit him where he lived, something for which he felt an instant affinity and which made him forget everything else such as the Veil of Tears. Julia had made him forget the Veil....

Like the imperious clap of a haughty queen, the slam of a car door summoned his attention. A feminine voice, filled with humor, arrested him in the act of rising from the glider.

"It's all your fault," Julia accused a bandy-legged man wearing peculiar green clothes. "You talked me into buying all these dust catchers. And these clothes! I can't wear them in public."

Alex couldn't believe what he was hearing. The too serious, too stiff and formal Julia, *laughing?* He stood back, remaining in the shadows for a few moments of fascinated eavesdropping.

The green man opened the trunk of the car and pulled out more packages to add to the ones he and Julia were already carrying. "Julie darlin', you've been wearing them in public all day. Mugsy will be your slave for life if you'd wear that and draw beer for him on a regular basis."

Alex's eyebrows rose. *Julia, drawing beer?* It boggled the mind.

The streetlamp flared to life, illuminating Julia as if it were a spotlight. Alex stared, unable to believe what he was seeing. Julia, of the conservative, touch-me-not suit, dressed in frothy scarlet gauze? Her face was flushed. A garland of wildflowers and streaming ribbons sat askew on her tousled hair, hair that wasn't simply brown, but a rich honey color streaked with gold. He sucked in his breath as she turned toward the house. An elegant feather was painted on one side of her face and tantalizingly disappeared into the off-the-shoulder neckline of her lace-trimmed peasant blouse.

She looked like an elfin queen accompanied by a lepre-chaun.

Alex wondered what magic had brought the stone maiden to life.

"Who the devil are you?" the green man demanded from the top of the steps.

Julia stumbled behind him and her gaze flew from Alex to her watch and back again. "Oh ... I forgot."

"I'm flattered," he said as he sauntered to the steps and rescued the bundles from her precarious hold. His gaze snagged on the feather and traced its path downward. It suited her—the whimsy and the froth, the soft fabric and vivid color of her dress.

She snatched the garland off her head and tugged the elastic neckline upward, looking guilty, as if she'd commit-ted a sin only she knew about. "Have you been waiting long?"

The group of future Hell's Angels rode by again, hoot-ing and whistling and offering Alex advice with implied ob-scenities on how to handle "his woman." Noting Julia's blush, he couldn't resist flashing the boys a thumbs-up in acknowledgement and—he hoped—dismissal. They rode away with a final cheer for the supremacy of men. His mouth quirked. "I've been here long enough to make new friends," he answered.

Julia almost smiled. *Darn it!* Why couldn't Alex act like a stuffed shirt or the arrogant bully she'd accused him of being? Then she might have been justified in making some sarcastic comment. Instead, all she could do was offer him the apology he was entitled to. "I'm sorry," she said on a sigh.

"Think nothing of it, Julia. I'm becoming quite accus-tomed to having you take potshots at my ego."

"Oh ... you must be Alex." Patrick's face cleared of confusion as he extended his hand.

Alex's mouth twitched as he watched Julia over her fa-ther's head, his eyes twinkling. "I see my reputation pre-cedes me," he said.

Julia couldn't look away from Alex, much less marshal her defenses against his charm. Seeing in his expression self-mockery heavily laced with humor, she felt something soften, stir and grow warm inside herself. And, she felt something more dangerous than attraction and physical desire. Hormones that had run amok could just as quickly settle down again, but emotions had a longer attention span. In that moment, she genuinely *liked* Alex.

Patrick observed Alex and Julia watching each other, and smiled as he led the way into the house. "Time for a cup of tea, I think."

Julia didn't notice. Alex's look gathered her in like an embrace, slow and lazy, with lingering touches and intimate promises, as if he had all the time in the world and wasn't about to waste a minute of it looking anywhere else.

"Would anyone like a cup of tea?" Patrick asked. When he received no answer, he shook his head and disappeared into the kitchen.

"I'll go change." Julia's voice was husky as she tore her gaze away from Alex, and set her packages on the table in the foyer.

He raised his hand and lightly ran his forefinger along the delicate feather painting on her cheek. The tip of her nose was red from too much sun. He felt pure male satisfaction as he heard her shaky breath.

"Please don't," he whispered. Unguarded and flustered, this was, he suspected, the real person beneath the facade—the woman who couldn't resist adding brightly enameled dragons and butterflies to negate the somber clothing and tough exterior she wore to fool the world, and perhaps herself.

Julia froze, not daring to look at him, willing herself not to react to his seductive touch and gentle voice. Her body wasn't listening. Nor was her heart. His touch kindled fires in the pit of her stomach. His "please" undid her. One by one, he was stripping her of weapons with which to fight the desire, the liking, the need.

Alex smiled at her, a private smile, as if he were sharing a secret with her. "See, I said please."

"I noticed," she whispered back, then caught herself. In another minute he'd have her coming to heel like a faithful puppy. *Ridiculous.* Alex was only a man, charming, good-looking and cultivated—a hothouse Casanova. Pugnaciously, she lifted her chin. "How long did you have to practice?"

"Not long enough, obviously." His expression sobered as he trailed his finger from her jaw down her neck, following the line of gold paint. A few granules drifted down and glittered on her shoulder. "Shall I try again?"

"Not on my account," she shot back. "Why don't you just be yourself?" Without giving him a chance to answer, she turned and started to climb the stairs.

Alex had a sneaking suspicion that she meant her retort to be an insult. In fact, he was sure of it. "Julia," he called as she reached the third step. "Don't change." His eyes praised everything he saw. "Just be yourself."

His meaning hit her full force and she clenched her teeth at the pain of it. *What happened to the girl who dressed to match the flowers in my garden?* When he had said that, her father had been asking about his daughter, a person who still existed. She had the feeling that Alex was asking for the same person, yet more—a woman honest enough to be herself, and confident enough to let the world see her as she was. For the space of a heartbeat, she wanted to be that woman.

Silently, with her back straight and her eyes fixed on the landing at the top of the stairs, Julia continued her climb and entered her room.

The smell of pipe smoke followed by the sound of silver against china reached Alex just as Julia disappeared from view. Sighing, he joined Patrick in the living room.

With his pipe clamped between his teeth, Patrick narrowed his eyes. "Why do I have the feeling we've met before?"

To cover his hesitation, Alex gestured to the tea tray. "May I?" At Patrick's nod, he helped himself to a cup of tea before answering. "To my knowledge, we haven't met."

Patrick shrugged, a look of age and weariness on his face. "You're right. It would have to have been too long ago."

Alex knew Patrick had sensed familiarity because of his resemblance to Nicholas, and felt weighted down by the knowledge. So much deception. So many victims. It felt like quicksand—this trap of his own making. He had sealed his fate the minute he'd walked out of Julia's office without telling her the real reason he had sought her out. Instinct told him that if he did tell her, there would never be a chance to discover why he'd experienced that sense of imminence when he'd met her, or to find a way to stop feeling so strongly about a woman who had been a stranger to him a day ago. For the first time in his adult life, Alex felt completely at the mercy of fate.

Patrick stood at the fireplace, his back to Alex, smoke from his pipe billowing above his head. "It's hard, letting my daughter go." His shoulders heaved. "I don't think I'll ever get used to seeing her with a man."

Alex winced at the heaviness in Patrick's voice, at the pain of a man who struggled with the knowledge that his daughter had grown up without him. "Would you like references?" he asked lightly, wanting to ease the sorrow of lost moments, surprised that it mattered to him so much.

"No. It's too late for me to have any influence over the course of her life." Patrick watched Alex stroke the tiny ridges of a leaf-patterned bowl on the mantel. "That's ivory Belleek."

The small bowl was eggshell thin and cool to the touch. Alex held it reverently and turned it over in his palm. "Yes."

"Hold it up to the light and it's translucent. You can see how fragile it is. The slightest pressure can shatter it into a thousand tiny chips and grains of powder."

"Yes," Alex said carefully. "This is a unique piece, one of a kind and irreplaceable if broken." He met Patrick's gaze head-on.

"It has a flaw or two," Patrick said.

"That's what makes it special."

"And more vulnerable."

They stared at each other, taking each other's measure in character-inches, weighing their respective first impressions.

Alex felt the quicksand closing around him, pulling him down.

"I've been in prison for the last fifteen years," Patrick said casually as he watched Alex from the corner of his eye.

Startled at the ready admission, Alex met Patrick's gaze. Was this the rope that might pull him out of the mire? *Slowly, Alex. Don't dig yourself in any deeper.* He smiled and indicated Patrick's costume with a wave of his hand. "For stealing gold, no doubt."

Patrick nodded. "Among other things."

"And, like the leprechauns, did you hide your booty?" Alex asked, lightly, trying to reduce the subject to small talk.

"They got everything back." The pipe had gone out again and Patrick fussed with it, tapped ashes out of the bowl, refilled it, and lit it, hiding the lie behind a wall of smoke.

Everything? Alex wanted to ask, but, seeing Patrick's conspicuous frailty and exhaustion, he knew he couldn't pursue the subject. Neither could he confront Patrick with his lie, without first confirming his ability to withstand such a confrontation. *Grasping at straws to pull you out of quicksand, Alex?*

Anything to buy some time.

Alex replaced the bowl on the mantel. "I'm sorry, but I can't seem to find anything to say that isn't a cliché."

Patrick raised a foot to the hearthstone and propped his elbow on the mantel as he fixed Alex with a hard look. "I'm giving you a chance to get the hell out of here gracefully, without hurting Julie too much if what I've told you makes a difference."

"I fail to understand why it should."

"My point exactly," Patrick said. "But some people are too nearsighted to see beyond my prison record."

"My vision is excellent." Alex drained his cup and grimaced at the taste of the cool tea. Setting the cup back in its saucer, he pinned Patrick with a hard stare of his own. "Mr.

Devlin, if you are trying to scare me into leaving, you're wasting your time. I don't scare easily."

Patrick smiled broadly around his pipe. "Good...and the name is Paddy."

Alex felt himself sinking further into the mire.

JULIA HURRIED THROUGH her shower. Her heart wouldn't stop racing and deep inside herself she felt a tremor of restlessness, apprehension, excitement. Alex had been a real sneak, approaching on her emotional blind side and appealing to her heart and body, bypassing the protests lodged by her rational mind. His looks had nailed her to the floor when they'd met, but he'd really gotten under her skin with a sheepish apology, his ability to laugh at himself and a fleeting glimpse of vulnerability in his makeup. Even his faults seemed more like attributes.

The man scared her silly. Scott Richmond had broken her heart, but she'd mended and survived. A woman could bleed to death over Alexander St. Ives.

With a towel wrapped around her body, Julia scanned her closet for a garment suitable for the occasion. Unfortunately, she had nothing that remotely resembled armor plate. She reached for an evening version of the traditional business suit, conservative, well-made and about as sexy as a cardboard box. Something told her that was exactly what Alex expected. She could almost hear him laughing at her.

She had a mad urge to knock his socks off.

Surrendering to a latent sense of mischief, Julia dug into the boxes she had yet to unpack from her shopping spree of the day before. She had just the thing....

AS GRAND ENTRANCES WENT, hers wasn't bad, Julia thought. The curved staircase was a perfect prop. Draped loosely over her arm, her black silk cape trailed along each step as she descended. She kept her other hand on the bannister, her fingertips barely brushing the wood. To look at her, no one would have the slightest inkling that her stomach felt like a football field at halftime.

She felt Alex's eyes on her before she actually saw him.

Alex watched Julia descend the staircase—first her feet
shod in leather pumps, then her legs encased in a long, slim
black skirt, her torso draped in soft folds of fabric in a che-
mise line, skimming rather than hugging her body. He resisted the urge to lean over so he could see all of her at once.
Anticipation afforded its own stimulation, and he relished
every millisecond of her emergence more than a man
watching a skilled striptease. He was delighted at the way
she trailed her cape behind her like a forties movie queen.
Finally, she cleared the last three steps. *Oh, Julia,* he
thought, *you are so easy to read.*

Her silk gown was matte black, covering her from the
horizontal slash of neckline across her collarbone to the tops
of her black evening shoes. The dolman sleeves tapered
from the padded shoulders to her wrists. Her hair was ele-
gantly upswept, her makeup subtle, concentrating on her
eyes and drawing attention away from the peeling red spot
on her nose. Back was the woman who wore her image of
uncompromising reserve like a suit of armor, disguising—or
protecting?—the realities of Julia Devlin. She presented an
image designed to repel the most tenacious of men...unless
he'd seen glimpses of the girl who covertly fraternized with
leprechauns and drew beer for a man named Mugsy.

"Julie darlin', you look beautiful." Patrick blinked rapidly and pulled hard on his pipe.

"Thank you, Father." She kissed him on the cheek, then
handed Alex her wrap. His expression was cocky, arrogant.
She chose her moment well and flipped him a challenging
smile. *So smug, St. Ives, so positive that you know what's
going on.*

His eyebrows arched in surprise as she turned around to
slip her arms through the side openings of her cloak. The
gown, so conservative in the front, was blatantly seductive
in the back. Actually, from the waist up, there was no back.
It was a creation designed to flirt and reveal one thing while
inspiring speculation on another, to seduce the imagination
rather than the eyes, a creation as contradictory as the
woman wearing it.

Julia spoke to him over her shoulder with a bland expression on her face that had a hint of the diabolical around the edges. "You'll have to forgive me for taking so long, Alex."

Her wording wasn't lost on Alex. Provocatively, his gaze swept her from head to foot, lingering on the strand of pearls reversed to fall down her back, and the long slit of her skirt that revealed teasing glimpses of silk-clad legs. "Yes," he murmured thoughtfully. "I believe I must."

With that, all of Julia's planning came to a dead halt. What had she expected from Alex? An argument? Whatever she had expected, it hadn't been the sensation of being completely seduced by a single pass of his gaze over her body and five whispered words. In all her scheming, she really should have figured out how she was going to handle the rest of the evening.

"Are you ready?"

"Oh. Yes." She smiled brightly, first at Alex, then Patrick. "We won't be late, Father." She would see to it. Somehow.

"You're a big girl, Julie. No curfews. Just have fun."

No curfews. Didn't he know there never had been? Julia wondered. Her adolescence had been lived by a very loose set of rules—not because Aunt Chloe hadn't cared, but because she had the idea that Julia could take care of herself. By the time they'd both found out otherwise, it had almost been too late. Given her reactions to Alex, her ineptitude in dealing with him, Julia was beginning to question whether she'd learned anything from the past.

The walk out to the car was silent. Julia drew her arms inside her cape to avoid Alex's hand at her elbow.

He chuckled.

Gathering the cape around her as if it were a cocoon, she slid into the passenger side of the car.

Deliberately, he folded his topcoat over the back of the seat before getting in. "Nice night," he commented, challenging her efforts to lower the chill factor in the car. "It must be at least sixty degrees."

Julia stared straight ahead, responding with cool politeness. "I'm cold-blooded." *Don't be defensive, Julia.* The Rolls was a big car, yet she felt crowded, surrounded by Alex. He was sitting sideways, relaxed, as if he were settling in for a nice cosy chat. She pointedly looked at her watch.

"You are stunning," he whispered, his voice as seductive as his gaze.

"Thank you," Julia responded coolly. *Always be gracious, Julie,* Aunt Chloe had taught her. *Never argue with or ignore a compliment.* Normally she had an indifferent attitude toward compliments, but she was having a hard time ignoring the heat and pleasure turning her insides to mush.

Reluctantly, Alex started the car...switched on the lights...adjusted the mirror...checked for oncoming cars, then stared straight ahead without moving. "Julia," he said abruptly.

Julia pretended she hadn't heard. He was up to something. She just knew it.

Alex waited patiently in the tension that was as thick as San Francisco fog.

"What?" Julia finally snapped.

"Relax," he said deadpan as he shifted into first and pulled away from the curb. "You're as stiff as a whalebone corset."

Julia blinked.

"You might hyperventilate."

Her mouth twitched.

"You could have an attack of the vapors."

She averted her gaze to the window, not wanting him to know that he was getting to her. That would leave her wide open to the invasion of his charm, and she was determined to keep the drawbridge shut tight and firmly barred. A few sharks swimming in the moat wouldn't hurt, either.

Alex leaned over slightly and reached to open the glove compartment. His hand closed over a brown paper bag and pulled it out. "Will you close the glove box, please?" he asked politely.

Julia pushed the door shut. Paper rustled and, curious, she stole a glance out of the corner of her eye. Alex had turned the bag upside down. A small roll of breath mints dropped out. She couldn't help it. She just had to get a closer look.

Breath mints? For Alex? She gaped.

Glancing down, Alex picked up the roll of mints and slid them into his pocket. "Would you like one?"

"No, thank you ... *yours?*" It was hard to grasp—Alex St. Ives, the man who didn't even get marshmallow on his lip when he drank hot chocolate, feeling insecure enough to stop at a drugstore to buy breath mints. "Yours?" she repeated.

The car glided to a stop at a traffic light. Alex kept his eyes on the road. "Arrogance does have its limits, Julia."

Julia shut her mouth, trying to contain her chuckle. It was no use. A sputter escaped her, then a full-throated laugh.

"Are you sure you wouldn't like one?" he asked drolly. "You never know when you might need extra confidence."

The image of a television commercial showing a man and a woman embracing and kissing stopped her laughter as suddenly as it had begun. And then there was the magazine ad with the same man and woman, gazing at each other as she and Alex were doing now, their lips slightly open, moist ...

A light flashed. Julia swallowed and coughed. "Alex, the light is green," she said, dragging her gaze away from him.

A car pulled up behind them, honked, whipped around the Rolls, leaving them alone once more. She felt it then: an electric thrill at his touch; the sudden rush of warmth through her veins; the pressure of his fingers as he lifted her hand. His thumb caressed her knuckles, then his lips, brushing over them, stealing a little taste....

"You can go now." She couldn't stop the tremor in her voice.

Alex's mouth quirked as he shifted gears and accelerated. "I don't think so, Julia. Not yet."

Not yet? Julia snapped her head around to concentrate—hard—on the view outside her window. She didn't even try to pretend that she didn't understand what he meant. The man was too much...of everything. *Not yet.* Hah! Did he expect every woman that met him to fall over like a wooden duck at a shooting gallery? Unconsciously, she slid a little lower in her seat, propped her elbow on the armrest, and cupped her chin in her hand. Of course he did, she answered herself. She herself had given him no reason to believe otherwise.

There were never any sharks around when she needed them.

Music drifted through the car as Alex slipped a cassette into the tape deck and began humming along with a Tchaikovsky piano concerto. His fingers tapped on the steering wheel, and once in a while, his hand would lift and move as if he were conducting the orchestra. Clearly, he was through talking.

Oddly enough, she felt at ease with the silence—probably because when Alex's mind and vocal chords were occupied elsewhere, she could delude herself into believing that she was still in control of the situation.

Outside the window, signposts and landmarks went by. She hated this particular route. No matter how many times she took it, she always relived the ride fifteen years ago, the one through the city that had ended one way of life and had begun a new one.

A shiver ran up her spine. That drive had taken her through a security gate where admission was denied to all but a select few. In the few days after that, she'd learned all about alarms, armed guards, attack dogs, and locked fences. She couldn't help but think that she, too, had been thrust into prison, a tight, closed place where the outsiders were treated like criminals, and private property signs and thick walls isolated the individual Julia until she, like everyone else, became nothing more than part of an elite crowd.

Alex slowed and eased the car to a stop at a small gate house, spoke to the guard, waited while the guard checked a list attached to a clipboard and waved them on.

"I should have known," Julia muttered, as her gaze followed the lines of a structure that was more than a simple house, but fell just short of being a mansion, a familiar structure whose grounds bore the unmistakable stamp of her father's talent. It was a place as flamboyant and individualistic as its owner. "I really should have known."

Chapter Five

"If I were you, Alex, I'd avoid me like the plague."

Alex tried to look innocent. "You didn't ask."

"Yes, I did, but you were too busy humming along with the radio to hear me." Julia quelled a hysterical urge to laugh. The signs had been there. Why hadn't she paid attention?

She hadn't thought twice about Aunt Chloe's call that morning, announcing her unexpected arrival in the city. Julia's thoughts on Alex St. Ives had been kindly then. He'd given her a legitimate excuse to refuse Chloe's invitation to her impromptu party that evening. And though Aunt Chloe knew that her niece only attended social affairs when they might benefit her professionally, Julia had been feeling guilty about refusing. She truly loved her zany relative with the twenty-four carat heart. It was Chloe's life-style she couldn't handle.

Shaking her head, Julia lamented her lack of critical thinking. How obvious it had all been: Alex suddenly requiring a companion for an equally sudden party; his long-term friendship with Chloe; the absence of her aunt's usual arguments; the satisfaction in Chloe's voice when Julia had told her she already had an engagement for the evening... with Alex.

"You're surprised," Alex said as he opened her door and cupped her elbow to help her out of the car.

"Only for the first five seconds," she agreed. "No wonder you and Aunt Chloe get along so well. You're both sneaky—" His expression stopped her. He seemed surprised that she had been surprised. And then she remembered his waiting on the porch, and the taunts of the neighborhood boys. "You thought that I knew and was late on purpose?"

"Ah . . . no," he said as he tried to steer her up the walk.

Julia refused to budge, forcing him to look at her. "You thought I had stood you up."

"A thoroughly enlightening experience."

"So that's why we didn't see you at first. You were hiding."

"Julia, I wouldn't want you to leave me with any dignity," he said deadpan.

"Oh, I think you have enough to keep you going for a while."

"Shall we go in?" The pressure of his hand insisted that they move on. "Chloe has been waiting at the door since we drove up."

Chloe was indeed standing in the open doorway watching them, but Julia barely noticed. "You mean I would have been the first?"

Alex glanced sideways at her with a devilish grin.

Brilliant, Julia. "I mean the first to—"

"Destroy my innocence?"

Enough was enough. Julia didn't have the stamina to trade double entendres with him. This kind of teasing was too sophisticated for her and she was smart enough to realize it. "You know, you shouldn't use a word unless you know what it means."

"Innocence?"

"It can't possibly exist in your vocabulary, Alex."

"It did until I met you."

She absolutely refused to ask what he meant. Crying "uncle" seemed the better part of valor. "Give it a rest, Alex," she said irritably as they reached the door, and Aunt Chloe.

"Alex! You haven't lost your touch. And Julie! You've definitely lost yours, letting him railroad you into coming. And to think I almost put money on you, darling." Chloe, a small and top-heavy redheaded woman dressed in urban cowgirl sequins and leather presented her cheek to Alex and whispered, "Thanks, King. Usually, I have to make an appointment to see her."

"King?" Julia asked as she unfastened her cape. A gentle tug from behind slipped it off her shoulders. Cool air hit her back. A feather-light touch adjusted the strand of pearls and lingered, heating her skin.

"Anything for you, Rusty," Alex said.

"King?" Julia repeated. *"Rusty?"*

"Just a pet name, darling," Chloe said with a wink.

"Pets should be kept on a leash," Julia muttered.

"I heard that," Alex said mildly. "Chloe, tell her I'm tame."

"Only when faced with a whip and a chair," Chloe said absently as she fixed a critical eye on Julia. "Alex, go away while I hug my niece." She waved him away and opened her arms wide.

Automatically, Julia walked into Chloe's embrace. She hadn't known how much she'd missed her aunt until this moment, hadn't realized how very much she needed her until now. Chloe's hug was no less tight, no less needing. Julia understood. For a while, Chloe would forsake her life of spontaneous improvisation and take her place in the family circle. She would be there for Patrick, for Julia, and for herself. And then, she would take off in fast forward in an effort to leave her sorrow behind.

"Good grief, Julie…" Chloe's hand patted Julia's back. "You're showing some skin."

Sighing, Julia stepped back and silently swore that she would never, *ever again,* act impulsively.

"Turn around," Chloe ordered, then walked around Julia in a slow circle. "Alex not only hasn't lost his touch, but he's improved on it."

"What does Alex have to do with it?"

"Darling, you didn't wear that dress for them." Chloe pointed to her odd mixture of bohemian and ultra-high society guests. "You've been buttoned up to your chin for years, and you avoid my parties like I avoid my birthdays. I'd say Alex has a lot to do with it."

"Well, you know what they say, Aunt Chloe. The best defense is a good offense." Smiling brightly, Julia feigned interest in scanning the crowd for familiar faces, found a group of several people she knew, and sauntered off in their direction.

Alex met her halfway with a glass of champagne in his hand.

She barely broke her stride as she accepted it and spoke to him over her shoulder. "*Rusty* is waiting for you. I'll be—" she gestured vaguely to the room in general "—somewhere."

An hour into the party Julia realized she was enjoying herself. The champagne was excellent, the company lively and interesting. Aunt Chloe's decor was an icebreaker in itself. Only Chloe could mix Art Deco with antiques, oriental treasures and high-tech brass and glass and make it work. The wood and rice paper *shoji* screens that partitioned the rooms were thrown open. Two high-backed wooden chairs from China, heavily lacquered and inlaid with mother-of-pearl, sat on a raised dais like elegant thrones. Lacquered occasional tables from the thirties and forties were placed conveniently near a modern conversation pit and period chairs were scattered around the room. The walls held a mixture of everything from paintings bought at "starving artists' sales" to Japanese scrolls and a four-panel seascape by Gregg.

Julia easily deflected the advances of an aging Romeo and walked away with a silly smile on her face. His compliments had been trite, but nice just the same. She couldn't quite quench the high spirits left over from her day at the Renaissance Festival. Memories came to her like tentative touches on the shoulder. She hadn't always hated parties. Once upon a time, she had seen them as magical and exciting, times and places where anything could happen. The problem now was that too much was happening all at once.

No matter what she was doing or how much distance separated them, she couldn't concentrate on anything but Alex. Their gazes kept colliding across the crowded room. Like now. She could feel his attention. Looking up, she found his gaze on her, steady, intense. The room was much too warm. Her clothes felt heavy. The music from Chloe's fifties jukebox vibrated through her body. Alex's attentions were persistent reminders of her femininity. A soft and melting femininity.

She beat a hasty retreat to the powder room when she spotted Alex heading in her direction. Mercifully, it was empty. Mirrors paneled the walls, reflecting her own image from every conceivable angle. Flushed skin, sparkling eyes, lips curving upward in a smile that refused to go away. The powder room was like her life lately—no matter where she turned, she saw facets of herself that were better left hidden. Two days ago, she would have sworn she'd have better sense than to allow a man—any man—to get to her in this way. Now, all that was in the past. Two days ago. Before Alex. Before everything.

Her reserve seemed to be a little on the flawed side. The day had gotten to her—too much sun in a fantasy setting where everyone had been having a good time and letting it all hang out. For someone with no experience in hanging out, she had taken to it like a natural. But, believing herself a woman capable of handling the transient desires of a man like Alex was an entirely different matter. And he did desire her. The signals he kept sending her way were in a language every woman past puberty understood. She didn't know how to turn him off. She wasn't sure she wanted to.

When she returned to the party, she saw no sign of Alex and relaxed. Five minutes later, Alex's stare was again lighting fires along the exposed skin of her back and a few other unmentionable places. Those moonstone eyes of his were really doing strange things to her. She kept having the oddest feeling that they were the only two people in the world and there was a bright, juicy apple dangling right in front of her just begging to be devoured.

It was so much more difficult to fight herself than to fight Alex. She couldn't seem to convince herself that she was not attracted to him. The man was nothing more than a handsome face and sexy body. If she repeated that to herself often enough, she might even begin to believe it. Failing that, she could only hope that he was receiving the message more clearly than she was.

Evidently Alex was tuned into the wrong frequency. For whole minutes nothing happened—no vibrations, no tingles, no sudden bursts of heat. Then, it happened all at once.

"More champagne?" a deep, mellow voice whispered from behind her. Her breath tripped. She could feel the back of her neck turning red. Alex seemed to always be catching her by surprise in one way or another.

Composing herself, she turned to face him. "You really should wear a bell around your neck." Needing something to do with her hands, she accepted the glass he held out to her.

"You're falling down on the job."

"See how irresponsible I am?" Julia took a sip from her glass. The champagne went straight to her head. As Alex did.

"I see something else entirely."

Like what? she wanted to ask, but she had better sense. "I just had a wonderful idea, Alex. Aunt Chloe is going to be climbing the walls inside of two days. Why don't you have her help you with the gallery? She can certainly handle it."

"I don't want Chloe."

You have exactly what I want, Julia. Her heart pounded once, hard, then seemed to stop. Yesterday, in her office, he'd used that same tone of voice, intimate, seductive, confident, as if he knew something she didn't want him to know. This was getting too complicated for comfort.

"Then I suggest, Alex, that you be satisfied with what you already have or you might wind up with nothing at all."

With that, Julia handed him her glass, excused herself, and joined another group several feet away.

Alex found himself standing alone in the middle of the room with a glass in each hand. Was this what it was like to be a wallflower? he wondered as he followed her every move.

Her inventiveness in finding ways to avoid him hinted at a healthy, if repressed imagination. In fact, it was the repression that fascinated him the most. All those bits and pieces of Julia—so carefully tucked away—kept peeking around the edges of the image she projected, intriguing him, enticing him, a treasure waiting to be unearthed, claimed, enjoyed.

He smiled grimly. Her reflexes were good, but not quick enough to hide those little betrayals of her true reaction to him. Like now. She was flitting from person to person, with a fresh glass of champagne, and chatting with an animation that had to be exhausting. Suddenly she stilled, cocked her head, then glanced over her shoulder. With a lift of both glasses, Alex saluted her.

Julia caught his gesture, and slammed her glass down on the nearest table. Champagne was the last thing she needed. If Alex didn't stop stalking her, a sedative would be the first.

Exhausted, Julia sighed as she sank onto a sultan's couch covered with jewel-toned silk pillows and surrounded by plants. A patron of the arts had Alex pinned down with a monologue on his latest protegé. Aunt Chloe was holding court from one of the Chinese thrones. If she was lucky, Julia thought, she might have at least fifteen minutes of rest and relaxation. Slipping off her shoes, she tucked her feet under her, focused on the seascape and willed herself to think of nothing. An old recording of "Moonlight and Empty Arms" filled the air.

"Our song, Julia. Shall we dance?" She blinked drowsily. Alex filled her vision, speaking to her in a voice more felt than heard, like a stroke of breath on sensitive places. His hand on her elbow burned away years of coldness as he led her out onto the dimly lit patio. She didn't have time to protest as he effortlessly picked up the rhythm of the music and took her with him on a slow glide around the polished terrazzo floor.

Was there anything he wasn't good at? His right hand was properly placed at her waist, but his fingers were inside the boundaries of cloth, moving in barely perceptible circles over her exposed skin. She should have worn an asbestos jacket. His left hand held her right one in the prescribed fashion, but her fingers wanted to flirt with his. She was doing a credible job of keeping at least three inches of space between their bodies, yet that three inches of air felt palpable.

The music filled her, moved inside her. Instincts she'd exiled years ago were back, playing catch-up with a vengeance. It became more and more difficult to think first, react second. She had the uneasy feeling that she was about to burst into flames at any moment. Tingles and quivers and firecracker bursts of heat resurrected all sorts of fantasies. If she didn't do a better job of remembering why she'd become a coward, she was going to revert to being a fool. Again.

Alex held Julia as close as caution would allow, caressed her skin as much as he dared. He leaned back to look at her as he felt her stiffening, straightening, chilling. The ocean breezes were playing with her hair, drawing tendrils out of their restraints to flow around her face. Her expression was detached, a little sad. Shadows cast by the luminarias bordering the patio emphasized the strength and grace of her features. She looked like a warrior queen facing her greatest enemy, defying him, wordlessly asserting her refusal to be conquered.

Without realizing it, he verbalized his thoughts. "There are legends of an enchanted veil...gold mesh, studded with pearls to reflect the glow and heat of a woman's skin...a crown and veil in one, suggesting power and vulnerability at the same time...a headdress for a queen, barbaric and incredibly beautiful. It would suit you."

Fighting the hypnotic vision he evoked, Julia broke the spell before it gripped her too tightly. "Are you so accustomed to dressing your women?" she asked, then bit her tongue as another, more erotic vision filled her imagination: of candlelight and soft shadows; strong, masculine hands skimming the valley of her spine and over, up and down her sides, easing her gown forward and off her shoulders; his body guiding hers in an elemental dance; music building in the background to a stirring crescendo....

Chivalrously, Alex declined to comment. He'd seen her bite her tongue, seen the resignation as she closed her eyes and turned her head away in embarrassment. Though she hadn't uttered a sound, Alex cupped the back of her head and gently urged it to rest on his shoulder, and suddenly, her body relaxed against his, flowing, gliding with his. Contentment was an alien feeling for Alex, but he felt it then, as his sigh followed hers and he rested his chin on the crown of her head.

And he was inexplicably pleased to note that his mention of the Veil of Tears had meant nothing to Julia. It shocked him to realize that he'd rather not find the Veil at all than learn that she was just a good actress willingly participating in her father's schemes. Sometime between yesterday and today, his priorities had shifted. How much easier it would have been if he hadn't seen that core of softness in Julia that was slowly dying for lack of exposure. If only he hadn't related that vulnerability to his own.

"Julie, are these yours?" Chloe asked from the doorway. A pair of black leather pumps dangled from her fingers. Her gaze was on Alex, narrowed and eloquent. *I want to talk to you.*

Pulling away from Alex like a guilty teenager caught necking in a closet, Julia looked down at her feet. She'd done it again—let Alex catch her with her shoes off. Angling her chin upward, Julia squared her shoulders and marched sedately toward her aunt. She didn't try to put on her shoes there, in front of Alex, but kept right on walking through the crowd, down the hall and back into the powder room.

Indulgently, Chloe smiled after her niece. "That's my Julie—class all the way. She always leads with her pride while I always lead with my boobs." Sighing, Chloe glanced down at her voluptuous figure. "Oh well, if you've got it, flaunt it." With a typically Chloe change of mood, she traded nonsense for her you-can't-put-anything-over-on-me disposition. "Ten minutes, Alex. In the library."

Alex's eyebrows rose as Chloe made her exit. Only Chloe talked to him that way. Only Chloe could make him listen and comply. He respected her too much to do otherwise. Ten minutes. Usually it was only five—Chloe's way of making a person sweat before she revealed the formidable woman beneath the ditsy behavior. Of course he knew what—or who—she wanted to talk about. He'd known the minute he'd seen her standing on the patio watching him and Julia that she was in protective overdrive. Ten minutes. Was it, he wondered, long enough to come up with some answers that made sense? Not likely. Flicking open the button to his jacket, Alex put his hands in his pockets to keep himself from loosening his tie. Ten minutes was just long enough to stroll through the garden and work up a good sweat.

SHUTTING THE LIBRARY DOOR behind the maid who had delivered a tray of coffee, Chloe poured herself a cup. She hadn't had anything alcoholic to drink, but she was jet-lagged and emotionally run-down. No matter how fast she lived or how many times she moved, she just couldn't seem to keep one step ahead of life anymore. In fact, her life was becoming more and more of a caricature lately, exaggerated and mocking.

The room smelled of old leather and antique furniture and polished wood. She could almost smell the smoke from her late husband's customary Saturday night cigar. With cup in hand, Chloe walked around the library, pausing here and there to read the title of a book. Every one of them was a collector's item, classics, leather bound, rare. The collection had been Robert's pride and joy and she just hadn't been able to part with it. She'd never read even one of them. Her tastes ran to paperback potboilers and, once in a while, romances—just to remind herself of what it had been like, before the disillusionment and the weariness.

She didn't mind that people called her eccentric and she never lost her temper—in public. She and Alex were alike in that way, not trusting anyone to understand their pain so they kept it private and walked through their own personal hells alone.

Like when she'd kicked the bottle.

No one had known that she'd had a three-year love affair with booze after Robert, her third husband, had died. They wouldn't have cared any more than they would have understood why she'd dried out when Julie had come to live with her. She hadn't known Alex then, but when Julie had left to make her own way, Alex had been there, a new friend who understood and cared. She'd fallen off the wagon, hard. Alex had locked himself up with her, held her hands when they shook, held her head when she'd been sick, held her down when she'd gone crazy, and held her together when she hadn't cared whether she fell apart or not. Alex, her friend. Julie, the daughter she'd inherited, and loved, and cried for...in private. Both of them had validated her, made her count for something.

She had been carefully observing Alex and Julia and was alarmed by the obvious attraction between them. They were like two stripped wires coming together. Sparks flew, excitement crackled between them, and it was easy to imagine lightning striking in the same place over and over again. Chloe had never seen Julia so tense or so seductive. Around Alex, her movements were soft, feminine, aware of every nuance of his presence. And, Alex—she'd never seen him so charged and restless. Not Alex, who had earned his reputation for ''cool'' in the toughest and biggest poker games in the world.

Chloe checked her watch and grimaced. Five minutes to go. She should have known that her ''bait and wait'' strategy would fail this time. This time, the problem hit her where she lived. Julie had too much experience with heartbreak. Alex hadn't had any experience with love. After Alex's call, she'd started to worry. She'd caught the next plane out of St. Croix and literally thrown together this party just so she could have a better look at what was going on.

By the time Alex arrived, Chloe was on her third cup of coffee. He didn't bother to knock. With an expression of polite interest, he wordlessly crossed the room to lean back against the old library table.

Chloe confronted him with all the subtlety of a flame-thrower. "I didn't have the sense to worry until after you called me, Alex. When I tried to reach you through your London office, I found out that you've taken up residence at the Alexander estate. Another call confirmed that Gregori Petrov is still running things out there so it's unlikely you don't know about my brother." Chloe didn't bother beating around the bush with Alex. "This whole thing stinks of calculation. What are you after?"

"A new gallery," Alex replied blandly.

Chloe's look would have sent a lesser man running to the nearest air raid shelter. For all her sultry looks and ditsy behavior, she could level buildings when it came to protecting her own. Until now, he'd considered himself to be one of that elite group—a stray she'd adopted, like Julia.

"Don't put on your poker face for me, Alex. You might be good, but I've played and lost more games than you have. And you learn a hell of a lot more by losing. You might as well show your cards now and tell me why my niece is part of the ante."

"I'm not out to hurt your family, Chloe."

Neither Alex's statement nor the signs of conflict that briefly flickered across his face reassured her. "I know you Alex. You never turn down a challenge and you can't resist a dare. Julie is both to a man like you. You use women. They know it, don't care, and use you back. There's nothing wrong with that as long as both parties are willing, accept the rules of the game, and can afford to lose. Julie isn't, won't and can't. She's been used enough."

Alex didn't need names, dates, places. He had a good idea of what Julia had been through. At an age, which was painful at best, Julia had lost her father under the worst possible circumstances and had been given over into Chloe's loving but haphazard care. To a certain extent, he could empathize with what it had been like for Julia. He could imagine what a target a woman like Julia would have presented to opportunists who rode through life on other people's coattails. How many had seen her as the way to get to Chloe's wealth?

He had been weaned by those who wanted to use him for their own ends. The result had been his refusal to be a victim or, the other side of the coin, a user. In her own way, Julia had done the same. But, she was more vulnerable and less cynical than he was, and more defensive, less willing to trust. He was fully armed against living in the modern world. Julia, he suspected, didn't trust her defenses enough to take her chances on what life had to offer.

As if she had read his mind, Chloe broke the silence. "Alex, your scars are just that—scars. Julie is still bleeding, especially now," she said quietly.

"Chloe, I am not in the habit of taking advantage of women and you know it, so why don't you say exactly what you mean and save me the trouble of having to interpret what you say."

"I'll engrave it in stone if you like," Chloe snapped. "Julie's experiences with men have been brutal, thanks to me and Paddy. Damn it, Alex, if you don't plan to take Julie seriously, then please don't take her at all."

"I can't imagine any man not taking Julia seriously," Alex responded gravely.

Chloe believed him, and had the odd feeling that Julia wasn't the only one who was vulnerable. Still, she couldn't help but worry. "What exactly are you looking for?"

He gave a short bark of mirthless laughter. "I'll have to let you know, Chloe."

Distressed, Chloe stared out of the French windows. It rocked her world to see the uncertainty, the rawness in his expression. He was strong and always so damn sure about what was right and honest. He was the best man she'd ever known, but that didn't mean he was the best man for Julie.

Chloe turned back to him, abruptly, before she could change her mind. It was so hard taking sides between two of the three people she loved most in the world. She'd forgotten how much Alex *needed*. He was standing there, patiently, with some unnamed conflict betraying the chinks in his armor. Placing her hands on her hips, she spoke quickly, before she could talk herself into walking away. "Okay, Alex. You won't use Julie. I can see that."

"But...?" he asked, resigned to either alternative, lying or telling her the truth.

"But..." Chloe nodded. "There are still five too many coincidences here. When you set out to meet Julie, you had something on your mind other than..." She threw up her hands.

"Being enchanted?"

Chloe blinked. "Is that what they're calling it nowadays?"

"The term fits the occasion." Pushing away from the library table, Alex helped himself to a snifter of brandy from the cabinet against the wall.

Angry now, Chloe began pacing and using her hands as she talked. "If you're trying to tell me you're a victim of love at first sight, forget it. You're not the type and you're not that spontaneous with your emotions."

Alex didn't believe love was that selective, but he wasn't going to argue the point with Chloe. The brandy swirled in his glass as he stared at the lights reflected in the amber liquid.

"You're in big trouble, King."

Poker-faced, Alex appreciatively sniffed the brandy and drank as if nothing but small talk was passing between them, certainly nothing that required a response. Once again, he became the man people expected him to be rather than the man he really was.

Stopping in front of him, Chloe gave him a direct stare. "There's something else going on here besides love in bloom."

His eyebrows rose.

"I'm not going to get another thing out of you, am I?"

Alex emptied his glass.

Clearly exasperated, Chloe sighed. "Okay, I'm going to keep trusting you, Alex... for a while."

The warning was implicit and stayed with Alex long after Chloe had stalked out of the room. His snifter was empty, the library was silent, and he was chasing circles around himself by thinking too much. A sensualist by nature, Alex knew when to take his cues from instinct and human nature. His senses inevitably led him to Julia.

Alex almost missed her. He'd searched the nooks and crannies for her, expecting her to be curled up somewhere to avoid the noise and the crush. Instead, he found her sitting side by side with Chloe on the twin Chinese thrones. It caught his fancy—the contrasts and the similarities between the two women, though they shared not a single physical characteristic. Chloe had a leather-encased leg thrown over the arm of her chair. Julia's knees were together, her back straight. Chloe was animated and her eyes sparkled while Julia's smile was mellow and a little absent, her eyes drowsy and soft. Leaning his shoulder against the wall, Alex watched broodingly as Julia fought exhaustion. Her head nodded, jerked up, then nodded again. The arms of her chair supported her elbows and her hands were relaxed in her lap.

In that moment, Alex noticed the little things: her lipstick was worn off and her blusher had faded; tendrils of hair had come loose and were lying against her cheek; small runs began on the bottom of her stockings and disappeared beneath the hem of her dress—from dancing barefoot, no doubt. Her eyelids drifted shut again. It was time to take the lady home.

"Alex," Chloe said as he approached the dais. "Will you please get Julie out of here before everyone gets the idea that my parties are boring?"

Julia stiffened at the sight of him. There was nothing wrong with her response time, he noted wryly. The starch might have gone out of her, but the whalebone was still there. Without a word to him, she bent and kissed Chloe's cheek and said her goodbyes.

Chloe waved them toward the door and rejoined the conversation going on around her.

The night was damp and foggy, the car warm and cozy. Alex gave up on making small talk and pushed a cassette into the tape deck. Julia had answered his every attempt at conversation with monosyllables, her well-frosted voice making it obvious that she had convinced herself that nothing had happened between them, no awareness, no lapses into vulnerability, no magic.

Determined to reduce all that conviction to dust, Alex flashed her an intimate smile. "Would you like some toothpicks to prop your eyes open?" he asked politely.

She kept her gaze locked on the view outside the windshield, her eyes wide and unblinking. "No thank you."

Exasperated, he shook his head. "Julia, you can go to sleep if you want. I'm much too busy driving through this pea soup to engage in an attack on your person."

An attack was the last thing Julia was worried about. She knew how to defend herself against unwanted physical advances. It was his assault on her emotions that had her digging in for a long siege. "Thanks for the reassurance," she said, her tone dry, her expression as straight as a Kansas highway. "I really was worried about that."

Now that he had mentioned it, she began to notice the coziness of the car, the sense of isolation created by the fog, the other-worldly quality of the deserted, fog-enshrouded streets. Her body couldn't decide whether to be relaxed or excited. The music stirred up embers. Alex's nearness fanned flames deep inside her. She wanted to shed her cape, curl up on the seat, lay her hand on his thigh. At the same time, she wanted to shout at him to hurry so she could shut the door, block him out, escape unscathed from a night of pure folly.

Well, relatively unscathed.

She breathed a sigh of relief when they finally turned down her street. Relief didn't stand a chance against suspicion when she noted that he had pulled up into the driveway instead of parking in the street as if he planned to stay for a while.

Chill, damp air hit her as Alex opened her door and held out his hand to help her out of the car. His palm was warm and dry, his grip firm. Suddenly the fog felt like an electric blanket. She stood there, refusing to move one inch closer to the house as long as he was still attached to her hand.

"Well!" she said brightly. "Thank you for everything...." Her voice trailed off at the end. He was giving her that look again, a look that burned through fog and layers of pretensions with equal intensity. It made her feel naked—not bare skin, but bare soul—and she didn't like it one bit. In desperation, she marched toward the porch, not caring if she dragged Alex along behind her or not.

He fell into step beside her.

Under the soft yellow light beside the door, Julia delivered a brisk good-night and a tepid handshake. As soon as he released her hand, she fumbled in her purse for her keys. She was almost home free. But not quite. She felt his nearness before she looked up.

Alex had raised his arms, placed his palms flat against the door, one on either side of her, holding her close, yet not touching her. Her breath caught and held. Julia watched him advance, her gaze locked to his. Everything, from the moment she'd looked up to see him standing in the doorway of her office, had been leading up to this moment. Every fantasy she'd ever had flashed before her eyes and they had his name on them.

With maddening slowness, Alex lowered his head, his lips barely brushing hers, teasing her with the promise of a kiss. She wanted him to keep that promise.

He hovered for a timeless second, waiting for her denial, pleased when it didn't come. He would have been hard-pressed to honor it. She was like the brandy he'd drunk earlier, filling his head with her essence, heating his blood with her taste. Intended to be gentle and brief, the kiss became more, intoxicating, stimulating. His hands cradled her head. His thumbs caressed her cheeks. The very air around them seemed effervescent, alive.

Julia clenched her hands against the need to wind her arms around him, hold him, touch him. Her mouth opened under his. Unconsciously, she bent her knee to rub her foot against her calf. She felt a distinct purr coming on.

Her shoe slid off her foot and landed with a clatter on the wood floor of the porch. Startled, she swallowed the whimper in her throat and jerked away. The door met her back. Alex stilled, but did not move away. She couldn't meet his gaze, knowing that if she did, he would see too much in her eyes—her desire, her need, the dreams he'd resurrected in so short a time. And, he would see that she would not resist his touch. She didn't want to resist.

Alex crooked his finger under chin, urging her head up. Her eyelids lowered. "Coward," he accused her softly and kissed the tip of her nose.

"Yes, I am," Julia replied just as softly.

Disarmed, Alex awarded her full marks for being able to resist what he clearly couldn't and admitting so frankly to her fears. Did she think that would end things between them? Her admission encouraged him, egged him on. If she could be honest about her vulnerability, she could be honest about her feelings.

He stepped back and bent to retrieve her shoe. His fingers stroked her arch as he slipped it onto her foot. Her toes curled, impeding his progress, giving him the perfect excuse to caress her toes and gently straighten them out. Rising, he saw that she had won the struggle with her composure.

"Good night, Alex." Her voice was firm, final.

He shook his head. "Julia, we can't start at the end. We'd both spend the rest of our lives wondering what we'd missed." Not giving her time to argue, which she was clearly gearing up to do, Alex tucked a stray lock of her hair behind her ear and walked away.

By the time he had cleared the steps, the fog had faded him out as if he had been a dream. The sound of him walking away was muffled, wispy. Julia felt as if she'd stumbled into a fairy tale and Prince Charming had taken her to the ball. It was midnight and she should be seeing pumpkins and mice. Instead, she saw nothing but Alex as he'd been yesterday in her office, lounging in a doorway, daring her to cross an invisible line on the floor.

She opened the front door and drifted across the foyer, up the stairs, into her bedroom. The lingering memory of his kiss had the bittersweet taste of regret. She'd more than liked the kiss. In spite of herself, she more than liked the man. If only she didn't have so many other memories reminding her that happy endings were only make-believe.

Chapter Six

"Good morning, Dina." Julia's voice was no-nonsense brisk as she strode into her office at a determined pace. "Do I smell coffee? Good. How does my schedule look for to-day?" She whipped the appointment book around to read it herself.

Dina gaped at Julia's suit, a conservative black skirt with a vivid red jacket that had a sassy V-neck, tucked-in waist and flirty peplum.

"No appointments? Good. Don't schedule any. Has the realtor called, yet?" Julia reached for the pink telephone message slip her secretary held out to her. "Oh, wonderful! She's found something." Dina handed her a packet of in-formation on the property.

"She sent this by courier? That was fast work. I just talked to her an hour ago."

"No," Dina said. "She dropped it off herself—said she had an unbreakable appointment with her divorce lawyer, but she'd meet you at the location as soon as she could. Here are the keys."

"Good. This will certainly speed things up. I may be out most of the day." Julia dropped the keys into her purse and ripped open the envelope as she pushed away from the desk.

"Julie?"

"Hmm?"

"I like the duds."

"Huh? Oh, thanks. You know, Dina, this property has real possibilities." Absently, Julia swept off her hat, a glamorous wide-brimmed black straw trimmed with a red silk rose.

"Good," Dina said dryly.

"I'll be in my office. No calls, please," Julia said as she breezed through the door, and tossed the hat on the credenza. She made a spot check of her makeup in the bathroom mirror. The suit was nice, the V not too high, not too low, and the chunky red and black jewelry really added pizzazz. She'd felt great ever since she'd seen herself in the mirror at home. Amazing what new clothes could do for a woman's confidence. There was armor, and then there was silk, perfume and good jewelry. The latter definitely gave her a greater feeling of power and control, and oddly enough, protection.

If she was going to make a fool of herself with Alex, then she ought to look her best.

It was wonderful how much difference a little time and distance could make. It put things into perspective, made life's little problems seem just that—little, easily solved. She'd spent all day Sunday convincing herself that Alex wasn't really the perfect date or the ideal man. He had faults, his arrogance, for example. And he had weaknesses: hot chocolate and marshmallows, raw silk and bare skin.

Such a man would spend his life looking on the other side of the fence for something better than what he already had. If she remembered that, she'd be fine. It shouldn't be too hard. She'd been around more than one block. Alex wasn't any different; his landscaping was just more attractive than most.

By Monday morning she'd managed to convince herself that her dreams weren't overlapping into the daytime. Dreams belonged behind closed eyelids, in the dark. All night long, for two nights, the campfires he'd set everywhere he'd touched her were still burning bright, illuminating those dreams. During the day, sanity prevailed over hormones. She'd made her bed and, for three months, she would have to lie in it. As long as she didn't wind up in Alex's bed, everything would be fine.

"Fine!" Julia said to her image in the mirror.

"Julie. Coffee and rolls," Dina said as she pushed the door open with her hip. The tray she carried was loaded with an insulated pot, two mugs, and a plate of petite pastries.

Dina set the tray down, poured both of them a mug of coffee and sat in the chair alongside Julia's desk. "Okay, how was it, Julie?"

"How was what?"

"Chloe's party. Alexander St. Ives. Saturday night. Your weekend in general. All of the above?"

Julia drank from her mug as she flipped through the real estate folder. "The same, exhausting, better than I expected, productive, and not necessarily in that order." Let her nosy secretary figure that out. "Who told you?"

"Alex called just before quitting time Friday—wanted your home number," Dina said between bites. "Naturally, I had to know why."

"Naturally."

"Then, Chloe called to invite me and Will to her party, but we had a house full of teenagers. I have to hand it to her—she doesn't discriminate between the idle rich and the working poor."

A light on the telephone blinked and Julia grabbed for it just as Dina reached over to answer it. Shrugging, Dina added NutraSweet to her mug, helped herself to a slice of cream cheese crumb cake and waved as she returned to her desk.

Julia took a deep breath before bringing the receiver to her ear. "Image Design . . . yes, hello Alex. I did call earlier . . ." She pulled off an earring and shifted the receiver to her other ear. "Can we meet? There's a property I think you should see . . . yes, an hour." She gave him the address, quickly said goodbye and hung up the phone. There! That had been easy. She was herself again and Alex—well, he was just a client.

THE RENOVATED UPTOWN MANSION was perfect and unmistakably "San Francisco," the structure predating the earthquake and fire of 1906. According to a whimsical note in the file, ghosts had been sighted roaming the halls for twenty years. Wondering if Alex was superstitious, Julia wandered around the old mansion, making notes about possible changes and complementing decor.

The air smelled musty, damp; everything looked gray and lifeless under a thick coat of dust. Her footsteps echoed back at her from every room, like the rattling of old bones. The walls and floors were bare, the rooms stripped of their identity, giving the old mansion a feeling of emptiness and suspension, like a lost soul waiting for a heart to bring it to life.

A loud crash made her jump. A high whine seemed to come from all the rooms at once... and gusts of cold air... and little dust devils whirling up from the floors.

Of course, Julia knew there had to be a rational explanation; perhaps it was wind blowing through the chimneys, doors slamming, poor housekeeping. Rational explanations didn't help. Her breath stalled in her throat. Goose bumps raised on her skin. She didn't know about Alex, but as of now, *she* was definitely superstitious.

And scared—too scared to move. All her blood seemed to have frozen and dropped into her feet, making them impossible to lift. She felt as if she were being watched from every corner, every crack and mouse hole. Everything dimmed at once. It had to be the sun sliding behind a cloud. It had to be.

Clutching the folder to her chest, Julia shuffled backward, toward the door. She wanted to scream, but her vocal cords refused to work. Something stopped her, something solid, large, unyielding, with two large hands— they had to be hands—gripping her arms. Did ghosts have a grip? As far as she knew, if they breathed at all, it was bone-deep chilling. But what she felt at her ear was warm... very warm. Her back connected with something solid and bigger than a bread box. She smelled mint.

"Ouch!"

Ouch?

"Julia, don't move anything but your foot," a wicked voice whispered in her ear. She knew that voice. It was the one that had been haunting her dreams for the past two days.

Fright quickly turned to relief. Spinning around, Julia found herself body to body with Alex. His smile was as wicked as his voice. His body was sending unmistakable signals to hers. Awareness was like a narcotic, turning her muscles to air.

Alex's smile dropped as soon as he saw her face. "Julia? What is it? You're as white as a sheet." He enveloped her hands in his to stop their sudden trembling.

Julia closed her eyes and shook her head. "A ghost." She sagged against him, just for a second, a minute. It felt good, being held this way, nothing sexual or threatening about the embrace, nothing to demand or frighten. His arms were tight around her with a gentle fierceness, protective, comforting. It had been so long since she'd been held against a body stronger than her own, strong enough to slay dragons and willing to do so...for her. She could hear it in his voice, feel it in the movement of his chin on her head as he scanned the room for possible dangers.

"All right, Julia, you're as white as a ghost. Why?"

She had to move away from Alex—now—before she wrapped her arms around his waist and never let go. Inside she felt incredibly soft and vulnerable. Suddenly, she wanted more than his gentleness and comfort, a different kind of pleasure. She wanted to break into a million tiny pieces, crumble at his feet, show him the softness, trust him with the vulnerability and the need . . . such a need to have someone to lean on once in a while, someone who didn't care that she wasn't rich or beautiful, or that her past was colored in shades of gray.

But it was a foolish thought, a weakness of the moment, not at all characteristic of her. She raised her head to look at him, angling her upper body away from his, and forced a light smile. "A silly thing. The place is supposed to be haunted and I overreacted to the usual creaks and groans of an old building.''

Alex regretted the change in her. It had been good to be needed, even for the purpose of warding off imaginary spirits. Such a simple thing, yet it had made him feel as if he were somehow *more*. Others had needed him in one way or another, but this time was different, special. This time it had been Julia, who always made such a point of not needing. He was beginning to understand how much he wanted from her, how much he wanted to give. All his needs were suddenly centered on Julia. Elusive dreams were taking form. Julia's form.

It wasn't supposed to happen this fast or be so overwhelming. He hadn't expected to feel this certain, no questions, no doubts, no arguments. He knew what he felt, accepted it. His imagination had spent years playing tricks on him, telling him what ''the'' woman would be like. He'd thought it would happen gradually when he found her, a kind of growing on one another. Julia didn't match his fantasies, yet she'd grown on him instantly.

Julia, he noted, was panic-stricken, and not by the possibility of ghosts in the vicinity. Her expression was haunted as she pushed away from him and her frantic gaze was everywhere but on him.

He hated it—knowing that Julia's past experiences were not kind ones, that his attentions caused such anxiety. What would it take to convince her that history didn't always repeat itself?

His voice deliberately light, Alex took her arm and guided her out of the room. ''Tell me about the ghosts. I have a fascination for old legends.''

''Oh, these are quite ordinary, noting to compare with enchanted veils and royalty in long-ago times.'' She sensed a sudden tension in him and looked up at his face. What had she said to make him stare at her so oddly?

Alex reminded himself that he had mentioned the Veil to her. There was no reason to suspect that she knew more than what he'd told her. There was every reason to tell her more. He didn't like deception, by omission or otherwise, no matter how well-intentioned. Those good intentions could very well lead him to hell.

He heard Julia talking—very fast—about the mansion, its good points and drawbacks, the price, the layout, ideas for restoration. He couldn't care less. His mind had already been made up when he'd first walked through the building.

"Julia," he said abruptly.

Her step faltered, then she turned toward him, her expression one of cool, professional interest, her gaze directed at the air beyond his left ear. She was taking little steps backward, as if she were trying to sneak away. "Of course, you really need to talk to the realtor, Alex," she continued as if he hadn't interrupted her. "But, I think this really has possibilities. The structure is sound—I have a report right here. It will need very little in the way of renovation and the price is good, though you can probably offer less and get away with it. Evidently the ghost stories have scared off several buyers."

"Ghosts can be dealt with, Julia." He paused and gave a crooked little smile. "I promise."

Julia wondered what Alex could possibly know about ghosts. What bitter experiences qualified him to make such a claim? A business deal that got away? It was difficult to imagine that this self-assured, successful man might have painful memories. And, knowing about them would involve her too intimately in his life. Still, she was tempted to take him at his word, to share with him, to pin too many dreams on that sharing, and on his promise, a promise that offered too much hope. "Well, I don't think you'll have to worry about it, Alex. If there are any ghoulies here, I have the feeling that they're just lonely and depressed."

Bemused, Alex cocked his head, as if to listen. "Ah. *The lonely one offers his hand quickly to whomever he encounters.* They're just rattling their chains because they're hungry for signs of life." He nodded. "I think you're right. We'll have to see that their hands are never slapped away."

The lump in her throat kept Julia from speaking. She pivoted and walked to a window, her eyes blinking furiously. Darn it! Alex was getting to her again. Just then, she recognized in him a wisdom that came from experiencing too much too young. Who, she wondered, had slapped his hands away? She cleared her throat and made the effort to speak lightly. "The quotation—I take it you've studied Nietzsche."

"Not studied. I *attempted* to read him during my 'intellectual' phase in high school. I was trying to impress a girl who was reading Colette."

Kindred spirits? Julia wanted to ask. Lonely people often found companionship in books. She knew all too well the comfort of reading about emotions and knowing that someone, at sometime had understood. It was so much easier to cry over a printed page than it was to cry on someone's shoulder. And, it was so much safer. "So what were you really interested in, besides the girl?"

"Doc Savage, The Man of Bronze. I had my hair in a crew cut, lifted weights, and went through gallons of artificial tanning lotion trying to look like him. My mother was appalled," Alex said, smiling easily. "And you?"

Julia couldn't help but smile back. "I traded Nietzsche for a Chilton auto repair manual to impress the son of a race car driver."

"Did you?"

She shook her head. "I would have been better off reading *Jack The Ripper*. He now produces horror movies." Sunshine and a spring breeze caught her by surprise. They were outside and headed toward Alex's car. "Alex, we're supposed to meet the realtor here."

"We'll call her from the car and arrange an appointment."

"All right." Julia held out a business card. "Here's her number. Let me know what you decide." She felt like the rope in a tug-of-war, torn between wanting to prolong the moment and hear more about Alex St. Ives, ordinary person, and wanting to make a quick getaway before she did exactly that.

Alex steered her toward his car. "Lunch first, I think. Then we can meet with the realtor."

This Alex—arrogant and presumptuous—was easier to resist, easier to walk away from. Julia dug in her heels. "Oh, I'm sorry, Alex, but I can't. Dina rearranged my morning schedule so I could meet you here. It will take all afternoon to make up for it."

"Are you always going to refuse my invitations?"

"Invitation? Now that's an interesting concept," she shot back. "You might try it sometime, Alex."

Intent on his purpose, Alex let her comment go over his head. "Julia, we need to talk." He watched Julia back away. Perhaps he should try a different approach. *You see, Julia, there's this lie weighing on my conscience.* But Julia wasn't in a listening mood. She had a remarkable talent for making quick exits.

"Call me after you've settled things with the realtor. Enjoy your lunch." Julie threw him a parting smile and made a beeline for her car. She had the engine going before her door was even shut all the way. It surprised him that she hadn't rolled up the windows, locked her door, and held up a cross to ward him off.

Frustrated, he climbed into his own car and stared into space. Was it relief he felt at having her foil his plans? His good intentions were fine, except he couldn't decide what they were. Where was his skill at hard, on-the-spot decision making?

Starting his car, Alex drove halfway up the driveway and stopped. Since Lady Luck had obviously jilted him, there was only one thing he could do. He placed a call on the cellular phone as he watched Julia's car disappear through the gates. Thirty-six seemed a damned odd time to start asking for advice on his personal life, yet he was about to do just that.

Julia waved and drove out the gate before she could change her mind. She wanted to change her mind and therein lay the real danger—herself, not Alex. So much for courage and new resolutions but, darn it, some resolutions should be worked up to gradually. Obviously it was going to take longer than a weekend to convince herself that she wasn't attracted to Alex, and didn't even really like him.

First, of course, she would have to start believing her own lies.

Alex hadn't tried too hard to persuade her to have lunch with him. Her brakes grabbed the road as she slammed the car a little too forcefully into her parking space. Maybe he was losing interest. The thought depressed her when she should have been sighing with relief.

Alex made rainbows seem close enough to touch, the pot of gold within sight, dreams more than soft whispers in the night. As she entered the privacy of her office, Julia made a sound of impatience. She knew for a fact that, while rainbows might be visible and dreams might seem close, they were also forever out of reach.

Deciding to treat herself and Aunt Chloe to an extravagant lunch, she picked up the phone. A few seconds later, she hung it up again. Chloe had just left for a luncheon engagement.

In defiance of her sudden need for companionship, Julia made a reservation for herself at an elegant restaurant nearby. She'd never minded eating alone before, yet the minute she sat down at the banquette, she wondered what she was doing there—the only person in the place eating solo. She wasn't a defiant little island floating on calm seas anymore. Too many shake-ups below the surface had rocked that island off its pedestal and tossed it right back into the mainstream of life. Funny, but she couldn't seem to feel regret. She was scared, and excited, and confused, but she wasn't sorry.

Out of habit, she pulled her organizer out of her briefcase and flipped it open to the "notes" section. The wine steward approached her. The last thing she wanted was wine, but it would take up some time, choosing, ordering, tasting. It took all of five minutes. Her pencil wandered over the page, making doodles. Then, restlessly, she dropped the pencil and opened the menu again, dawdling over it, reading every description, every footnote and price.

Then something changed. Her senses perked up, reached out. Out of the corner of her eye, she'd seen a couple enter the restaurant, and she'd heard the murmur of voices as the maître d' greeted them. She turned her head and stared, feeling awareness first, then tension, electricity, panic.

The woman was middle-aged, auburn-haired and what was euphemistically known as stacked. The man was tall, golden and gorgeous. And, they were coming her way. Julia dipped her head, using the menu to hide from view—a foolish strategy since her red suit-jacket and wide-brimmed hat weren't designed to blend in with the woodwork. Peeking around the edges of the menu, she saw Aunt Chloe leading Alex toward her banquette. He looked frustrated, or annoyed, she couldn't tell which.

A beautifully manicured hand pulled the top of the menu down. Green eyes raked all that was visible of her above the table. "Good grief, Alex was right," Chloe said. "It is you."

The menu cut off Julia's view as it sprang back up in front of her face, but not before she'd seen Alex's amused smile. Whatever had crossed his features before was gone. She'd preferred the whatever. His amusement was aggravating. Still behind the menu, she dredged up a smile before coming out of hiding.

Never one to stand on ceremony, Chloe hustled off to catch up with the maître d'. Still smiling, Alex leaned over and spoke, his voice low, seductive. "Ah, Julia, it's a waste of energy to hide. I can sense your presence in a room."

As lines went, it was on the corny side. All of a sudden, corny had the power to touch her, move her, turn her into a believer. "Did someone else say it first, or is it an original?" she asked, knowing that she was baiting him, waiting for him to trip on that golden tongue of his.

Alex straightened. "You decide, Julia. I'll wait."

Ghosts can be dealt with . . . I promise. He might as well have said, "Trust me." But, her trust had been used up so long ago that it lay dormant like a field in winter. Her desire to trust again was like the pain of heat on frostbite, searing, overwhelming, unbearable.

"Scoot over, Julie. We're blocking traffic." Chloe waved her hands to punctuate her remark. The maître d' stood patiently in the background, menus in hand.

"Perhaps Julia is waiting for someone, Chloe. Our table is still free."

Julia's smile slipped. Her eyelids lowered to hide sudden pain. It had been annoyance and frustration she'd seen. Alex, it appeared, preferred to have lunch with Aunt Chloe alone, no matter whose presence he could sense in a crowded room. So much for corny. The cloaked-in-courtesy rejection felt like a hard fist slamming into her stomach.

Chloe scanned the table. "Well, if she was expecting someone, it looks as if they've been unavoidably detained. Julie's been here long enough to kill a glass of wine."

"Julia?" Alex's voice did more than ask her a question. It pulled at her, demanded that she look up at him, beguiled her into believing she'd heard consideration rather than rejection. "Are you waiting for someone?"

From deep inside herself, Julia tapped into one of her most highly developed talents—faking poise in awkward situations—and addressed her aunt. "You're welcome to join me," she said, her smile as bright as a spot of new paint on an otherwise drab wall. "In fact, Aunt Chloe, I called to invite you to lunch, but you had just left."

"Oh, well that makes me feel better," Chloe said as she slid in next to Julia. "I'm Alex's second choice for a lunch date. At least I'm breaking even in popularity." She opened her menu. "What I don't understand, Julie, is how you could turn Alex down for me. Maybe you should go in for analysis."

Julia's gaze flew to Alex, asking a silent question. *You told her?*

His eyes twinkled. "Chloe, behave. Julia was obviously having a working lunch." He tapped his forefinger on a corner of her organizer. Julia snapped her notebook shut, hoping he hadn't seen the silly doodles she'd drawn all over the page.

Things progressed from awkward to humiliating when Chloe minutely inspected every detail of Julia's suit, her jewelry, the hat. "Red is definitely your color. It's still too conservative for you, darling, but at least you're being more creative."

"Thank you," Julia said, deadpan. "I dressed this way just for you." From anyone else, her aunt's remark would have been just short of an insult, but from Chloe it was a stamp of approval. Julia took in Chloe's own ensemble. Only her eccentric relative could mix secondhand with gaudy and still radiate chic. Only Chloe would dare try.

Feelings of fondness turned to thoughts of homicide when Chloe gave Alex graphic verbal pictures of Julia as a child. "She was the most amazing child, Alex—gregarious, quixotic, and with her own ideas on color, style, and life in general. The stories she made up! And she devoured books on myths and legends and magic."

The color of Julia's face was a perfect match to that of her jacket. She kicked Chloe under the table.

Chloe shot her a frown. "Stop kicking me, Julie. You know I'm not going to shut up." Without missing a word, she picked up where she'd left off. "I took her shopping one day and she fell in love with the oddest conglomeration of clothing. I tried to talk her out of it, but she wouldn't listen. She said that if she wore that outfit to school, everyone would say that her aunt must love her very much to buy her such neat clothes. That ensemble was anything but neat, Alex, but I bought it for her anyway."

Alex was hanging onto every word, and showing no surprise at Chloe's disclosures. His smug smile made Julia want to bury her head under the table. She would have felt less exposed if Chloe had showed him photos of her as a naked baby on a bearskin rug.

She glared at him, as if to say, *If you were really a gentleman, you'd change the subject.*

His eyebrows rose and his expression was innocence itself. *A gentleman? Where?*

Julia's fork clattered against her plate, a discordant note in the refined setting. "Okay, Aunt Chloe, I'm completely mortified. You can stop now."

The sudden silence was worse than Chloe's hundred-mile-an-hour chatter. What on earth had she said to make Chloe's mouth drop open, and Alex to find a sudden interest in his lunch? It was as if they'd been confronted with something alien. And then she knew. Neither Chloe, who knew her so well, nor Alex, who thought he had her pegged, had expected her to say anything that honest or revealing about herself, not even in jest. She'd been dead serious.

"Has the world ended?" Chloe asked.

Julia sighed. "No, Aunt Chloe, the world hasn't ended."

"Just checking."

"You know, Chloe, the property we looked at this morning is haunted," Alex said, effectively closing the subject of the habits and hang-ups of Julia Devlin.

For that, Julia would have given him a Boy Scout merit badge.

The conversation took a turn for the better. Ghosts and goblins and things-that-went-bump-in-the-night seemed a safe subject. Relaxing, Julia sat back and played with her wineglass while Chloe launched into a dramatic account of every paranormal experience her friends had ever related to her.

Maybe it was the glass of wine. Maybe it was Alex. Julia suddenly felt languid, unconcerned about his nearness, the way his thigh pressed against hers, and how his gaze never left her for very long. She listened to him describe the old mansion without hearing the words. Participation seemed too much of an effort, yet she heard herself making comments, and even laughing as she related her fright in the deserted building.

And, as she laughed at herself, Alex's finger lightly brushed her cheek on its way to tuck a stray curl behind her ear. Laughter died. She couldn't drag her gaze away from him. He seemed to have the same problem. Nothing existed but the moment, magical, out of time and place, a moment that had to end so that anticipation could build for the next one. Julia wasn't ready for any of it, yet it was impossible to pull her attention away from him, focus on the table, the room, anything but Alex.

The waiter removed their plates. Businessmen and women on fixed schedules had been replaced by a crowd of more leisurely diners. Chloe asked Alex questions about the property. Alex cleared his throat before describing the mansion, Julia's ideas, his plans. Julia was having a terrible time concentrating on what they were saying. There wasn't a bolt hole in sight, and suddenly she needed one.

Realizing that Chloe had wound down for the moment, Julia spoke to the air above Alex's shoulder. "I have to go. Can we discuss this in my office later this week?" She had no idea what "this" was. Because she'd been too busy concentrating on keeping her heart from doing a tap dance on her sleeve, she hadn't paid much attention to what her nods and uh-huhs were responding to; it seemed reasonable to assume they'd been talking about the gallery.

Alex's raised eyebrows cast doubt on her assumption. He laid his hand over hers. "At your convenience, Julia. And it is I who must go." He folded his napkin and placed it by his plate as he stood up. "Why don't you stay and have dessert with Chloe?"

If Julia had tried to speak, she knew she would have sputtered in indignation. Since when had Alex taken her convenience into account? What really bothered her was Alex's X-ray vision, always seeing right through her, always spotting her little white lies. Her cool, challenging look was wasted on Alex. He was leaning over to buss Chloe's cheek. It bothered her, that little kiss, probably because she wanted one, too. Badly.

He extended his hand to her. The handshake she expected never came. His thumb caressed the back of her hand as he lifted it, paused, slowly bent over to bestow an old-world kiss on her fingertips. That gesture sent tingles up her arm, heat through her bloodstream, enough heat to melt concrete walls. And then he left her, just like that, to cope with vagrant thoughts, renegade emotions.

With a distinctly hungry look in her eyes, she watched him walk out. "It's either feast or famine with Alex. There is no such thing as a light snack," she said musingly.

"If you're still hungry, darling, I'll order dessert," Chloe suggested innocently.

"That's just it," Julia sighed. "I haven't been hungry in years. Not like this. Now, all of a sudden, I'm ravenous."

Chloe ordered lime pie for both of them as she tried to cope with this new Julia who was speaking and acting like a grown-up version of the old Julie. And, Alex—he was behaving like the young man he'd never had a chance to be.

Chloe had three reasons for coming to San Francisco. It was too late to do anything about the two she'd just had lunch with. Whatever Alex's reasons for wanting to meet Julia had been, there was obviously only one thing on his mind now. Whether she knew it or not, that one thing had a softness in her eyes and an animation in her voice that hadn't been there for years.

For the first time in her life, Chloe felt the urge to interfere, but she didn't know whether to play matchmaker or hire someone to shanghai Alex on a slow boat to China. If Alex hadn't engaged in so many trivial pursuits over the years, Chloe would celebrate his attraction to Julia. If Julia were as tough as she'd like to believe she was, Chloe wouldn't be so worried. If she had a magic wand, she'd wave it and give each of them a clean slate so they could start out even. Alex and Julia really would be good together... *if.*

"What am I going to do, Aunt Chloe?" Julia asked as she stared at the back of her hand, still feeling the touch of Alex's lips on her fingertips.

"You really want me to answer that?" Chloe asked with a catch in her voice. She was absolutely sure that Alex had wanted some advice, even though they hadn't had a chance to talk before spotting Julia. A lucky guess would be that her niece was the intended subject. Alex never asked for advice. In fact, he'd never discussed his private life with anyone, except for that week a long time ago when he'd talked her through the d.t.'s. Julia never discussed her private life, either, yet here she was... asking for advice. For such a momentous occasion, Chloe wished she had something really profound to offer... like an answer.

"What do you want to do, Julie?"

Julia's look was more explicit than a book in a plain brown wrapper. "I'd really like to follow my instincts, except that my instincts have always led me down the Yellow Brick Road." She spoke quickly, as if she recognized the danger of not talking. "Aunt Chloe, I've been to Oz. It's full of visitors, but nobody lives there. And tour guides like Alex are exciting, but there's always someone else waiting in line to see the sights."

"Julie, did it ever occur to you that even tour guides in Oz retire? I should know. I married three of them." Chloe grimaced. "I think I'd better quit while I'm ahead." Finishing her pie, Chloe couldn't resist adding, "Julie, you've spent a lot of years asking negative 'whys' when it came to getting involved with people. That kind of question doesn't leave much room for positive responses. The little girl I told Alex about always asked 'why not?' with an I-can-do-anything defiance."

Chloe had mastered the art of keeping others from slipping words in edgewise when she didn't want them to. She employed it now, saying all the things she'd been holding in for years. "No one dared tell you that something you wanted to do might be more than you could handle or that anything you believed might not be true. You had trees to climb and if you fell out of one because it was too high, you'd dust yourself off and insist that next year, when you grew a little more, you *would* make it. But, Julie, you stopped growing before you'd climbed all the important trees."

Putting her napkin down, Julia slid out of the banquette. "There's a big difference between a broken arm and a broken heart, Aunt Chloe."

Chloe followed her out of the restaurant. Rarely did anyone have the last word with Julia. Chloe was determined to be the exception to the rule.

Julia was standing by her car, looking lost, bewildered. Biting her lip, she kept staring at the back of her hand and rubbing it. Her voice was low, barely discernible from the sound the breeze made as it rustled through the budding trees. "Aunt Chloe, I need a hug."

Inside, Chloe cried. And, she rejoiced. How long since Julia had made that particular admission? How many times had she wished that her niece *could* make such an admission? Chloe gathered Julia close, and stroked her hair as she used to do so long ago.

Julia's hat tipped and began to fall. With a quivering breath, Chloe caught it and stood back to set it on her niece's head at a jaunty angle. Her smile was bittersweet, reflecting a lifetime of memories, both good and bad. "Remember, broken hearts mend, Julie. Untouched hearts wither and die."

Chapter Seven

Aunt Chloe had failed to mention that there was untouched and then there was untouched. The difference was of mammoth proportions when choice was involved. Without realizing it, Julia had made her choice. Any suffering that might come along as a result, would be self-inflicted, asked for. A lot of old sayings like *Too little, too late* came to mind as she sat in her office trying to be productive. If a three-day acquaintance with some heavy breathing thrown in could be counted as too late to stop herself from falling headlong for a refined rogue... or too little for that matter. Julia didn't count the four days that had passed since she'd last seen Alex.

Budding relationships—even mild flirtations—needed some fuel to get them going. Alex's ardor, it would seem, had been running on fumes right from the start.

After lunch on Monday, Julia had decided that she could either follow the Yellow Brick Road one more time and see if there was a residential section in Oz, or she could buy a dog and settle in Kansas. On Tuesday, she'd admitted that she'd been letting old memories pollute her view of the world. Maybe it was time to clean off her grime-tinted lenses and take another look.

By Wednesday, Julia had accepted that the child Chloe spoke of was very much alive, heard but not seen in the shadows where Julia had tried so hard to keep her. Since walking into her father's hospital room, she'd been having a devil of time keeping her there. On Thursday, she'd come to the conclusion that she couldn't move forward until she quit looking back.

But, now it was Friday, and Julia was at a dead end. After all that agonizing and firm decision making, she'd gone nowhere all week except to work. After his gentle and sensual persuasions, there had been nothing from Alex except a cryptic message relayed by Petrov that Alex was "out" and would contact her as soon as possible. She could translate that to mean anything.

It seemed possible that Alex had claimed equal rights in the mind-changing department. Either that or he hadn't been sincere in the first place. Neither possibility thrilled her. To be fair, if she discounted her response to his kiss, she'd done everything but dump a bucket of ice water over his head. "Of all the times for a man to take me seriously," she muttered.

Vowing not to waste any more time agonizing and making decisions unless she was absolutely sure it was necessary, Julia stayed in her office during the lunch hour. Her staff had better things to do than remain there and mope along with her.

The light on her telephone flashed. She punched the line button and picked up the receiver. "Image Design...yes, this is Julia Devlin...oh, hello, Don Juan...yes, I know you want your girlfriend to be part of your...uh...team, but I'm not sure it'll work. Miss Elizabeth has the sweet-and-innocent market cornered. Then you have Scary Sherry for the mean-and-nasty slot—"

Frowning, Julia picked up her pen and doodled on her desk blotter as she listened. "All that's left is a mother figure, an intellectual...what? No, I can't see Sharon in either of those roles...of course she's intelligent...I'm sure she'll be a wonderful mother...you're missing the point. Sharon is very feminine. Furthermore, she has a lot of quiet dignity. I went to the last Bash of the Titans. No one there was quiet, and dignity was left at the door—"

Julia rubbed the bridge of her nose. "Yes, I suppose Sharon is sort of like Rocky's wife. Quiet strength, yes. But, she's not your wife. You're Don Juan, remember? It would ruin your image. If you really want to do this, I think we should make her a woman of mystery... yes, very dramatic. No one will know who she is or even if you two have anything going. She'll just show up every time you're in the ring... her clothes? High society, sophisticated, pearls, not diamonds...a cigarette holder? No, wrong image. We want silk stockings, not black fishnet.''

Julia closed her eyes, counted to ten. Don Juan the Destroyer was one of her favorite clients, and the most trying. "I'll work up some ideas before you come in next week. You're welcome...and Don Juan? I think the spotlight and fanfare might be a little much. Subtlety is the key here. Yes... goodbye.'' After replacing the receiver in its cradle, Julia propped her elbows on the desk, bent her head, and massaged the back of her neck.

Something intruded into the silence, electric, charging the air. Something exhilarating and dangerous. Her nerve endings began to twitter like those of a teenage girl at the receiving end of the quarterback's smile. She could feel the back of her neck turning red as she looked up...

He still took her breath away.

Tall and elegant in a casual suit of linen and silk, Alex leaned against the door frame, watching her as if he were discovering the secrets of the universe. His hands were in his trouser pockets as if he had personally put the universe on indefinite hold. As he had put her on hold for a week.

"How long have you been standing there?" she asked.

"Not long." His caressing gaze felt like a mist of exotic perfume, sable next to her bare skin, a wild ride in a Lamborghini, luxurious, decadent, breathtaking. She forgot the universe altogether. His slow, lazy smile said hello, then spoke to her in a silent, intimate language that conjured images of a caviar-and-champagne snack shared on silk sheets....

"Am I disturbing you?" he asked in a tone that conveyed his pleasure at the idea.

Actually, yes, she wanted to say. Caution and rational thought were distant memories. The further he sauntered into the room, the less air there seemed to be. She really should be worried about that, but she felt too alive, too aware and aroused.

"I know for a fact that you only see your clients by appointment, Alex," she said pointedly, somehow managing to keep her voice cool and calm, as if she was still in possession of all her faculties. She'd even managed to keep her hands marginally steady.

Alex smiled faintly. "I do."

No snappy comeback or corny line? Just once, Julia wished that he would be predictable, offering white lies for the sake of pride, black lies for the sake of self-delusion, unscalable walls for self-defense against emotional intimacy. She should know. Alex obviously didn't know. He was always honest—about what he wanted, and what he was willing to give. *We can't start at the end, Julia. Ghosts can be dealt with. You decide, Julia. I'll wait.* His promises were building up, like rungs on a ladder.

He was waiting now, as if he knew she was making heavy-duty discoveries about herself, about him, about them. "You're driving me crazy," she said. Honesty was catching.

"Yes?" Alex looked pleased, a little cocky. "Shall we go crazy together?"

Why not? The thought sent a shiver up her spine, as if she'd walked over her own grave. Clearing her throat, she frowned at Alex. "Umm, about that appointment—"

"Don Juan?" Alex interrupted her, ignoring her efforts to establish ground rules. "I'm intrigued."

She gave up for the moment. "World Champion of the United Wrestlers Federation. He's tall as a mountain and built like the proverbial brick outbuilding. I don't think he has a central nervous system. He's also dark and handsome—makes his entrance in a black gaucho hat, black cape, breeches and knee-high boots."

"Let me guess," Alex said, his mouth twitching. "His theme song is 'Bolero.'"

Julia grinned. "It was. Now it's the adagio from the 'Concierto de Aranjuez.'"

"Your idea, no doubt."

"Mmm."

"A good choice. It's much more dramatic and powerful, more stirring."

"Alex—" Julia didn't want to talk about stirring. Don Juan the Destroyer had nothing on Alex in that department. She knew Don Juan for what he was: a quiet, gentle man with a Ph.D. in Philosophy. Employers weren't beating down any doors for doctors of Philosophy. So, Don Juan made a bundle wrestling and, she suspected, acting out the fantasies of an ex-nerd. Alex, on the other hand, was exactly what he seemed: lethal to repressed twenty-eight-year-old women.

"And, what is the Bash of the Titans?" He stood on the other side of the desk, looking down at her, waiting.

Sighing, Julia waved toward the chair. Obviously, he had no intention of making an appointment. "It's like the Pillsbury Bake-off, only for wrestlers—lots of violence and snarling, a totally tacky affair." She smiled and cupped her chin in her hands. "The showmanship is appalling, the noise deafening, and there's usually standing room only."

"You enjoyed it."

"Every minute of it," she agreed, giving a puckish grin. "You can get rid of a lot of angst at a free-for-all like that." Before he could ask the next question, she straightened in her chair and folded her hands on the desk. "Now you must have important matters on your mind, or you'd have made an appointment." Eyeing his relaxed posture in the chair, Julia noted that his hands were busy again, stroking the upholstery on the arms and down to the wood insets on the sides, up to press gently into the softness of thick padding. Mercy! Everything he did was sexy, subtly graphic.

"No, nothing urgent," he replied casually. His eyes, however, expressed something else. *Nothing, except to see you.* Those eyes were stroking, too, a lazy, sensual caress that reached down deep, and touched her from the inside out. Apparently, he was in no hurry to do any more than laze away the afternoon in her office.

"Okay, Alex, I'll bite. Why are you here?" *Where were you?*

"You called me."

"Oh…yes, I did, but that was earlier in the week. All you had to do was call back."

"Yes, I could have." His eyelids were lowered, his face relaxed. She noticed the circles under his eyes. He was giving a good impression of a man about to fall asleep.

"Alex, maybe you'd feel more like doing business after a nap."

He shot up out of the chair and paced the length of the office. "No business. I've had a bellyful the last seventy-two hours." Even his voice was weary. "I'm sorry, Julia. I'm not fit company." He returned to the chair, and sat down heavily.

"Problems?" She'd opened a door with that question, inviting confidence, intimacy. A door she'd kept firmly closed for years. Oddly enough, she had no desire to slam it shut again. She had the feeling that Alex needed to be invited in—somewhere.

"Not mine exactly." He stretched his legs out, crossed at the ankles. Invitation accepted. "There was an earthquake on the ocean floor in the South Pacific."

Apropos of what? Julia wondered, but instinct kept her silent. In her business, she had to know when to talk, and when to listen between the words. Body language said a lot. Alex's spoke of exhaustion—he didn't like it—and frustration born of helplessness—he wasn't used to it. Alex was captain of his ship, and in the habit of weathering storms. That must have been some earthquake to have the contained Mr. St. Ives foundering.

"Do you own part of that, too?" she asked, meaning to lighten the moment.

"Yes, an island."

It took a second to register, and she couldn't keep her eyes from widening nor could she stifle the questions inspired by such a revelation. "Oh…any damage?"

"No. Not to Sandcastle. But a friend of mine, a retired freighter captain, lost his island. It sank."

Bemused and fascinated, Julia snapped her mouth shut and cupped her chin in her hands again. She couldn't grasp the reality of what he was saying. And, then she had a horrible thought. "Alex, your friend, he wasn't on the island when—"

"No, thank God. But, still, he lost everything."

"He called you?"

"Yes. So did the mortgage company, and Lloyd's of London."

Julia knew that whatever she heard from that point on would decide whether her feelings for Alex would take a turn for the better, or the worse. She was almost afraid to discover the outcome, but better now than later. "Why would they call you unless your name was on the mortgage, and the insurance?"

"No reason." He rolled his shoulders, as if to ease the tension there.

"Have you lost a lot?"

He leaned forward, clasping his hands between his knees. "Not a damn thing. Jack, however, had lost the home he built with his own hands, and the lifetime of memories he had inside it—photographs, mementos, logbooks, a manuscript he was working on."

"The insurance?"

"Adequate. We've made an offer on another island and it's been accepted. It's suddenly a buyer's market in the South Pacific."

"Are you selling Sandcastle?"

"It would have to sink first."

"I see." And, she did see. Alex's island meant more to him than a simple luxury or a good investment. The fact that he'd given it a name, and a fanciful one at that, implied as much. "I hope, Alex, that your Sandcastle never washes out with the tide," she whispered and mentally rolled her eyes. Talk about corny.

His head jerked up. His gaze was penetrating, intense, searching for lies. And it was naked, making it clear that she'd touched on a fear of his, a weakness. She wanted to look away but didn't dare. Seeing his vulnerability hurt.

There ought to be some invincible people in the world. Alex was not one of them—if they existed at all. He just seemed to deal with life's big disappointments better, handle them with more ease and acceptance. And, most of the time, he kept his vulnerability vacuum-packed, as she did.

The doors were wide open now. With his admission, Alex had taken a giant step inside . . . his trust, and he knew it, accepting that, too. It was her turn to either cut and run, reject what he'd just given her, or to go forward, no looking back.

Her own little island was foundering badly, but not giving up just yet. Trust could swallow her up, drown her in idealism, then release her to cope with the resultant emptiness of lost hope. She wasn't as brave as Alex, or as strong, to take what came with such resilience. She just couldn't seem to forget her past. Her steps would have to be smaller, more tentative than his.

In an attempt to ease the tension, and to break away from Alex's stare, she shook her head. "Mercy! Privately owned islands . . . Lloyd's of London . . . a millionaire gambler turned renowned art dealer who makes a dream come true for a retired sea captain—Toto, I don't think we're in Kansas anymore."

Alex's expression was whimsical, his mouth quirked in a suggestion of a smile. "Try Papeete."

"I'd love it. Tahiti. Palm trees. Lazy ocean breezes. Pastel drinks in coconut shells with paper parasols—"

Alex sat back, at ease once more. "Thatched huts. Hammocks that cradle your body, sway with every movement. Soft sand under a magic moon—"

Julia sat bolt upright, definitely not at ease with the erotic images he was conjuring up. "Alex. If there isn't anything more to discuss—"

"Sunday," he said abruptly.

"What about Sunday?" Was that a note of hopefulness she detected in her own voice, excitement thumping in her chest?

"Do you have plans?"

"No. Why?"

His grin was spontaneous and roguish. "I have a strong urge to play..." His pause was just a little bit naughty—not at all consistent with his usual sophistication. "...tourist."

Flustered by her sudden impression that Alex was, yet again, letting her in on a secret about himself that he kept from society at large, Julia dropped her gaze to her hands and cleared her throat. The situation held more than a little irony. "Are you asking me to be your guide?"

"I'll leave the itinerary to you as long as you include as many bona fide tourist traps as can be seen in one day."

Before she could find an excuse to say no, Alex left the office with a lightness to his step and weighty thoughts on his mind. He was surprised at himself for telling Julia about Sandcastle. He'd always been so careful to keep that part of his life—the part he considered real—private. Julia represented a host of firsts in his life. Important firsts. Like the kiss after Chloe's party, begun so casually and ended years before he'd been ready for it to end. A kiss that hadn't shaken the earth. It was enough that it had shaken him.

Four days away from Julia, missing her, thinking about her, remembering every detail of her, assured him that she wasn't just a novelty in his jaded existence. She was necessary to sweeten a world that for him had grown increasingly sour. He needed a lifetime of those kisses and more. Much more.

Julia stared at the empty doorway long after Alex had strolled out of her office. She could swear that Julie had just found a kindred spirit—

Dangerous thinking, Julia. Cynicism made a last stand, telling her that men like Alex played in boardrooms and boudoirs, and that trolleys, souvenir shops and crowded sidewalks were much too plebeian for a citizen of the world like Alex.

Her eyes gleamed with a mischievous light that was pure Paddy Devlin. Tossing down her pencil, she stuffed papers and files into her briefcase and headed for the nearest bookstore. Like most natives of a city, she rarely frequented the areas designed to attract and entertain tourists, but if Alex wanted to play tourist, who was she to disappoint him? And, while she was at it, she would take him on another tour—through her past.

THAT EVENING, Julia absently rubbed at the back of her neck, her temples, then her neck again as she sat hunched over her dining-room table, catching up on the work she hadn't been able to concentrate on all week. Familiar with her work habits, Patrick brought her a carafe of coffee and an oversize insulated mug with the name of the local grocery printed on the side.

"Thanks, Da'. Just what I need."

"Are you still working on that wrestler?" he asked as he cocked his head to read the name on the open folder in front of her.

"I wouldn't dream of working on Don Juan the Destroyer."

Patrick grinned around his pipe. "Too much for you to handle?"

"He's too much, period." She kept her pencil moving across the page in an effort to discourage conversation. Patience was not her strong suit when she was working, and especially not when her father caught her working exclusively on Alex's account. She really couldn't take any of his teasing tonight. Not when Sunday loomed so close. Not after the decision she'd made to meet Alex's honesty with some of her own. Confession was good for the soul, or so it was said, but it was sheer hell on the nerves.

"Alex again, I see."

"Uh-huh." She wrote faster. It was always Alex. He'd brought her idealism back to life, but it was still on the critical list. Sunday would bring the moment of truth. She couldn't put it off any longer. If Alex was going to be turned off by her background—and her father's—it was better to know now, before she became too attached to her idealism. And to Alex.

Dread of his reaction made her sick. So what if Alex was kind and gentle and sensitive? Everything had a limit. Alex seemed to value honesty, in his emotions, in his business, in acknowledging his needs. The Devlin family, including herself, was a little short on honesty. She may not have a criminal record, but she was the world champion at lying to herself.

"Isn't this job a little out of your field?" Patrick asked. Idly, he picked up the file and read the address on the tab.

"Not according to Alex."

Patrick frowned, and dropped the file like a hot potato. "You never did say how you met him."

Julia laid down her pencil and turned to face him. "As in the case of any other client, he was referred to me."

"Who referred him?"

"Aunt Chloe. Why?" The smell of freshly poured coffee finally registered on her senses. She sipped carefully from the steaming mug.

"Does Chloe send you a lot of clients?"

"Every chance she gets."

"You're seeing him Sunday."

"I told you that I was." Her break was over. The pile in her briefcase wasn't growing any smaller while she chatted. "Don't you have a game of darts or pinochle at Mugsy's?"

"Julie darlin', you shouldn't be so subtle. If you're trying to get rid of me, just say so." He paused, his eyebrows drawn together in concentration. "As a matter of fact, I do have a game at Mugsy's. I'll be home early."

"I'll drive you."

"No," Patrick said quickly and glanced at his watch. "Ben is picking me up in a few minutes. I'll wait on the porch for him."

"Okay. Have fun, and thanks for the coffee." Julia was bent over her work before Patrick had made it out the door.

As soon as he was out of sight, Patrick's movements became quick, agitated. He felt a heaviness in his chest that had nothing to do with his heart, not physically at least. But, the past was a claw tearing at him, punishing him. He'd deserved punishment for his actions, but not Julie. Never Julie, who had suffered too much, paid too much for being his daughter. It had to stop. With his unlit pipe clamped between his teeth, he walked the five blocks to the nearest pay phone and called for a cab.

No wonder Alex seemed familiar, Patrick thought as he gave the driver an address. Suspicions hardened and turned to stone in his chest. Old memories were resurrected. Old curiosities were transformed into new insights: a room at the Alexander estate filled with toys and books—never used, never out of place, always dusted and shiny new—suitable for a boy in various stages of development; photos of a boy growing and changing with the years hung on the walls of that same room; letters arriving regularly from Philadelphia with L. St. Ives above the return address. Why hadn't he remembered the name sooner? And then there were Nicholas's frequent trips back East, his despondency upon returning and his sailboat named *The Lorna*. Either his imagination was playing a practical joke on him or there was a snake in their midst. He muttered a prayer, thankful that his patron saint was proficient in dealing with snakes.

A thousand memories tormented him. He remembered Julie's reactions to Alex, the flush on her cheeks when she'd come home from Chloe's party, the sparkle of mischief and excitement in her eyes when she'd come home from work, her arms full of guidebooks. He cursed under his breath. He only hoped that he was not too late to prevent his daughter from paying too dearly for his sins.

"Sir?"

Alex swiveled his chair around to face his housekeeper. "Yes, Mrs. Hall," he answered wearily.

"A Mr. Patrick Devlin to see you... I can tell him you're already retired for the evening. You really should, you know."

"Don't tempt me," he said with grim resignation. "You can show him in. And, Mrs. Hall? I won't be needing you tonight. You have plans, I believe?"

"Yes, sir. Thank you for remembering."

Having no illusions concerning the reason for Patrick's sudden visit, Alex stared at the doorway as if doom were waiting on the other side. With a morbid sense of irony, he thought of his quick trip to Sandcastle. His idealism was never stronger than when he was on the island, his dreamer's soul never more evident than when he sat on the powder-soft beach at dusk. In that short visit, he'd never been more aware of all the vacant, waiting places in his life.

He'd come to terms with the fact that the Veil of Tears was merely a symbol of what he really wanted—permanence, devotion, love. He regretted nothing except his cocky assumption that, because he'd dismissed the Veil of Tears as a priority, it would cease to be an issue altogether. It was the worst judgment call he'd ever made.

The door opened and the housekeeper showed Patrick into the study. "May I get you anything before I go, sir?"

"No, thank you."

"Good night then." She paused on her way out, as if to say, *Are you sure?* Her frown favored Patrick, whose stance and glowering silence suggested a volcano about to erupt.

"Enjoy your evening, Mrs. Hall, and please close the door on your way out."

Upon hearing the door click shut, Patrick didn't waste time beating around the bush. He faced Alex belligerently, his fists clenched, his expression tight. "You know who I am. I know who you are...or close enough that what branch you occupy on Nicholas's family tree doesn't matter."

Alex nodded as he poured wine into two glasses. Surely the wine would be better for Patrick than the full head of steam he was building. "I was hoping you wouldn't make the connection," he said calmly, hoping his composure would transmit itself to Patrick.

"You're after the Veil of Tears, aren't you?"

"I was."

Ignoring the glass of wine Alex held out to him, Patrick placed his fists on the desk. "I won't have you using Julie. She has nothing to do with this. As far as she knows, everything was recovered fifteen years ago."

Alex washed down a lump of anger with a healthy swallow of wine. He was getting damn tired of being accused of using Julia. "I'm aware of that. For the record, Mr. Devlin, I have no intention of using your daughter. And, whether I acquire the Veil or not is irrelevant at this point.''

Patrick snorted. ''Then leave my Julie alone.''

''No.''

''You can have the blasted Veil.''

''No. Taking it from you was never my intention.'' Alex pushed the glass of wine across the desk. ''I would appreciate it, Devlin, if you would sit down. We have quite a bit to discuss, and I'd rather do it in comfort.''

The last of Alex's irritation escaped on a sigh as Patrick sat in the chair across from him. ''Now, frankly, I'd like nothing more than to forget the Veil exists, but at this point, you're too suspicious of me to take that at face value.''

''You're damn right I am.''

Alex continued as if Patrick hadn't said a word. ''I am prepared to purchase—''

''I said you can have it.'' Patrick snapped. ''I knew what it was and had a fair idea of how Nick got his hands on it. I kept it for Julie's future, except that she wouldn't touch it if she were starving and homeless.'' He downed his wine in one swallow. ''She has more honesty than the last two generations of Devlins put together. If giving the Veil to you will ensure that you stay away from her, then I guess it would be serving a good purpose after all.''

''This is absurd.'' Smiling without humor, Alex shook his head. ''You stole the Veil from Nicholas who stole it from Hitler who stole it from God knows whom. It's unlikely the Veil has had a legitimate owner in centuries. My intention has always been to purchase it from you in a simple business transaction.''

Patrick narrowed his eyes. ''And Julie?''

Alex's expression hardened. ''Money in exchange for the Veil. Period. No other terms are acceptable.''

Packing and lighting his pipe, Patrick sat back in the chair and studied Alex thoughtfully. ''In the interest of easing a father's fears, you'd better spell it out for me. I wouldn't want to misunderstand what I'm reading into this.''

Alex, too, relaxed. Patrick's color was returning, and his breathing had steadied. Later, he would probably think it odd that he was concerned for the well-being of the man who had entered his home looking and acting as if he'd find great pleasure in using a shotgun to keep him away from his daughter. "As you said, Julia has nothing to do with the Veil. Of the two, she has by far the greater value ... to both of us."

Patrick's mouth curved upward into a smile of cherished yesterdays when his dreams were ahead of him instead of lost in the shuffle of time. "If I hadn't married my Elise only three days after I met her, I wouldn't believe you. Those three days were the longest of my life. The seven years we had together were the shortest." This time he drank his wine more slowly, savoring it as he did his memories. "Julie reminds me of her mother—capable of making a man lose track of time...."

He cleared his throat and glared at Alex. "I liked you from the start. Chloe tells me you can be trusted. The devil himself could show up wearing wings and a halo and my sister wouldn't be fooled. But, if you hurt Julie, I'll haunt you into eternity."

Accepting the warning with all due respect, Alex gave him a solemn nod of understanding. "A thing to be avoided at all costs." He held up his glass in a toast.

Patrick met it with his glass and they drank, each measuring the silence, the ease with which they welcomed that one small moment to order their thoughts and alter their perspectives.

"Do you have any brilliant ideas as to how we're going to get out of this mess?" Patrick asked.

"What will it take to put your mind at ease?"

Smoke billowed around Patrick's head. "Proof that your designs are on Julie, and not that blasted piece of gold."

"We could melt it down, reduce it to nothing more than a piece of gold far less valuable than it is in its present form."

Patrick blanched. "Faith man, do you know how old the Veil is? It's a treasure." Once again, he abused the vintage by gulping down his wine. "The legend places it in the Old Country, you know. Near my parents' home."

"A legend only, Devlin. It seems more likely to have originated in England."

"Bah! Only an Irishman would have the sensitivity and patience to make such a piece."

"So, we will not destroy the Veil. Shall we give it away?"

"And, who, besides you and me, would appreciate it for what it is, what it stands for?" Patrick asked seriously.

"Good point," Alex again saluted Patrick. "The only solution seems to be for you to sell it to me."

"And how would I know that you weren't going after Julie so you could get your money back?"

Alex was hard put to contain his amusement. Patrick Devlin was a born haggler, and Alex suspected that he'd never closed a transaction in his life without a certain degree of negotiation. "Then I suggest we set a price between fair and outrageous and you can donate the proceeds to charity."

"What charity?"

"A retirement home for ex-convicts?" Alex said tongue in cheek. "Or...you could put the money in a trust fund for Julia, to be administered by Chloe so that blackguards like me can't touch it."

"Hmm. I think I have a better idea." He rubbed his hands together. "Now let's get on with it."

The haggling began in earnest and continued for a half hour before they agreed on a price—less than Alex considered fair, more than Patrick wanted to accept—for the Veil of Tears.

Patrick nodded in satisfaction as they shook hands on the deal. "It's done. If you keep seeing her after this, I'll know it's because of what she is and not because of what she has."

"I'll write you a check now as a sign of good faith. You can bring the Veil here on Monday, and Petrov can witness the transfer." Alex picked up the phone to call for a cab.

"Petrov," Patrick said as he folded the check and slipped it into his pocket. They left the study to wait in the foyer. "Now there's a man with his priorities straight. He was more concerned about the wine I'd stolen than the art."

Alex chuckled. "From what I understand, a few of those bottles were almost as valuable as the Veil. Gregori will never forgive you for drinking it all."

"I'll never forgive him for not warning me that some of that 'fine' wine wasn't fit to drink," Patrick muttered, then stared down at his feet. "By the way, this is to be a confidential business deal . . . between you and me."

Foreboding prickled the back of Alex's neck.

"There's no need to tell Julie. If she knew about the Veil, she'd also know that I would have already given it back if I'd intended to. I've disappointed her so much already . . ."

Alex disagreed with Patrick, yet sympathized with his reasons. He understood Patrick's need to keep anything from complicating what time he had left, much less admit to any further wrongdoing. From Patrick's point of view, it was finished business, and enlightening Julia would serve no purpose. In Alex's opinion, deception could cast a very dark shadow over a relationship. And he had every intention of beginning a long-term relationship with Julia. "I should have told Julia right away, Devlin. Now, it's a lie between us. I plan to rectify my mistake immediately."

"If you tell Julie about the Veil now, after not telling her in the past week, she'll see it as a lie anyway—mine and yours. She'll never trust you after that." Patrick's sigh shuddered with regret. "Alex, there are some secrets that belong in the grave. Right or wrong, I'm selfish enough to ask you to let this one be buried with me."

Because Alex wasn't absolutely sure that Patrick's request was wrong, he reluctantly agreed—with a proviso. "Burying a secret doesn't necessarily mean that it is dead. If this one surfaces in any way, I will not lie to Julia."

Patrick nodded. "I'll ask no more of you and hope that my grave is very deep." Patrick's steps were slow, his body bent as he walked out the door.

As he watched the taillights of the taxi disappear from view, Alex wondered if his silence would prove to be an involuntary act of wisdom or the greatest of deliberately committed follies.

Chapter Eight

The spring rains had given the flowers in Patrick's garden an added lushness as they danced in a sprightly breeze. Blossoms mingled pastels with brights, their foliage every conceivable shade of green. The buzz of insects soothed while bird song added cheer to Saturday-morning chores.

"Aha!" With zinc oxide stripes on her nose and beneath her eyes, Julia wrestled a tenacious weed from a flower bed. "I told you that you'd be dead meat if you so much as looked cross-eyed at my peonies!"

Patrick smiled and breathed deeply, a sigh of contentment. Julia still talked to plants as if all the years between yesterday and today had never happened. It felt as if it were yesterday, full of quiet conversation and wistful thoughts, the best of the past recaptured. In the past, they'd always begun their Saturdays working in the garden as they had today, as Julia had done since Mrs. Penny had moved away, as he had longed to do while pacing the length of a dusty prison yard.

He looked up at the sound of footsteps on the walk, and smiled in greeting. He hadn't known how he would react to seeing Alex again, but his presence here seemed natural, right. He really did like the younger man, and felt at ease with his instinct to do so. Alex had an air of authenticity about him that reassured paternal concern. The check Alex had given him helped, further assurance that he wasn't here to con Julia out of more than a fancy piece of jewelry. And,

Patrick saw something in Alex only another dreamer could recognize and respect. Alex didn't need to see beauty to know it existed. He could feel it with a sensitivity and appreciation for all its variations, tangible or otherwise.

Alex breathed in scents that teased at first and then darted away on capricious currents of air. His gaze wandered over grass and trees and flowers, and his mouth curved at the busy flight of insects, the lazy slither of a caterpillar. The garden was like another world in a gentler time, full of the smells and sounds of life.

"You're history, you miserable, no-good parasite. Nothing chokes my peonies and gets away with it."

Alex turned his head in the direction of Julia's voice.

"Come out of there or I swear I'll burn you out."

Alex smiled at her vehemence. The weeds didn't stand a chance.

Patrick observed Alex's expression as he spotted Julia, the concentration with which he focused every sense on her, absorbed her existence, nakedly displaying his need to be a part of it. That kind of wanting and needing produced its own torment and magnified the loneliness of a man's soul.

Julia felt a subtle shift in the breeze, a different pitch to the bird song. Glancing over her shoulder, her gaze latched onto Alex. The weed slipped her grasp and she sprawled seat first into a snowball bush, its petals drifting around her like confetti.

Alex restrained the laugh building in his chest and sauntered over to help her up.

Patrick leaned on the handle of his shovel and chuckled. From the expression on his daughter's face, he knew she had fallen for Alex in more ways than one.

Leaning back on her elbows, Julia blew a strand of hair out of her eye and glared up at Alex. The man's timing was brilliant, inspired. Her eyes narrowed suspiciously. "I'm beginning to see a pattern here. Your appearance always seems to land me in awkward positions. Is it fate or do you plan it this way?"

Bemused, Alex shook his head. His gaze busily explored the bare length of her legs below the cuffs of her khaki

shorts, the outline of her breasts under a coral polo shirt.
"A lucky fate..." he responded, homing in on her face,
"...to always find you in such delightful positions."
Crouching beside her, he plucked flower petals from her
nose and brushed them from her hair.

Julia drowned in sensation, Alex's touch, his admira-
tion. Her blood had turned to champagne and every fantasy she'd ever had flashed before her eyes. His gaze, so
intent on her barely clad form, should have made her acutely
aware of every bulge, lump and ripple that shouldn't be
there, every curve, hollow and feature that wasn't. Instead,
she felt impossibly feminine and powerful and wicked.
Alex's expression was telling her that nothing was impossible; wicked was a lot more fun than safe, sedate and sane.

Patrick cleared his throat to remind them of his presence.

"Julia, you are a dangerous woman." Rising to his feet,
Alex offered his hand to help her up.

Dangerous? Alex was a walking definition of the word.
In so many ways he'd given her glimpses of storms and secrets and passionate emotions beneath the laid-back elegance and refinement. She'd always been fascinated by
storms, yet she'd spent years avoiding the rain, being afraid
of the wind, running from fire.

Alex brought back all her old dreams, dreams of being
swept away to exotic places where passions were never
mocked, needs were never ignored, love was always returned. She'd been such an idealist once upon a time. Reality was that much more painful to an idealist, striking from
behind, disabling and maiming, but not kind enough to kill.
Idealists didn't die. They just learned not to believe, not to
trust, not to dream. But, dreaming was like swimming; you
never forgot how.

Her leg came in contact with his, hard muscle encased in
taupe linen. Her hand splayed against his chest, equally hard
beneath a sweater of butter-colored ramie. Feeling she might
melt into a puddle at his feet, she stepped back.

"I'd swear you said Sunday," she said.

"I couldn't wait."

Suddenly, Julia couldn't wait, either. She wanted to be a part of the storm instead of merely watching it from a safe distance. And, she wanted to ride the waves Alex was making in her life. Only a fool would reach out to him. Only a coward would stand back and deny the excitement. Only a dreamer would ignore the safe choices and take a chance on the endless possibilities.

Yet, still she resisted. "As you can see, this isn't a good time, Alex. I'm busy."

"Julia, if I were to wait for you to find a right time, the devil would be serving frozen daiquiris to the hired help."

"Heaven forbid."

"Exactly." His gaze mapped out the garden. "I could help you, instead. It's been a while since I puttered in a garden."

Her hands on her hips, Julia took in his clothes. "Alex, even Ralph Lauren wears jeans when he's home on the range. Those—" she pointed to his trousers "—do not qualify." She cocked her head. "Don't you have a garden on Sandcastle?"

"One of Mother Nature's finest. I wouldn't dream of tampering with it." He tucked the errant curl behind her ear in an easily accepted gesture. "These are just clothes. They can be replaced."

"Is it so easy to replace the things in your life?"

"These are cloth, Julia, mass-produced and inconsequential. Treasures of exceptional rarity are another matter entirely." *Like you,* his look said, but it was too heavy to be voiced, too much from the man who walked an isolated beach and dreamed of a different life for himself, full of shared moments in a garden, on a beach. Julia was too skittish, too suspicious to believe him. Yet. He jammed his hands into his pockets. *"Will* you come with me today? Or, *may* I stay and help?"

He looked as if he expected to be rejected, and was braced for it. The way he'd asked told its own story—of loneliness, a need for companionship and sharing. His expression was a stark pronouncement of her culpability. Again, Julia felt a sense of power, the same power he held over her.

The balance of it reassured her, gave her courage to do what she really wanted to do.

"No, you may not help in the garden," she said as she dusted off her hands. Power felt good. She knew she ought to be ashamed of herself for pausing, but for once, Alex seemed at a loss for arguments. For once, she had the upper hand, and she wasn't above taking advantage of even this small victory.

Calmly, Julia picked up her shoes and sauntered toward the house. At the door, she glanced at him over her shoulder. "Father will keep you company while I shower and change. There's ice tea in the fridge, coffee on the stove and fresh juice on the counter."

"Sassy," Patrick muttered, then fixed his gaze on Alex. "Are you going to let her get away with that?"

"She already has," Alex said easily, enjoying Julia's victory over him. He, after all, had also won.

"I wouldn't have thought a man like you would take to being backed against a wall."

Alex stooped to pull a weed, then another. "That depends on who is doing the backing and why."

A pungent aroma drifted through the garden as Patrick ripped open a bag of fertilizer. "Do you know what you're getting into?"

"Not entirely," Alex replied. "But, I'm sure you'll tell me."

"I could, but I won't." Lifting his face to the sun, Patrick breathed deeply. "There's magic in the air. You and Julie feel it—the suspense, the discovery, the excitement. You have to experience it all, or you'll deprive yourself of memories."

"Yes?" Alex cocked his head, listening to the cadence of Patrick's voice, absorbing his meaning, knowing it was true.

"Memories keep the magic alive, make you want more." The shovel sliced through soil. Pushing with his foot, Patrick sent it deeper and winced. He waved Alex away, refusing help, hating the knowledge that even the simplest pleasure brought him pain.

"Even the bad ones?" Alex's voice was light, casual.

"Ah, the bad ones are only bad if they end that way. Good memories encourage us to keep that from happening."

Alex looked up at the house, as if he might see Julia through the walls. Life had given him precious few good memories. He was hungry for them, ready to accept them. And, magic? He'd always believed in it; in fact, as a child he had lived in a world of magic because reality had been too much to cope with. Magic thrived in his imagination, creating both the dreams and the ways to realize them.

"Have you ever seen rainbows in the dark, Alex?"

Alex stared at the sky as his hand absently stroked a leaf. "No," he said, his attention captured by the idea. "I would think that it would take a special person to have that kind of vision."

Patrick nodded. "Rainbows you can see in the dark are a grand sight. Julie has always been able to see them, even when she didn't want to. Someday, you'll have the vision, too—when it matters the most."

"Rainbows in the dark," Alex murmured, his gaze attracted to the house. Visions and dreams were forgotten as Julia opened the screen door, descended the porch steps, walked toward him. Her skirt and tank top were laundered white cotton piped with navy. The sleeves of her navy blazer were pushed up, its collar flipped up in back to give her a jaunty look that matched her walk.

"I'm ready," Julia called as she fished around inside her oversize purse for her sunglasses. "Father, don't stay out in the heat of the day. I'll check in from time to time."

"You certainly look ready." Patrick nodded toward her bag. "Julie, if you carry that around, your shoulders will be lopsided by the end of the day."

Julia wasn't listening. She was too conscious of Alex curiously looking at the items she pulled out of her bag, too aware that they would be together all day without business to buffer her responses to him. This was definitely a date, a time for emotional intimacy and personal conversation. The conversation she planned, however, was not the kind you had while holding hands.

She'd planned it so well—Alex's enlightenment on the truth about Julia Devlin, and her father. It was her secret weapon, intended to repel Alex before he came any closer. Would he be repelled? Her doubt worried her. It meant that it mattered, that she had already begun to trust him. She was only prepared for rejection, even as she hoped for understanding and a clearing of her name for a crime she had not committed.

"Sunscreen, guidebooks, folding umbrella, towelettes—you're definitely prepared for any eventuality," Alex said.

"Absolutely," she replied and wished it were true.

Patrick watched them leave, then bent to lovingly tend the rose he had bred and named for his wife. His hands stroked the white buds tinged with delicate streaks of rose and palest yellow, thinking of sunrises never shared and promises they hadn't had time to keep. There was only one promise now. A promise to right a wrong and protect his daughter the only way he knew how. Soon, he would keep that promise. And soon, he would take a single bloom to his Elise and see her smile again.

"JUST WHO IS LEADING WHOM?" Julia demanded as she leaned against a lamppost to remove a stone from her shoe. "I can get this kind of workout by letting a Great Dane walk me."

"You don't like exercise?" He crouched down and reached for her shoe.

"Oh no, you don't." She snatched it away. "If you want to play with shoes, you have a pair of your own." A small pebble dropped to the ground and rolled away, but she continued to shake her flat-heeled pump and kept her gaze averted. "I'm beginning to think you have a foot fetish," she muttered as she slipped the shoe back on and hopped once to keep her balance.

Alex propped his arm on the post above her head as she straightened, his gaze lazy, his voice pure seduction. "Did you know that your big toe is crooked?"

"What?" At the very least, she'd expected a smooth line, a heavy dose of charm, an improper suggestion.

He leaned a little closer. "Your big toe. On your right foot. It's crooked."

Biting her lip, she sidestepped away from the lamppost, and from Alex, the heat of his body, the caress of his breath on her cheek.

"Didn't you know?" he asked, falling into step beside her.

Yes, she knew. She'd broken the toe in question twice—while climbing trees. "Okay, so it's a toe fetish," she said lightly.

He watched, with interest, the way her shoe flip-flopped against her heel. "Julia, you didn't fasten your strap."

"I know that." Stopping abruptly, she raised her foot to buckle the sling strap. Without something to hold onto, she accomplished nothing more than a graceless stumble and lurch.

"Allow me." Several feet separated them and Alex made no attempt to shorten the distance. His arms were angled away from his body as if to prove that he was neither armed nor dangerous.

But, Julia knew better. Alex had enough of an arsenal to reduce any woman's defenses to smoldering ashes. With a resigned sigh, she stood on both feet once again.

"I'm merely looking after my own best interests," he said conversationally as he leaned over, placed her hand on his shoulder for balance, and bent his head to watch what he was doing.

"I know I'm going to hate myself for asking." Tingles danced up her leg at his touch. "Okay, Alex, how so?"

"If you turn your ankle or lose your shoe, I'll have to carry you . . . Julia, I can't get up unless you let go of my shoulder."

She jerked her hand away. The idea of being carried by Alex sent Julia's imagination on a spree. He managed to wind up right in front of her as he rose. They weren't touching, yet his nearness drew her, pulled her face closer to his, held her there with a thread of anticipation.

His expression itself was an improper suggestion. The light in his eyes burned hot with desire. "If I carry you, Julia, it will be to the back seat of my car."

Her fantasies produced a tremble, more anticipation. Alex never provoked her usual responses to a male come-on. It never seemed practiced with him, every word sounded brand-new, invented just for her. With Alex, she didn't feel as if she were the bait in a hunting match or another notch on his belt. With Alex, she felt valued.

"I'll settle for a bench at Fisherman's Wharf and a paper cup full of shrimp." Alex's eyebrows rose, and she could almost see the wheels turning in his head. She'd done it again—tossed out an innocent statement and invited Alex to lead it astray. Slinging her bag over her shoulder, she glared at him. "Don't you dare, Alex. I don't want to hear a single smart remark."

Alex's smile said it all.

TWO HOURS LATER, and six since they'd left her father fussing over his roses, Julia groaned and called time-out. Her senses were on overload from the mixed odors of Fisherman's Wharf, the textures and graceful lines of the jade and wood and cloth they had examined in Japantown, the rich flavors they'd sampled at Ghirardelli Square, the high-decibel confusion of Chinatown, and the unsettling motion of driving down Lombard, the most crooked street in the world. She needed a roll or two of antacid and a tranquilizer.

Alex's idea of playing tourist was to see, and taste, as much as possible in the shortest period of time. She'd watched in disbelief as he'd sampled the food offered by every street vendor in sight, coaxing her to do the same. The man who had given every impression of being slow and languid was anything but. The man she'd accused of not taking life seriously, did just the opposite—passionately, completely. Even his indifference was intense; he'd passed art galleries and museums as if they didn't exist.

"You're not interested in checking out the competition?" she'd asked after they'd passed yet another gallery.

He shrugged. "Either I work or I play."

And, Julia thought, he did both full-out, no half measures, no compromises. She had the impression that, to Alex, each new experience was unique, and he accepted each as a challenge; he took all he could from it while he had the chance. It was as if he were a child who saw more trees than he could count and was determined to scale them all before they were cut out from under him.

When they entered the Japanese Tea Garden in Golden Gate Park, he visibly appreciated the grace and serenity of its landscaping and architecture and altered his pace accordingly. She sipped a cup of jasmine tea and wished she could put her feet up. Cherry trees surrounded them, their blossoms like fine lace draped above their heads. Everything was a whisper—the breeze, the conversations of the sightseers, even the exuberance of a game of touch football in another part of the huge park.

"You don't play very often," she observed idly as she stared up at a towering red and black pagoda.

"More so than you, I think," he answered. "I work hard at my business and just as hard at making time to relax." His wording told Julia a great deal. If she were to believe his lazy walk, his frequent smiles and dry observations, she'd also have to believe that he was relaxed. But that walk covered a lot of ground and his smiles didn't once grow into laughter. The storm she sensed in him was very real and unrelentingly constant. Alex was a prime candidate for burnout. Or blow-out. One left nothing but a shell filled with cold ash. The other left peace in the wake of unrest. "You're still working hard, Alex. Didn't you play as a child?"

Alex avoided her gaze. "Doesn't everyone?"

Something dark and heavy in his voice gave her the disturbing feeling that she'd found his secrets, touched them, violated them. His smile was raw, and painful to witness. She felt as if she'd caught him in the altogether and seen the scarred human being beneath the veneer of strength and confidence and arrogance.

His hand cupped her elbow, and he guided her to yet another attraction in the multifaceted park. Silence enclosed them within their individual thoughts. Alex stopped often to smell a flower, touch the rough logs of an old pioneer cabin, watch children playing while their parents cleaned up the debris from a picnic lunch. Normal things, yet Alex made them seem extraordinary.

Like people slow-dancing on a crowded floor, rental boats bobbed up and down and gently bumped one another in their moorings on Stow Lake. The wood creaked and water gurgled against their sides. Some boats glided on the lake, occupied by couples of every age, some making new memories, others reliving old ones.

"Shall we go to the island?" Alex asked as he grabbed her hand and led her toward the rental concession.

"Alex, there's a bridge. We can walk across."

He didn't seem to be listening. Money changed hands and the attendant pointed out a craft. Before Julia knew it, Alex was standing in the boat and holding out his arms to her. "Alex, the bridge is right over there. See—" She pointed toward the bridge, then looked down at him. In a flash his expression had gone from little-boy excited to man-of-the-world smooth and controlled.

She glared at him suspiciously. "You don't expect me to share the rowing, do you?"

His eyebrows rose. "There are some pleasures I never share."

"Pleasure? You've got to be kidding." Automatically, she grasped his shoulders as his hands tightened at her waist, lifting her clear of the dock, then lowered her into the boat. Suspended above him, she looked down at him and parted her lips, moistened them with her tongue, drew a shaky breath as he brought her closer in the long stroke of two bodies sliding against each other.

Her feet touched wood. The boat bumped the dock and swayed from side to side. Alex raised his hands to hers, guided them around his neck, then slowly lowered his arms, his fingers skimming down her sides to her waist. He paused, his gaze never leaving hers. She couldn't move, didn't want to move, ever. He wrapped his arms around her, holding her closer, tighter. His head lowered. His mouth closed over hers, withdrew just enough to nip teasingly at her lower lip, tasting, sipping, and finally drinking deeply, drawing from her all that she was willing to give.

"Hey mister, if you're into contact sports, this ain't the place." The attendant stood on the dock, a cigarette dangling from his lips. "You fall in the lake, I ain't gonna be responsible."

Julia jerked her arms from around Alex's neck, tried to move away from him. He wasn't letting go. Jumping in the lake seemed to be a good idea. She tried to twist away from him, but the boat rocked violently and Alex tightened his hold.

"Lady, you do that again and you'll get a dunking fer sure. I told you, I ain't gonna be responsible."

The pressure at her waist increased, urging her to sit.

"Julia," Alex whispered, "Unlock your knees."

"Let go," she whispered back.

"That ain't no dance floor, you know. Either sit in the boat or git out." The grizzled old man tossed his cigarette into the water.

All of Julia's attention focused on the hiss of extinguished flame, the sight of the cigarette floating in the water. The tension ebbed, then centered on a new object. She calmly sat down and arranged her skirt before glancing up at the man. "What is that for?" she asked pointing to a long-handled net leaning against his little shack.

"Huh?" the man looked from her to the shack and back again.

His mouth twitching, Alex sat on the seat facing her.

"The net ... I assume it's for cleaning trash out of the lake?" At his bemused nod she smiled. "Will you hand it to me please?"

Alex rested his arms on his legs and bent his head. His shoulders shook.

"Thank you." Taking the net, Julia calmly fished out the cigarette butt, swung the dripping net in a wide arc toward the man and dumped it at his feet, talking all the while. "Shame on you, sticking your nose in other people's business, and using the lake as your personal ashtray." She turned back to Alex. "I'm ready anytime you are, Alex."

Alex pushed off from the dock and began rowing. The twinkle in his eyes made her face flame. She stared him down. "Alex, if you say one word—"

"You ain't gonna be responsible"? he supplied.

Julia's mouth dropped open. The sound of exclusively American vernacular uttered in precise, cultured tones—Philadelphia mixed with London—sounded odd, almost as if it were a foreign language.

Her embarrassment was forgotten as they stared at each other. Alex chuckled. Julia smiled.

They broke into laughter at the same time, gut-level deep and honest. When, she wondered, was the last time she had been so spontaneous? When had she last found pleasure in absurd moments and off-the-cuff banter?

The answer was loud and clear in her mind. *Every time you're with Alex.* She sobered, pleasure faded, laughter died. The truth was that she had never felt such a richness of emotion, never experienced such pleasure in the company of another person. Too many such moments were building between them, like a bridge without a solid foundation. Her fault. Only truth could build such a foundation. Only the elimination of doubt could give it strength. Only courage would give her the strength to reveal the skeletons in her closet, shake them free of dust, present them to Alex. Being a coward had been so much easier.

Alex rowed easily, powerfully, completely absorbed in what he was doing. Obviously, he was in seventh heaven, even on a small lake rather than on an ocean. Conversation was unnecessary. The day was bright, the air carrying just enough coolness to keep them comfortable, and all around them, sounds of happiness carried over the water. The gentle glide and rock of the boat coupled with Alex's rhythmic motions were drugging, giving her an excuse to put her thoughts to rest for a while longer. If she'd had a pillow, she'd lean back, close her eyes, trail a hand in the lake.

But, she'd done that before, with another man, a handsome man, sophisticated, wealthy, charming. A man she had loved. The memory intruded, reminding her that the past was still there, would always be there, a part of her. She had secrets which, if she had learned anything from the past, needed to be told. Better to know now whether Alex wanted all that she was or just what he could see.

Fretfulness set in, destroying the contentment she'd caught from Alex. She lowered her head and massaged her temples, trying to soothe the tension creasing her forehead. She shifted position, fussed with her skirt, glanced around, seeking escape. The past had caught up with her, and she had no choice but to deal with it.

"Julia? Don't you like the water? Are you ill?"

She saw his concern, and knew the moment had come.

Chapter Nine

The hull scraped on sand as Alex beached the boat on the island in the center of the lake and helped Julia back onto land. "Better?" he asked, all gentle concern. "It never occurred to me to ask if you were a good sailor." He walked slowly, and spoke to her in a voice as rich and soft as a nocturne. "I just naturally assume that everyone is like me, a throwback to our ancestors who called the oceans home. The water gives me peace, serenity."

Julia smiled absently. "I'm fine really." She stared pensively at the view from the top of Strawberry Hill. Not far away was the garden where her father's prizewinning roses had once been displayed. She could see the towers of the Golden Gate and Bay bridges, and Alcatraz Island was a dot in the bay, a reminder that there was no place to hide, no way to avoid what she must do.

She would never understand what had driven her father to steal. There was no way she could excuse it, but she had forgiven him. Forgetting was a little more difficult. He had paid his debt, not only from the pockets of his soul, but from hers as well. Would it now cost her the magic of Alex's presence in her life?

Alex sensed the change in Julia's mood. Her arms were crossed over her chest, her hands rubbing them as if she were cold. More than a mild case of *mal de mer* was at the root of her unrest. For the first time in his life, he wanted to ask, to know the intimate thoughts of another person. But, he never asked for something that only had value if it was given without prompting or suggestion.

In the past, he'd always paid for what he wanted, whether in business or pleasure. Life had been less complicated that way. He'd always received exactly what he'd paid for and never paid more than he could afford. If it was true that everyone had a price, then Julia's was patience and understanding. And so, he waited, locked into his own thoughts and his own insecurities about his ability to handle the situation in which he found himself.

Julia's earlier question about his childhood had made him disturbingly aware that having all of Julia meant giving all of himself—past, present and future. He'd lived the last eighteen years as if Alexander Sinclair existed only on paper. Alex St. Ives had been born the day he'd left Jeffrey sprawled on the parlor floor with bruises as blue as his blood and as black as his heart. He had walked away and he'd never looked back. He didn't want to look back now, but when Petrov had come to Sandcastle, he had brought the past with him, making it an indisputable element of the present.

Julia was conscious of Alex standing next to her, watching her, waiting. It was hard to speak after so many years of silence, learn to trust after so many years of suspicion, feel so intensely after not feeling at all. She was having a hard time getting the words out, afraid of what they might begin . . . or end. And she acknowledged another fear. A fear of herself and of how much she was willing to give this man. Fear that he would do nothing but take.

Julia took a deep breath, feeling Alex's attention shift and center on her. Her gaze met his and clung. She found her voice. "I thought you would have lost interest by now."

Alex smiled at that. "Impossible, in spite of your best efforts. I am neither bored or indifferent to you, Julia. Surely I've made that obvious."

Julia refused to be moved by his assertion. Words were easily spoken, but she had yet to know a man who could live up to them. Fatalistically, she was prepared for him to prove once and for all that Prince Charming didn't live up to his name.

"What if I told you that my father is a convicted felon, a repeat offender?" Without giving him a chance to reply, Julia allowed the words to tumble out and pile up between them. "He'd served two sentences before he met my mother. He managed to stay clean for six years after she died. His next 'caper' was to rob Nicholas Alexander, his employer. The courts aren't sympathetic to three-time losers." Tuned into every nuance of expression, she watched Alex closely for signs of cooling interest, repulsion, rejection, signs that her former fiancé hadn't bothered to hide.

Alex hadn't turned a hair, raised an eyebrow or backed away from her, mentally or physically. Everything about him bespoke a total lack of interest in her skeletons: his relaxed stance, his unclenched hands, a look that said he wouldn't be discouraged by her disclosures. His gaze moved over her, as tangible as the caress of soothing hands, a comforting embrace, a loving, tender kiss. More than she'd ever wanted anything in her life, she wanted to believe what his body language was telling her, wanted him to be all that he seemed.

Alex claimed her hand, covered it with both of his, looked down at her fingers as he stroked them. "Is this a test?"

"A test?" Julia's expression was dazed, as if the world had changed and she didn't know what to do, where to go, how to act. "Yes, I guess it is."

He closed the small distance between them and crooked his finger under her chin. "Julia, I already knew about your father. How could you think I didn't?"

"Aunt Chloe," she said on a sigh.

"And Petrov and your father. They all seemed to think I might be scared off by events over which you had no control." He grimaced. "Not very flattering to me, but understandable."

"I wouldn't have blamed you—not really," she whispered and tried to lower her head.

Alex wouldn't let her. "If you want to scare me off, you'll have to do better than that. On the other hand, I might send you running with a few stories of my own. Shall I tell—"

She placed her fingers over his lips. "No! Don't."

"Why?" he challenged with a hard expression.

"Because it doesn't matter." Her reply had required no thought, no careful wording, no self-examination. It was a simple truth that she had no trouble voicing.

"Well, that's a relief. Relating my sordid past would have blown the entire evening."

"Alex," Julia's moment of truth had gained momentum. While she was at it, she decided that she might as well touch every base. "I have nothing to offer you."

His mouth tightened as he released her abruptly and turned away from her. "Nothing but insults," he grated, shoving his hands into his pockets. "Time to go, I think."

"Alex—"

"Not another word, Julia. Not now."

The warning in his voice stopped her. Though his expression was wiped clean, Julia knew he was angry. She couldn't blame him. The tact she used so well on her clients failed her with Alex. But then Alex was more than a client. Much more.

The boat skimmed through the water as Alex rowed around Strawberry Hill with power in every stroke, his silence like a condemnation. She cleared her throat. "Alex..."

He ignored her and rowed faster.

She clenched her hands around the edge of her seat. "Darn it. Will you do whatever you do with oars to put them away and listen to me?"

Alex shipped the oars, and flexed his fingers, saying nothing.

She wanted to cower in the face of his calm, and it infuriated her. "Don't patronize me, Alex. Lose your temper, yell, walk away, but *don't...patronize...me*."

"Would you like me to walk away, Julia?"

"No!" His calm grated on her frayed nerves. "But, now that you mention it, I'd like to know why you haven't."

"So would I." It was a bald pronouncement, a confession, a question. "Especially since you have nothing to offer me."

"Darn it, Alex, you know what I meant."

"I don't think so, Julia. Why don't you tell me why you assumed it would be important to me?"

"Because it's been important to everyone else who—" She stopped herself before she revealed too much, committed more than she felt comfortable with, promised more than she could deliver.

"I see." Alex leaned slightly forward, propped his elbows on his legs and clasped his hands. "Julia, you've been running with the wrong crowd," he said solemnly.

Julia's posture was ramrod straight. "It was the same crowd you run with, Alex. You probably know most of them."

"Well, that explains it. As I said, you've been associating with the wrong people."

"But, they're your friends."

Metal creaked as Alex released the oars and began rowing again, but slower than before. "They are acquaintances, clients, business associates and enemies, not friends. Why do you think I spend all my free time on an isolated island in the South Pacific?"

She was afraid to respond, but had to ask the next question. "Aunt Chloe?"

"The exception to the rule. Chloe has been my friend and companion, my support system and on occasion, my conscience." Alex knew he was telling Julia more than he'd ever told another person. He also knew that he was going to tell her more, making an emotional commitment to her that would irrevocably change his life.

"Oh." Nothing in Alex's description of Chloe's role in his life answered Julia's question, but it didn't matter. Deep down, she already knew that her aunt was exactly what he'd said, nothing more, nothing less. Judging from Alex's silence, it appeared that he had no intention of offering further explanations. *Take it or leave it, Julia* was the message his silence conveyed. She took it because his refusal to compromise his relationship with another by "talking" reinforced her impression of his integrity. Besides, there was another question she had to ask, a question whose answer would determine the course of her immediate future.

"Alex..." It was hard to give away so much of her feelings after years of giving nothing of herself. She cleared her throat. "What exactly do you think I have to offer you?"

He held the oars out of the water, let the boat glide on its own momentum, and watched her with nothing in his expression to show how her question had affected him. It always unnerved her—the way he kept himself in such strict control, giving away neither anger nor displeasure. In fact, she mused, the only emotions he freely displayed were pleasure, amusement, contentment. The rest of Alexander St. Ives was a complete mystery.

"Friend, support system, lover," he said seriously.

Lover. The word had snagged her attention, and held fast, evoking images—of his hands finding intimate flesh, his mouth provoking reckless responses, his eyes seeing everything about her, fears, inhibitions, secrets. The prospect seemed all too real, and much too electrifying. "You don't want much, do you?"

"In time, Julia, I have a feeling that I'll want a great deal more." With that, he turned the boat toward shore.

Julia watched the dock loom closer, like the inevitable moment of magic and reckoning when dreams and reality would meet.

"WOULD YOU LIKE ITALIAN, Chinese, French or Russian for dinner?" Alex asked, letting Julia know that he considered their next meal far more important than talk of friends and lovers and fifteen-year-old news. And while they strolled down Clement Street, they sampled the offerings of some of the neighborhood's more than fifty ethnic restaurants, in a progressive dinner consisting of everything from antipasto to Russian piroshki.

By nine o'clock, Julia was staggering under the fifty or so pounds she was sure she'd gained. Her feet were killing her and she felt as if she could sleep standing up, if Alex would only allow her to stand still for two seconds. When they arrived at Mugsy's Tavern for Irish coffee, all she wanted to do was climb up on Mugsy's hundred-year-old bar and fall into a stupor.

"Julia, you're not listening," Alex said indulgently.

"Be quiet, Alex. Don't you recognize a coma when you see one?" She hiccuped and peered up at Mugsy as he approached her with another cup. "No, I don't want more of that dreadful brew, Mugsy. You should be hanged by your toenails for selling that stuff."

She was in a dream world where magic was a natural element in the air and reality was a mixture of feelings too special to be denied—friendship and happiness, companionship and pleasure and sweet suspense. The word *lover* insinuated itself into all her thoughts, making her wonder what it would be like, making her want to find out.

A fine sheen misted her skin; tension was a seduction in itself. Her blood flowed through her veins like warm oil. She felt her heartbeat in every pulse, a slow, steady beat, building in intensity. Julia was intoxicated by desire, sensuality, life, and Alex was the narcotic. The complementing wines she'd had with each course at dinner had nothing to do with her state of euphoria.

The Irish coffee, however, had everything to do with her hiccups on the drive home. At regular intervals, her body gave a little bounce as she stared out of the car window. Beneath the streetlights the sidewalks had a golden glow, and the evening fog seemed like fairy dust. The city was enchanted, its skyscrapers and bridge towers rising from the mist like castle turrets against an indigo sky.

Alex turned into her driveway. She felt no unease or irritation. If he wanted to linger, it would be all right with her. She was too mellow to argue, too full of dreams to fight her instincts.

Cool air drifted over her as he opened her door and helped her out. She could have sworn her porch was more than two steps away. Butter-soft leather cushioned her body. It didn't seem to be important to ask why they'd moved to the back of the car or why Alex was sliding across the seat and pulling her onto his lap.

"There is only one foolproof method of curing hiccups," he murmured. The thought of resisting flickered briefly, then died. She didn't want to resist. His mouth closed over hers, stealing her breath. Tongues of fire followed the path of his hands.

His surefire remedy suspiciously resembled necking. One kiss led to another. His hands moved over her back, urging her closer, then ran up the nape of her neck and swept languorously down her spine to her waist. His fingers brushed intimate places, but nothing more. Nothing to push her into going further, nothing to force a physical commitment before she was ready for an emotional one.

Julia responded without inhibitions, reveling in the freedom he had given her. She didn't have to worry that every move she made was being interpreted as a promise to deliver more. Alex was asking for moment-to-moment honesty, not promises. There was no way Julia could lie, no way her body could deceive him, no way she could deceive herself.

The windows fogged quickly and the air inside the car felt heavy and warm. Tremors began at each touchpoint Alex discovered. Moisture gathered and pooled low in her body. She opened her mouth, inviting more, giving more. Alex accepted, his tongue making bold statements with every stroke. Julia shifted her position and her breasts pressed against his chest, wordlessly answering him with ideas of her own. The world narrowed to this one place, this one moment, this one man.

There was a certain magic in discovering recklessness at the age of twenty-eight, knowing that her father's bedroom was only a few feet away and her neighbors were probably peeking out from the edges of their draperies.

Light spilled into the car, dimmed by the fogged windows, but startling just the same. Alex pulled away from her just a little, not quite separating their mouths, not quite ending their embrace. His hand continued to move in slow circles on the small of her back. He whispered between teasing nibbles on her earlobe. "Your father is awake."

"Hmm?" Julia glanced out the window, saw a shadow move on the other side of the bedroom window, reach for a curtain draw, then drop from sight. She heard a muted crash, but it didn't register. The curtain rod gave way and fell. A chill raced up her spine. Everything seemed to be moving in slow motion as she pulled away and squinted through the window.

"No," she cried, the sound echoing over and over again in her head. "Oh no. Da'!"

Alex lifted her, set her on the seat, opened the door, and vaulted out of the car, his hand reaching for hers at the same time, pulling her behind him as he ran for the door. Prayers ran through her mind. "Oh, please, God, no!" She fumbled for her keys as she begged, pleaded, bargained. This couldn't be real, this fear, the panic that overwhelmed. It didn't feel real. Alex grabbed the keys from her and unlocked the door. Julia pushed it open and raced straight to her father's bedroom.

She paused in the threshold, somehow knowing what she would find, yet refusing to believe it. Hope was a living thing coiling in her chest, hope that all was well, and her father had simply stumbled. She stared, unable, for a moment, to comprehend what she saw, unable to accept the reality.

Moonbeams poured through the bare window, like a spotlight. Patrick lay on the floor beneath the window, his face colorless, his lips tinged with blue. The sound of his breathing hurt Julia's ears. She ran to him, sank to the floor beside him, raised his upper body, held his head against her shoulder. "Alex, call—"

Alex was gone. Dimly, she heard him in the foyer phoning for help. "It's all right, Da'. Alex is here. He'll make them hurry," she crooned, rocking back and forth.

And then, she heard Patrick's voice, faint, like a worn thread. "Julie, I'm sorry... too late... too many 'if onlys' dragging on my soul... no time to make it right... my secret...can't die now...too late..." His eyes seemed to fade, a field of shamrocks dulled by encroaching night. "Don't forget...a rose...Elise..." His breath left him, a sigh, the ebbing of a soul.

A siren wailed mournfully and then silence. She heard hurried footsteps approach. Alex led the way into the bedroom and stopped inside the doorway. The uniformed man and woman paused behind him for the space of a heartbeat, then pushed past Alex and ran toward Patrick.

Julia blinked. The world was out of sync, everything moving slowly, like a runner through quicksand. The paramedics set up their equipment, asked her to move. She felt Alex's presence, safe harbor in the midst of a storm. His hands were all she could feel as he helped her up, led her out of the way. His voice was all she heard.

"Julia, loosen your fingers. Come with me. The paramedics need room." He held her close, willing his strength to become hers. His throat was tight, blocked with emotion. Julia's skin was cold, her body stiff, her hands clenched around his as she watched the woman hold electric paddles to her father's chest.

"Clear...okay, now!" Twice more, the order came. Nothing happened. A small monitor sounded a steady, unrelenting beep. A straight line showed on the screen, going on and on, unchanging.

Alex didn't know what to do. Never had he felt so helpless, so impotent. Never had it been so important that he do something that mattered, that made a difference. He knew pain as never before. Pain because he felt as if he had failed her even though he knew there had been nothing he could have done to make that difference. Pain because he had just discovered what it really meant to love, and, through her, what it really felt like to lose.

The woman dropped her instruments, and looked up at her partner. Just that—a long look of utter despair and grief for a man she hadn't known. The man reached across Patrick's body and touched her hand. "It was already too late when we got here," he said.

Julia pulled away from Alex and dropped to her knees once more. Her hand squeezed the woman's. "It was too late, you know," she said calmly. "He told me so." Gently, she smoothed her fingers along her father's closed eyelids. She bent to kiss his cheek. A single tear slipped down her face, and she sobbed once, the sound escaping in a single syllable, "Da'." Her body began to sway in a gentle rocking motion. Raising her head, she looked up at Alex, the pain of an abandoned child in her eyes.

Chapter Ten

Aunt Chloe moved into Julia's home the following morning, issuing orders like a field marshal and taking it for granted that they would be followed to the letter. Julia was apathetic and indecisive, though she insisted on going to work during the next three days and, when she came home, she worked in the garden until her muscles did the screaming she didn't know how to do.

She hadn't accepted her father's death, yet. Maybe after the funeral it would seem more real. Maybe then she'd be able to cry.

Alex was always there exactly when she needed him. On Monday, he had arrived to take her to lunch just when she had begun to feel the silence of her office closing in around her, the emptiness smothering her in grief. That evening, he'd appeared on her doorstep with dinner. Seeming to know that she hadn't wanted to talk, he'd said nothing, letting the silence bring them closer in another way, telling her that he understood the privacy of her anger and grief, telling her he understood that hers was a battle only she could fight.

His silences were eloquent as he'd watched her work, mindlessly, sometimes obsessively. She clung to him as if he were a towrope that she trusted to pull her through each new wave of grief.

He'd driven her to work on Tuesday, then taken her home at the end of the day. She'd wanted to work in the garden again. It made her feel closer to her father, made him seem real again. Guilt and frustration nagged at her because she couldn't relate her memories to anything immediate. Her Da' only existed in her mind now, like a dream that faded in and out at odd moments.

And so she knelt in the garden and forced herself to remember, and perhaps to pretend that Patrick would come through the back door, rolling up his sleeves, and start tending the rose he'd named for his wife: *Elise.*

"Julia Devlin, just what in the hell are you doing?" Chloe stood on the flagstones with her hands on her hips. "Your father was an Irishman."

Julia sat back on her heels, laid down the hedge clippers, and glanced at Alex, who had removed his shirt as he helped her weed and fertilize. He stopped digging and rested his hands on the handle of the shovel, appearing to know what Aunt Chloe was talking about. Julia didn't have a clue. "I'm taking care of the garden, Aunt Chloe, and I know father was an Irishman."

"Then why does this look like a formal garden? Paddy hated formality. He liked his gardens to have a 'lived in' look," she explained patiently. "What are you going to do next? Dust the grass? Polish the trees?"

Stricken, Julia saw for the first time what she had done. Aunt Chloe was right. The garden no longer had the slightly mussed appearance her father had favored; it looked orderly, untouched, sterile. She stood up abruptly and dusted off the seat of her shorts. "I'll take care of it, Aunt Chloe. Alex, would you move that flagstone a little to the right so the walk meanders?"

"No." Alex dropped the shovel and walked toward her, the late-afternoon sunlight burnishing his skin with gold, emphasizing his long, sleek muscles. His expression was determined, while his gaze touched her with tenderness. "Tomorrow afternoon, Julia, I will make the walk meander, or I'll rumple the ferns, anything you want. But, right now, I am going to clean up." He met her gaze without repentance in his expression. His linen trousers were streaked with dirt as were his bare feet. Rivulets of moisture ran down his chest and a ladybug was crawling on his shoulder.

Julia blinked. "Alex, don't you have any grungies?" she asked as she watched him carefully nudge the ladybug into his cupped palm and deposit it into a flower bed.

"Not here," he answered lightly. "Business trips rarely afford me the opportunity to play in the dirt." He straightened. "I'm going home to shower and change. You are going to have a long soak and a glass of wine. By the time you finish, I'll be back with dinner." He waited for her to bristle, to shoot him down with the look he'd come to expect from her when he was being high-handed. Something had to shake her out of her calm, he thought, knowing that the silence had to end and Julia had to let go, cry, scream, rage—anything to finalize her loss so that she could go on with her life. In a way, he would miss the silence. It had given him the satisfaction and pleasure of experiencing another kind of sharing, another kind of trust.

"Not tonight, King," Chloe said, reminding Julia and Alex of her presence. "I'm perfectly capable of making dinner, and we're going to have an early night."

"I'll cook, Aunt Chloe," Julia offered quickly. Chloe's idea of preparing a meal was to set the table and wait for the delivery of a gourmet pizza. More effort than that on Chloe's part would result in the total annihilation of Julia's kitchen.

"The heck you will. It's wine, bubble bath and my chef's salad for you. Alex's cook sends over too many calories, and all that canned food in your cupboard makes me nervous." Turning on her heel, she waved at Alex and disappeared through the door.

For a moment, Alex thought he'd seen a spark of rebellion in Julia's eyes, but then she rose and carried her tools to the shed. "Aunt Chloe is right, Alex. You've been spending entirely too much time catering to us."

Alex kept his mouth shut. This was the first time Julia had shown signs of breaking away from him, and much as he had enjoyed her dependence on him the past few days, instinct told him that it wouldn't be long before she resented it, and him.

Julia watched him use his shirt to wipe the dirt off his chest; he showed a total lack of concern for the fine fabric. "What are you going to wear home?" she asked.

He shrugged his shoulders. "My skin. This is California. Anything goes." He winked roguishly and sauntered to the side of the house, his shirt hooked over his shoulder. "I'll see you tomorrow."

Alex's forced lightness faded with every step he took away from Julia, and once in his car, he sat unmoving, his thoughts troubled. The full weight of his promise had settled on him since Patrick's death. If he and Patrick had had time to finalize their transaction, the Veil would be out of their lives once and for all. He had a bad feeling about the mess he'd gotten himself into and he'd spent the past three days agonizing over whether to break the promise he'd made to Patrick or honor it.

Honor exacted a high price. Guilt ate at him like acid. What was a broken promise—especially since it had been made against his better judgment? That question had echoed over and over in his mind for three days. But, so had Patrick's logic about Julia's probable reactions to the truth. For once in his life, Alex was unwilling to take a gamble. The risk was too high.

His mouth twisted at the irony of it. The gambler had become too cautious, though he knew that too much caution could be just as fatal as recklessness. He'd indulged in the ultimate act of arrogance by thinking he'd made the right decisions simply because his decisions usually were right, and if not, the outcome was one with which he could live. Alex could live without the Veil, but he had the sinking feeling that living without Julia might prove to be more difficult.

Without realizing it, he'd made his decision to honor his promise. Patrick's secret was safe with him. The question remained whether his secret was safe with Patrick.

"GET THEM OUT OF HERE, Aunt Chloe," Julia said under her breath later that evening. One by one, Patrick's friends filed into Julia's house, each carrying bottles of wine and whiskey or snack foods or boxes of glassware and napkins. Gone was her talent for the civilized put-down, the gracious refusal. She wanted to scream at them, kick them out of her house and throw their offerings out the door after them. Instead, she kept her back straight, her chin up, and tried to ignore the joviality each man brought with him like the chant in a barbaric ritual.

Chloe shut the door after the last man walked through. "Mellow out, Julie. We're about to have a good old-fashioned Irish wake."

"No." Julia's voice was calm, without inflection. "It isn't right. They shouldn't be here like this."

Chloe grabbed her arm and marched her into the bathroom, which was tucked under the stairs. "You want sackcloth and ashes, Julie? How about some keening and wailing, candles on every table, those nine men in there suffering under tight collars and heavy black suits?"

"What happened to mourning and reverence?" Julia asked tightly. "They're in there singing bawdy songs and playing poker and...*celebrating.*" Her voice broke and faded to a whisper. The sounds of revelry appalled her. She'd heard of wakes and knew that they were still a tradition in some cultures, but not here, not for her father, not when she couldn't see him or touch him or simply know that he existed somewhere besides in her thoughts.

"Julie," Chloe chided. "This is Paddy's kind of party. He would have loved this. For all we know, he might be enjoying it."

"But he's not here. He doesn't even seem real anymore and it's only been three days. Mugsy and the others are acting as if they're glad he's gone." She pulled open the door and walked across the foyer.

Chloe caught up with her on the front steps, grasped her arms and gave her a shake. "Julie, the last thing Paddy would have wanted is tears. He hated them. He loved celebrations. He believed that leaving this life meant going to a better one—''

Jerking her arm free, Julia didn't want to hear about celebrations or toasts to Paddy's grand adventure. She wanted to cry. She needed to cry. How dare they laugh and tell jokes and play poker in her father's honor when she couldn't even cry for him?

Julia walked around her block, and then around another block and still another. It could have been five minutes or five hours since she'd left the house. For the last few minutes, though, she hadn't been alone. She'd felt Alex's presence as she always did, deep inside herself in the place she supposed was the soul. He had approached her with caution, announcing himself in a soft voice so as not to frighten her. Warmth had surrounded her as he'd draped a shawl over her shoulders, then fell in beside her, again giving his silent, undemanding comfort.

More than anything else, his silence had shown her that she and Alex were kindred spirits. Like her, he was accustomed to living in more silence than anyone should be. She sensed that Alex, too, grieved for something lost or perhaps for something he'd never had. Knowledge slipped into her awareness before she realized its importance. She not only liked Alex; she loved him.

And she needed him desperately, as a friend, companion, lover.

Passion had come almost immediately, with the crashing of trains and the bursting of rockets. Loving had come more slowly, a learning process taught by Alex's compassion and empathy, his wit and even his arrogance, his ability to see her as nothing more than she was, nothing less than she could be.

"Chloe is right, you know," he said casually. "Your father would have loved the party."

It was like a blow, hearing Alex support the madness of a party to celebrate death. She stopped under a tree and whirled around to face him. "You, too, Alex? Tell me, what is there to be so happy about? My father going to a better place? What if he's gone *nowhere* and he's *noth-*

ing...nothing at all?'' She dipped her head to hide the emptiness she felt inside.

Stepping closer, Alex took her in his arms, held her close, rested his chin on top of her head. He understood grief, had experienced it acutely after that fateful day eighteen years ago—the day he'd shed all remnants of a sense of belonging and family. The memory still hurt. *Nothing and nowhere.* He'd been there, and come back because he'd realized that dreams were hope and hope was faith and faith was strength.

"Perhaps you're right, Julia. But, then again, your father might be in a place where dreams become real everywhere he looks.''

She raised her head so quickly that she bumped Alex's nose. His head jerked back with the impact and he gave a muffled grunt of pain. Shakily, her hand lifted, hovered, then gently touched his nose, cupped his cheek, felt the warmth and vitality of his skin, the roughness of the beard he hadn't had time to shave. He was real, solid, a dream she'd been afraid to acknowledge. "Are you a poet, Alex? A philosopher?''

He breathed deeply, as if preparing to make a confession. "I'm simply a man who believes in faith and dreams and the miracles they can inspire.''

"Da' believed in faith and dreams, too,'' she whispered. "He just didn't know how to make them count for something until the end.'' She squeezed her eyes shut. "Alex, I can't cry for him.''

He took her hands in his, brought them to his lips, kissed each finger in turn. "He doesn't need your tears, Julia. He isn't the one who is suffering. You need to cry for yourself.''

Patrick's voice reached out to Julia from across the years, a memory of her father's faith, his own belief in miracles. *Julie darlin', your mother isn't dead. She'll always be alive and happy in the arms of the Almighty. Look at the stars, Julie. We can't touch them, but your mother can. It's a glorious thing to be able to touch the stars.*

"There are nine men at your house waiting to share a toast with you," Alex said gently.

Reading between the lines, she understood what he meant. Those men had been her father's friends. They hadn't stopped caring because Patrick had broken the law, and they hadn't filled his place in their hearts simply because he hadn't always been there to fill it with his tangible presence. They were friends who cared about the man even though they hadn't always cared for some of the things he'd done. Friends. She might not be too crazy about the way they chose to show it, but she respected the feelings behind their actions.

Wordlessly, Julia gazed up at the sky, then slipped her hand into Alex's and turned toward home.

A glass was thrust into her hands as soon as she walked into the kitchen where most of the revelers had congregated. She wrinkled her nose as she brought it to her lips. One sniff made her shudder and she lowered it again, untasted. "I don't suppose you brought any root beer," she asked hopefully. At Mugsy's horrified expression, she held her breath and downed a healthy swallow, scrunching her eyes shut at the raw taste and the fire burning its way down her throat. She hated hard liquor.

Petrov appeared and bent his head to listen to Alex before leaving the room. "Alex, what is he doing here?" Julia whispered.

"Back-up bouncer—just in case."

"Then, why is he leaving with Aunt Chloe?"

"I believe he and Chloe have developed a sudden craving for root beer."

"Do you think they'll bring enough back for me?"

"I guarantee it."

Relief was short-lived when Mugsy reminded Julia that she had drunk before the toast. Her glass was refilled. The men watched her expectantly as she shuddered again and raised her glass. "To Da' and the new garden he is undoubtedly planting." She drank, choked and hiccuped. The men cheered. Gasping, Julia glared at the stocky man ready to refill her glass. "Mugsy, I'll hold you personally responsible if I grow hair on my chest."

Petrov arrived with the root beer in the nick of time.

Mugsy reached over to spike her drink. "Julie, you can't toast Paddy with that. Just watching you upsets the mood."

"Pretend, Mugsy," Julia advised while holding her glass out of reach. "After a few more swallows of that stuff, you won't care what I'm drinking."

After the fourth imaginative and increasingly expansive tribute to Paddy, Julia's muscles relaxed and she flowed with the crowd, the mood, the acceptance of her loss. She was too tired to fight herself, too realistic to fight the truth. Her father was gone. She was not. Denying it wouldn't change a thing. Her anger was spent and her father was still gone.

Alex was never far from her. Her eyes bleary from exhaustion, Julia smiled brightly at him and stumbled against his side. His arm wrapped around her waist, pulling her closer, keeping her steady, letting her know that it was all right to lean on him.

"Alex, if you let go of her, she's going to land facedown in the potato chips." Chloe pried open one of Julia's closed eyelids. "How much has she had to drink?"

"Not enough to anesthetize her like this." He shifted her weight until he could ease her into a chair.

"Hmm. Internal shutdown. It's about time. She's worn-out."

"I'm fine," Julia said, her eyes still closed. "You were right, Aunt Chloe. This is Da's kind of party."

"It was," Chloe said as she climbed onto a chair, put her fingers to her lips and blew a shrill whistle over the din. "Time to pack it in, guys. Let's clean up this mess and go home to hit the sheets."

Glasses clinked and bags crackled as the men scrambled to obey. "My aunt the field marshall," Julia said as Alex led her to the sofa after several gruffly delivered complaints were registered that she was in the way.

Sweet, she thought. One of the men was actually mopping the floor where a glass had spilled. Another had started to hand-wash the dishes until Chloe pointed out the automatic dishwasher. Within thirty minutes, order was restored and all nine souls stood in front of her to say goodbye. Julia eyed them one by one. "Who's your designated driver?" Her voice ended in a hiccup.

Awkwardly, they looked at each other and at her, their expressions sheepish, their cheeks turning as red as their noses.

"I will drive them home," a sober Petrov volunteered.

"I'll navigate," Chloe offered.

Leaning over, Chloe kissed her niece's cheek. "I'll be back soon, love." She began herding the men toward the door like a drover on a cattle drive. "I'll steer, Greg."

Greg? Julia's eyes met Alex's, sharing a smile.

Petrov bristled. "Gregori, madam. And, I'm perfectly capable of steering."

"Not you, Greg—them." She nudged the last man through the door. "Somebody ought to rinse the starch out of your shorts."

"Perhaps, madam, they should wash your mouth out with soap at the same time." The door shut behind him, cutting off Chloe's reply.

Julia sat up. "Did he say what I think he said?"

"He did." Angling himself into the corner of the sofa, Alex pulled her back against his chest.

"Alex, I don't think that Aunt Chloe takes prisoners."

Freckles had blossomed on Julia's nose in the last few days. Fascinated, Alex traced his forefinger along their path. "Petrov fought the German army and escaped the Russian one. I think he can handle one redhead."

"I wouldn't be so sure about that."

"Julia, the worst that can happen with those two is that they will handle each other."

"Maybe we'd better duck."

Alex raked his hands gently through her hair, massaging her scalp. Her weight on his lap commanded his attention, ruled his body, turned his thoughts to those of a young man's fancy in the spring.

Suddenly aware that she and Alex were alone, Julia fidgeted in his lap, and wondered whether she should be excited or uneasy about the tension she felt in his body, the hardening. "I think I'm the teeniest bit whoozled," she confessed.

Alex knew better, but didn't say so. She had opened up, become more natural than he'd ever seen her. He didn't want to remind her that it was exhaustion making her punchy, or why. Alex leaned over to pour two cups of coffee from the tray Chloe had placed on the coffee table in front of the sofa.

A hiccup escaped her. "I have the hiccups," she said and snuggled deeper into his embrace.

He smoothed her hair away from her face.

"That isn't going to do it." Julia looked at him expectantly.

Alex kissed her forehead, the tip of her nose—he really liked her nose, the shape of it, the impudent tilt at the tip.

"Alex, we're talking radical hiccups here. I think aggressive treatment is called for."

Alex was tempted to do more than hold a cup of coffee to her lips. He shifted position.

She sipped obediently. "This isn't what I had in mind, either."

"Julia, would you be acting this way if you weren't the teeniest bit whoozled?" The excuse was convenient for both of them, and Alex used it unrepentantly. Julia concentrated fiercely before answering, "I have no idea. You make me want to do things I've never done before. Why? Am I embarrassing myself . . . or you?"

Her frown of exaggerated gravity encouraged his White Knight fantasies. Her serious candor made Alex aware that, right now, he was holding Julie the child rather than Julia the woman. More and more he was seeing the two merge. When the process was complete, he planned to be on hand. But instinct warned him that if he accepted what Julie was offering tonight, Julia wouldn't be comfortable with the results in the morning. It was essential that Julia be as comfortable with him as he was with her—if one didn't count the stressed condition of his body.

"No embarrassment, Julia. Not between us. Remember that."

"I'd rather have something else to remember, Alex," Julia answered him solemnly, honestly, clearly.

Alex tipped up her chin and brought her mouth to his, nipping her lower lip, laving it with his tongue, leaving her in no doubt that she echoed his own desires. Punchy did not necessarily mean immune from hurt. "Julia, my first instinct is to listen to my considerable ego and believe that I can make you forget everything but me . . . what I can make you feel." He stroked her cheek. "But, you won't forget. In the morning, you'll be fully aware of what we did—for all the wrong reasons."

As she opened her mouth to argue, he shook his head, stopping her. "I don't want any hangovers between us, Julia. This is too special, too important to happen because of desire on my part and despair on yours."

Julia caught her breath. "Is it going to happen?"

"Never doubt it . . . and when it does happen, I'll be expecting and accepting promises."

"How very arrogant of you, Mr. St. Ives."

"No, just sure. You're not about to allow yourself to indulge in that kind of relationship unless you have feelings to back up the actions."

Julia bit the inside of her lip as she thought about that. She couldn't doubt his assertion that he wanted her. Her position on his lap made her unmistakably aware of his physical condition at the moment. As for the rest, she just didn't see Alex talking futures unless he had a vested interest. "That's quite a talent you have." At his questioning look, she explained. "Your rejection sounded more like seduction."

"Not rejection, Julia. A postponement."

Yawning, Julia laid her head on his shoulder, feeling comfortable with him as she'd never felt with another human being. "I can live with that," she murmured and gave in to exhaustion.

Alex hoped that he could live with it without going mad. He'd never imagined a time when his heart and his mind would say no, while his body so emphatically said yes.

Julia nuzzled his neck. "Alex? Why me?" she asked, too tired and too secure in his arms to worry about what such a question might reveal about her hang-ups. Was there something about her that other men might have missed or that she might not be aware of?

Smiling wryly, Alex answered, "I have no idea—" he teased, throwing her earlier words back at her "—other than it feels right . . . you chase away the loneliness."

Staring at him owlishly, Julia felt a surge of pleasure. He had given her intangible explanations with intangible meanings that touched her deepest fears, soothed them, and sank into her all the way to her soul. Explanations so stark and honest, she couldn't doubt them, yet she felt no pressure or threat from them. Smiling, she slipped into sleep between one breath and the next.

Wondering when he had become so honorable, Alex leaned his head back against the sofa, closing his eyes—just for a minute until Petrov and Chloe returned. For the first time since they'd met, he and Julia were alone—really alone—no pretense, no memories, no suspicions. Her bottom was nestled firmly against his straining sex. Her breast conformed provocatively to the hardness of his chest. She made soft, sweet little sighs in her sleep, teasing his ear with warm puffs of breath. For the first time since they had met, Julia was relaxed, unguarded.

He was strung tighter than a bowstring. With a smile of self-mockery, he tucked an afghan around Julia and resigned himself to a long night.

TO JULIA'S SURPRISE, every last man who'd attended the wake was in sober and respectful attendance at the funeral. So was Dina and her office staff. Thirty people stood around the grave, a throat-clogging tribute to a man who had flouted the law and, as a result, had been out of circulation for fifteen years.

Mugsy's eulogy was short and infinitely sweet as he crumpled his notes into his pocket and gazed at the assembled company. "Paddy Devlin is gone, but he has left his mark behind—in the gardens he brought to life, the memories he has left with us, and the holes in my wall at the tavern because he never could hit the dart board. And, in his daughter, Julie, he has left all that was good and special in himself. May he rest in peace. Amen."

Alex bowed his head and added his own silent prayer that Patrick had taken his secrets with him, and that the Veil of Tears would remain a legend. He knew he was being selfish, but Patrick had been right. The time for telling Julia about the Veil was past. He should have told her about it that first day, before not telling her had become a lie. Julia walked forward to place a single flower on top of the casket—a white rose washed with shades of palest rose and gold, like the first glimmer of sunrise. She returned to Alex's side, her gaze clinging to him, and a single teardrop trailed down her cheek as a gentle breeze raised whorls from a mound of freshly turned earth.

Chapter Eleven

"He's late," Dina pronounced flatly as she staggered into Julia's office with an armload of catalogs and swatches. "If it were for anyone but Alex, I'd say this gallery job is a pain in the behonkus." She dumped her burden in a chair. "Where is he, anyway?"

Julia kept staring at an open file, her chin resting in her hands. "He's helping Aunt Chloe move back into her own house."

"I thought Chloe had a thing going with Petrov. Why doesn't he help?"

"He's playing hard-to-get." Julia looked up with a bemused smile curving her mouth. "I don't think he approves of Aunt Chloe."

"I'm not sure I approve of her, either, and I have teenagers. I *have* to be broad-minded." Dusting off her hands, Dina glanced out the window. "Gee, it's not the same without Alex showing up."

"I haven't noticed."

Dina rolled her eyes and muttered, "Uh-huh."

Julia suppressed a smile until Dina shut the door on her way out. The smile felt good, like a hug she was giving herself. It had been a bad day, poignant with memories. For the first time in the six weeks since the funeral, she felt truly alone. Chloe was moving out. Alex wouldn't be coming to take her to lunch. Her father wouldn't be waiting for her at home. Even the work on the gallery was winding down.

She'd spent so much time working on it that the opening would occur a month ahead of schedule. For the first time in over a month, she had time to think.

Her grief was like a stone wall, building upon itself, isolating her from everyone, even from herself. She functioned well, eating, sleeping, working. No one would guess that she felt rearranged from the inside out.

The door opened and Dina swung it back with her foot. She carried a tray with hot chocolate, cups, and extra marshmallows. Her look was determined as she served. "Okay, Julie. I can't stand it anymore."

Julia sat back in her chair, kicked off her shoes and propped her feet on an open drawer. "Dina, can't this wait? I spent four hours at the dressmaker's while Don Juan the Destroyer fussed over Sharon's costume and I have a lot of catching up to do."

"I've been waiting for weeks, and you haven't said a word."

A stab of pain stopped Julia's breath. Each day seemed to fade the reality of her father's time with her a little more. She met her routines just as she had before he'd been released from prison, as if he hadn't been with her for those few weeks, and nothing had changed.

Except that everything had changed, including herself.

Dina sighed in exasperation and threw up her hands. "You can't change your appearance and your routines without people noticing, and wondering."

Julia shrugged. "So I've bought some new clothes—"

"And highlighted your hair, and you've had a make-over, and you hum, Julie."

"Isn't that allowed?" Julia asked innocently.

"Of course it's allowed. Frankly, I'm tickled pink about it. You've been so quiet most of the time since your dad died."

"I'm pretty sure that's allowed, too, Dina." Julia swallowed a lump in her throat and changed the subject. "Now, if there's nothing else on your mind—"

"There certainly is something else on my mind." Hooking a chair with her foot, Dina pulled it closer and flopped down. "The most gorgeous man in two hemispheres is by your side at the funeral as if he belonged there—by your side, I mean. Your lunches have expanded to two hours and you've spent every one of them with *him*."

Julia bit the inside of her cheek. Dina always said "him" as if it were in boldface and underlined. "Do you mean Alex?"

Dina nodded and kept right on talking. "That man makes every woman he looks at feel good about herself, yet he looks at you as if you're a pearl and the rest of us are just so many pretty beads. And, you . . ." Dina snorted in disgust. "You act as if everything is business as usual. Nothing new. Nothing special. Are you blind? Are you deaf? Are you crazy?"

"Mmm. Crazy, I think."

Dina's mouth fell open, but she recovered quickly. "You don't seem too happy about it."

"I'm not sure," Julia said, a stark, raw note in her voice a reaching out, a sharing of herself, a need to become part of the greater whole that was friendship. Yet, she was still afraid to give in to it, afraid that she might be left empty once again.

The only reaction Dina gave was a thoughtful look, quick and penetrating, then a casual shrug. "So who *is* sure about these things? Julie, men aren't the most logical humans on the planet. When you think about giving one a big chunk of your heart, it can be pretty scary." As if she knew that pushing too much might make Julia bolt, Dina bounced out of the chair and headed for the door. "But then, so is breathing the air, living on a fault line, and eating anything but oat bran. It's all dangerous to our health, but we still do it." She glanced at Julia over her shoulder. "It's a matter of survival, honey. There are some things we just can't live without."

"Wisdom according to Dina."

"Nah. Somebody else said it before I did."

All humor left with Dina, and Julia sobered. It was scary, knowing you couldn't live without someone. Alex had become such an important part of her life. She and Alex were spending so much time together, they might as well be married. The only thing they hadn't done was share the intimacy of physical love. Evidently, Alex had been serious about wanting her as a friend, support system and lover—in that order. She didn't mind. The lack of pressure in their relationship kept her on an even keel. Working with him on the new gallery and seeing him almost every evening had given her new insights, new needs.

That was what scared her—the needs, the way Alex had become a part of her life, so that no thought was complete unless he was a part of it. Julia stared out a window at the walled garden she'd put in after taking over the property.

It didn't make sense. Their whole relationship wasn't following the rules. She and Alex knew nothing about each other, none of the minutiae that were supposed to be important in getting to know each other. Neither of them had offered, nor asked. Each of them had refrained from violating the privacy and memories of the other. Only that once, at Golden Gate Park, had Julia volunteered information and then only in a last-ditch effort to get Alex out of her life before he seduced her into believing he was different than the others.

Her knowledge of Alex consisted of fleeting impressions and quick flashes of insight, nothing palpable, yet she trusted her perceptions as if they were proven fact. *Not a good idea, Julia,* the voice of experience warned. *Alex doesn't fit any molds. He's an enigma. Face it—you don't understand him. You simply want him. If Dina asked about Alex, what would you tell her?*

Many things came to mind and she closed her eyes, focusing, concentrating, trying to put them all together.

The details of Alex's life seemed insignificant compared to what she'd discovered about the man himself, a man who didn't talk about himself, but rather showed what kind of person he was, with no fanfare, no efforts to convince. His elegance was innate rather than acquired. He was the ultimate in civilized man. Most so-called civilized men would have thought twice before stripping off a silk shirt and ruining expensive trousers for the dubious pleasure of working and sweating in someone else's garden.

He was gentle and kind. He was logical, as well as brilliantly creative in solving problems. Though worldly and jaded, he also had an unerring eye for the dreams beneath the realities. His calm disposition, his patience, the wisdom that seemed such a natural part of him, showed a man fully in control of himself, contained. Yet, his sensuality and passion—the sheer power of it—suggested a more primitive man who didn't hide on his island, but merely retreated there from time to time, to be rejuvenated, to gather himself together, to heal.

From what?

Resting her chin in her hand, Julia stared at the clock in her office. All she really knew about Alex was what he allowed her to see. Though he wasn't afraid to show his emotions, she knew he kept secrets that would reveal what had made him the man that he was. Yet she didn't rush it because she, too, had been holding back, using grief as an excuse to keep from taking the next step in their relationship.

Her emotions were on overload and her practical left brain seemed to be out to lunch. She hadn't been able to cry, or scream or rage—all the normal reactions to loss. What was wrong with her? Had she kept her emotions on ice for so long that she wasn't capable of feeling as most people felt? But, that couldn't be true, she thought. She did feel, acutely. For Alex.

The phone rang in the outer office, and Julia heard Dina answer. A light on her own console blinked as Dina's voice was magnified by the intercom. "Julie, it's Chloe."

Julia flicked on the speaker. "Hello, Aunt Chloe."

"I can turn right around and go back to your place."

"I'll be fine." A surge of panic caught Julia by surprise, and she had to remind herself of the reasons why she'd suggested that Chloe move back into her own home.

Her aunt was a wonderful person to visit for a while, but impossible to live with for any length of time. Chloe had rearranged the furniture, fed her a steady diet of rich delicacies, most of which Julia hated, and she'd constantly run tapes of Star Trek on the VCR. Chloe seemed to have a penchant for men with pointed ears.

"I think you still need me, Julie."

"Yes, but I can handle it, Aunt Chloe," Julia said quietly. It was becoming too easy for her to depend on others, cop out on the issues at hand.

"Julie, what planet are you on?" Chloe demanded.

"I'm listening..." A frown puckered Julia's forehead. "What did you say?"

"I said that Alex is on his way to pick you up."

"Oh. He is?" Movement from the side window caught her eye—a car pulling up to the curb. Alex's car. "Did he happen to say why he was picking me up?"

"Something about skinny-dipping in a swimming hole."

"Oh."

"What do you mean 'oh'? Julie..." Alarm raised Chloe's voice. "I thought Alex was kidding."

"I don't think so, Aunt Chloe." Mischief gleamed in her eyes as she reached out to put her finger on the disconnect button. "I'll talk to you later. Bye."

From the reception room, Julia heard Dina's voice, husky with just a dash of honey—a voice Dina had developed just for Alex. Anticipation curled in Julia's stomach, pleasure warmed her skin. As he walked into her office, she felt the jolt of excitement Alex always brought with him. Only now, that jolt kicked a little harder at the thought of skinny-dipping with him. Julia sat back, releasing her breath and telling herself that she was being ridiculous. He had been kidding, hadn't he?

ALEX'S VERSION OF HOOKY was to wander the acres of his estate as if it were uncharted territory. They walked through fern-carpeted woods and shared a picnic in a flower-speckled meadow that overlooked the ocean far below. The silences were there, comfortable and comforting, and Alex's hand was always within reach, to hold, to reassure, to lend strength when she needed it.

His version of skinny-dipping in a water hole was swimming in the huge pool at his estate without the "skinny."

Instead, he appeared from the bathhouse wearing the latest in European men's swimwear—formfitting navy briefs. Brief was the operative word. Actually, the stretchy fabric seemed as if it were just another color of skin, emphasizing every detail, drawing attention to the very parts of him it covered.

Julia took one look and kept right on staring. Every line of his tall, muscled body was beautifully symmetrical, his broad chest and broader shoulders, the hard ridges of his stomach, his long, well-developed legs, his tight, masculine buttocks. The more she looked away, the more her gaze was drawn back. She indulged in another sweeping appraisal. Startled at what she'd seen, she couldn't stop the momentum of her gaze, racing upward, colliding with his. Her blood became heavy, warm, responsive to the approval, the desire she saw in his eyes . . . and his body.

The suit he'd provided for her was a shiny maillot, white, with a conservative cut, supposedly modest. Alex's gaze told her otherwise. His body approved more boldly. Julia's responded in its own way, more subtly, but no less dramatically. She should have felt self-conscious, but she didn't have the energy. Her figure was far from perfect. All her makeup had worn off, and she'd tucked her hair under a frilly little bit of a bathing cap. Chlorinated water always turned the ends of her hair green.

Alex enjoyed watching her, the proud way she stood, without a trace of self-consciousness. She made the simple white suit look elegant. He'd been right about her figure. It was average, except for her long legs, her rounded hips and thighs, just the smallest bit out of proportion with her trim waist and narrow rib cage, her moderately large breasts. Those hips and thighs and breasts, the deep curve of waist made her that much more feminine and touchable, that much softer.

Alex held out his hand, smiled easily when she reached across the small space separating them, her fingers clasping first. He kept the pace slow, lazy, enjoying the sweet torture of physical urgency, hot need. Julia's obvious approval of him made him feel ten feet tall. A sense of power surged through him at the subtle signs of her own physical response, in the swelling of her breasts, her quickened breathing, the heat and glow of her skin. It was special, that power, all the more so because Alex knew it was shared. He'd seen it in the way she'd stood under his gaze, every part of her enhanced by an inner sense of pride in herself. As surely as he knew how he felt about Julia, he knew that only he had ever made her feel that pride and know her own sense of power.

"This place," she whispered, "is magical." The path wound among tress and bushes. The sunlight was diffused by a heavy canopy of green overhead, appearing misty, a little blurred, like a dream. Delicate wildflowers were cradled by the exposed roots of redwoods. The scent in the air was fertile, seductive. The sounds of leaves rustling, the muted roar of the ocean, ebbing and flowing on the beach, filled her with erotic rhythms.

The pool was large, free-form, with winding streams branching off in several directions and ending in small secluded coves. To one side was a hot tub, artfully designed to resemble a natural spring. Foliage grew lush and oversized, surrounding pool and streams and the coves like curtains. The trees were old and tall, their leaves draped overhead like the roof of a sultan's tent.

"At Sandcastle, there is a place like this, but it has a waterfall, too." He smiled musingly. "My own personal bathtub and shower."

Julia sighed. "So much for romance."

"Bathtubs and showers can be incredibly romantic depending upon whom you share them with."

"I am not going to ask." She stepped up to the edge of the pool and sighed at the silky feel of water gently lapping at her bare toes. It was neither cold or warm, but a mixture of the two, like a pool on a tropical island. She sighed again, a deep breath of contentment and banked excitement. "Nicholas must have been a complete sensualist."

"It would seem so." Alex abruptly turned away to unpack the sports bag he carried.

"He always seemed so sad and alone. It's a shame he had no one to share all this with."

His hands clenched. "Perhaps he chose not to share it."

Julia dropped her towel and waded into the water. "Do you think so? This whole place, the house, the woods, the pool, the stable and meadows—it all seems so perfect for a family. I remember once, when I was here with Da', Nicholas talked about building a tree house in the woods."

"You came with your father often?" Alex fussed with bottles of spring water, a widemouthed thermos filled with ice, a plastic container of lemon and lime wedges, another filled with sliced cheese and grapes. Something twisted in his chest. A tree house. He'd asked Jeffrey for a tree house once.

"Once in a while, not often." Julia's voice grew distant as she disappeared down one of the little waterways.

Suddenly feeling more alone then he ever had in his life, Alex dived in and followed her. He stopped and found bottom to stand chest-deep in the water, watching her, her absolute stillness in the cove. Her back was to him, yet he sensed her pain.

"Julia," he called softly, afraid to startle her.

She turned, her mouth trembling. "Alex, look, over there." She pointed toward a small clearing, her eyes unblinking. "It's a faery garden. Da' and I planted it the last time—" Her voice trailed off on a broken whimper, a note of anguish.

With long strokes, Alex swam to her. He'd seen her shoulders heave, her hand tremble as she tore the cap off her head. Pulling her back against his chest, he held her close, felt a shudder pass through her body, felt an ache in his throat, a tightness behind his eyes. "Julia, it's past time. Let go. The pain—it can't get better until you acknowledge it's there."

The tears came silently at first, streaming down her face and falling onto his arms where they crossed over her chest. Her body shook with her effort at control, her muscles quivering. Alex gripped her shoulders, pulled her around to face him, gave her a gentle shake. She blinked her eyes at him, bit her lip. "That's not good enough, Julia." He shook her once more, again gently, though his fingers bit into her shoulders. "Cry, damn it. Scream. Anything. Just... get... rid... of... it. Now!"

His hand cupped the back of her head, brought it to rest on his shoulder, stroked her hair. He heard the first sob, then another, deep wrenching sobs that shook her body. Tears bathed his shoulder and sank into him, gathering on wounds he'd thought healed long ago, burning, stinging, making them bleed.

He kept on holding Julia, sharing her grief, and knowing that this was one of those moments that enriched life and left a memory that would never fade, a moment that proved he was not alone.

Julia raised her head and looked up at Alex. A sound escaped her, different now, half sob, half laugh. "You wouldn't happen to have a handkerchief, would you?"

He smiled, as she'd intended. "Come with me." He lead her to the edge of the pool and pulled a large leaf from a bush. After washing it in the water, he handed it to her, then looked away, instinctively knowing that she was sensitive about such things.

Self-conscious, Julia blew her nose as quietly as she could, and threw it into a waste can camouflaged with foliage. She couldn't look away from him, his tender concern, his empathy, as he cupped her chin in one hand and bathed her face with the other.

His gaze was brooding, serious, too. "How do you feel?"

"Fine. A little weak. A lot foolish." She drew a trembling breath, let it out again, gazed up at the leaves overhead, then back at Alex. "I feel free." *Unburdened. Peaceful. Happy.*

Words for how she felt just kept coming, but she didn't voice them. She didn't have to. Alex understood. It was written all over him. Obviously, something terribly, terribly tragic had happened to him once. It amazed her that he didn't use it as an excuse to be cynical or bitter. Somehow, he had learned to compensate for the pain and handle the memories that went with bad experiences. She wished she had the right to ask what those experiences were, and share in his own walks through the past.

Her hand lifted to caress his cheek, her thumb rubbing across his lips. Her walls were down now, the gate open, inviting. She badly needed to be touched, held, loved. By Alex. Just as badly, as she wanted to touch, hold, love—only Alex.

He cradled her head in his hands, just that, as he asked a silent question. *Are you sure?* He gave her so much power with that question. She floated against him in the water, their hips cradled, their chests touching. She felt her power in his body, the growing, the hardness, the strength, the need.

She stood on tiptoes, her lips reaching for his, touching them, barely. "I'm fine, Alex," she whispered against his mouth. "In full possession of my faculties." He didn't wait to hear more, but displayed his own power by taking her mouth completely, telling her what he'd expect if they went on. She was ready. More than willing. And able? Yes, that, too. Able for the first time in her adult life to give, knowing it was right.

It was magic. Her body changed, swelling here, hardening there, turning hot and liquid under his hands and mouth. She wasn't afraid to stroke him. She wasn't shy about telling him where she liked to be touched, or about lowering the front of her suit, then touching the front of his. Boldness followed boldness. His arms wrapped around her tightly, his kiss plunged deeply, his hips ground into hers, out of control. His lips followed his hands as he slid her suit down her body, smiling when the wet fabric caught on wet skin. She smiled back, and played with the waistband of his suit, then ventured lower. Bits of navy blue and white floated away, undulating on the gently rolling waves.

Julia twined her arms around his neck and floated free from the bottom of the pool. Alex pulled her close, then closer still, urging her legs around his waist. She opened herself to him, accepting him, loving him, knowing that they were sharing the ultimate dependence upon each other.

Warm, silky water played over their bodies as they moved together, two parts becoming one.

She chased his mouth, caught it, nibbled his lower lip, soothed it with her tongue. She felt his muscles tightening, straining against her, and yielded to him. Trembling began, deep inside her and spread outward, caressing Alex in another way. He plunged into her once more. She met his thrust, losing herself in him, feeling the tension, the unbearable urgency that went on and on. Release came with a rush, overwhelming her, making her cry out with pleasure and tighten around him. Julia felt his own release, a giving way to her, a vulnerability she had created in him. And, her gaze locked with his, her lips parted, her breath suspended, time suspended, for that one small moment of magic.

Alex waded to the bank, still a part of her, wanting to stay that way forever. He found a small, grassy patch to the side of the garden, big enough for two, and sank to his knees as he took a kiss from her. Easing her onto her back, he followed her down. Another kiss and he rolled to his side, propping his head with his hand while the other wandered over her skin, tender, calming.

Her breathing slowed and her heartbeat returned to a gentler rhythm. Time passed around them, not touching the world they'd created for themselves.

"Tell me about the faery garden," Alex whispered.

Julia turned her head to look at the little clearing and the assortment of plant life, the bright splashes of color. Her smile was poignant with drifting emotions, her voice melodic. "We were weeding around the pool, and I found the faery ring . . . there."

"The mushrooms growing in a circle?"

"Yes. Da' told me that sometimes growths like that are centuries old. There were more varieties, but he weeded out the truly dangerous ones."

"What is a faery ring?"

Julia sighed, thinking of childhood visions and fairy-tale dreams. "It's where the faeries dance." Her gaze went back to the cove and its surroundings, the illusion of another world, wholly theirs.

"When we found the ring growing near the water, Da' told me the story of Urisk." Her voice thickened. "He lived a solitary existence near isolated pools. Sometimes, he even craved human companionship to ease his loneliness."

"He craved? I take it, he wasn't successful."

"No," Julia whispered. "He wasn't attractive, so people avoided him. Father and I planted the flowers and trees for him, to keep him busy." A bittersweet smile tugged at one corner of her mouth. "I hoped that other faeries would come here, too, so that he wouldn't always be alone."

Alex brushed the hair away from her face, kissed her at the tender spot just beneath her ear. "The garden is still here, Julia. Urisk has been busy and perhaps others of his kind do come to visit from time to time."

Her smile was real this time, a spark of pleasure at Alex's whimsy. "I used to imagine him sitting right over there."

"How did you see him?" Alex asked, not knowing why, but feeling as if her answer was important, an insight into the real Julia Devlin.

"He wasn't ugly at all, or frightening. He was just small, and withered from neglect, drooping with sadness, like the mansion." Her voice seemed to wither, too, like the lonely spirit. "Father...*Da'*...looked like that when he came home from prison."

"But, not later, Julia."

"No," she said, turning to Alex, curling into him. "Not later." Her hands ruffled through the lush grass and stilled. "Alex, look. A four-leaf clover." Her fingers pinched the fragile stem, then released it as Alex's hand closed around her wrist.

"Don't pull it."

"Why?"

"Because—" he kissed her fingers, her nose, her mouth "—it belongs here and it will die if you pull it."

She closed her eyes, wanting to cry for the man who understood so much. The afternoon had been theirs, precious hours when they belonged nowhere but here, and they had nothing but each other. A time when a man and woman had been given the freedom, and the courage, to dance with the faeries.

Chapter Twelve

'You will stay," Alex said, not a question, but not a statement, either. They'd paused at the edge of the woods, reluctant to leave their private moments behind. Even the early-evening light was different in the open, bright and shining like satin, defining everything sharply.

"Will I?"

"Yes."

Definitely a statement. Really, Julia thought, he was so cocky. She gazed at him with a challenging lift of her eyebrows. "Alex, rattling my cage is not the way to get what you want."

"You're not staying?"

"Of course I'm staying," Julia said as if there had never been any doubt, or any alternative. "But only because I want to."

"Of course."

"Who wants to drive home in rush-hour traffic on a Friday?"

"Especially since I'm the one who would have to drive."

"On second thought—"

"It's too late for second thoughts, Julia."

The words hit her like a swift kick from the past. Had the raw note in his voice been regret? Already? But, no, it wasn't regret she saw in his expression as he stared back the way they had come—the long way—from the pool. It had been Alex's idea to walk through the woods, rather than swim back to the main pool not far from the house. She'd had the feeling that he'd deliberately led her around in circles just to prolong their return. But it was a silly thought. Why would he want to do that when the whole area belonged to him? He could camp in the woods until hell froze over if he wanted to. In the back of her mind, a reason lurked, afraid to come out, afraid it would be laughed out of the realm of possibility.

Maybe, just maybe, Alex didn't want to leave the private world they'd created because it was a place where only they existed, two lonely spirits who had found a home in each other.

He looked back once more. "It's special, Julia, the day, the place, the memory."

Special. He'd said it as if it were foreign to him—the word, and the experience. "Alex," she said softly, "you're sentimental."

"On special occasions, yes." He rested his forearms on her shoulders, touched her forehead with his, a quirky smile on his face. "Like today."

Julia lowered her eyelids, unable to meet his gaze. The silence waited to be filled. But not by her. Deep inside herself, she knew there were words to fit the moment, yet she couldn't say them. It had been too long, and all this was too new. Everything that had happened since Alex had come into her life had too much unreality about it for her to trust it completely.

"You're panicking, Julia." Mockery angled Alex's mouth as he straightened and broke contact. "I am, too."

It startled her, his admission. And, she confessed to herself, it wore her down. How on earth was she supposed to be inhibited and wary with a man who so readily admitted to being as insecure as she was? First the breath mints, and now this—small, normal things, yet coming from Alex, they were making her very nervous.

Alex took her hand and stepped out of the woods. "Come on, Julia—one step at a time."

ID SHE REALLY have the energy? Julia wondered as she
ared down the curved staircase. It seemed twice as long
nd twice as steep as it had last night when she and Alex had
nally gone up to his room. But, then, last night Alex had
layed romantic hero to the hilt and staggered up the flight
ith her in his arms.

He'd stumbled on the landing and nearly dropped her.
hey'd spent a good ten minutes sitting on the stairs while
'd caught his breath and stolen hers. She'd fretted about
etrov and the housekeeper, but Alex had assured her that
Irs. Hall had the weekend off. When they'd entered the
buse, Petrov had taken one look at them and made a call
Chloe, agreeing to accompany her to the wrestling
atches, though he said he would have preferred the bal-
t. Alex had been sure that Petrov wouldn't return until
orning.

Alex had been right. Petrov had yet to show up. She
asn't ready to draw the obvious conclusions about that.

And, then, Alex had again insisted on courting a
rniated disk by carrying her the rest of the way. She smiled
she absently strolled down to the kitchen. The sophisti-
ted man of the world was a mixture of little boy and
negade from the "Manly Man" school of thought. As
'd carried her up to his room, he'd told her—of all
ings—every silly elephant joke he knew.

He'd told each joke with relish, as if it had been the first
ne in his life that he'd had the opportunity, or an audi-
ce that would appreciate his more outrageous side. What
nd of life had he come from that it would deprive a child
telling silly jokes? What kind of existence kept a man
om "cutting loose" until the age of thirty-six? Where had
come from that he chose a solitary island over going
me to family and friends?

Julia brewed coffee and rummaged in the kitchen for
eakfast foods. She found Pop Tarts, chocolate dough-
ts, and sugared cereals. She loved Pop Tarts. Since there
re several flavors, she assumed that Alex did, too. She
isted an assortment, and arranged everything on a tray.

The doorbell rang as she put her foot on the first step. Glancing down at herself, she decided that Alex's robe was decent, covering her from neck to knees. It had to be Petrov. But Petrov would know the codes that opened the security gates. The sweet old bear. Only he would be considerate enough to ring the bell when he had keys.

With a welcoming smile, Julia balanced the tray on one hip and opened the door.

A small, elegant woman with a short, sleek cap of hair stared back at her. Her suit was French, her shoes Italian, her honey-blond hair and sharp gray eyes were pure St. Ives.

From the corner of her eye, Julia saw movement at the stairs.

"Who is it, darling?" Alex asked as he reached her side.

The woman's eyebrows rose in true St. Ives fashion.

Julia's gaze bounced from the woman to Alex and back again. His mother? Sister? Aunt? Since no one offered her any clues, she relinquished her place to Alex. Whoever the visitor was, she wasn't quite meeting Alex's eyes. A cousin come to ask for money?

"Hello, Alex." Her voice was cultured, brittle.

"Mother."

Julia stepped back farther and clutched the robe together at her neck, feeling chilled. *His mother.* No hug or greeting, not even a kiss on the cheek, no pleasure expressed by either of them at seeing each other. Amazement widened her eyes as Alex's mother brushed past him as if he were the butler, her glance raking Julia once—very thoroughly—then traveling over the foyer to linger on doorways, as if she expected someone to be there waiting for her.

"Come in, Mother." Alex shut the door and walked straight to Julia to take the tray from her hands and set it on the receiving table. His expression was smooth, stark in its emptiness.

Barely hearing him make the introductions, Julia watched Alex. He was so polite, so distant, so odd. Lorna Sinclair—not St. Ives?—was equally polite, equally distant. Julia had the feeling that she had just walked into someone else's nightmare. It disturbed her to witness such a cold plete lack of a relationship, as if all emotions between them had been canceled long ago.

It hurt her to watch Alex, so controlled and rigid, so resistant to the quick flash of vulnerability in Lorna's eyes. Alex, who took the time to be gentle with a ladybug, took the crude ribbing of young boys with equanimity, and found pleasure in the simplest of things, now looked like the man she had first thought him to be—hard, cold, arrogant. Like his mother.

Now she understood how he had learned to live with loneliness.

"How do you do, Miss Devlin?" Lorna said smoothly. "And you are...?"

The woman's tone rubbed Julia the wrong way, like stroking a cat against the nap of its fur. She released her hold on the robe and held out her hand for a bare skimming of palms. "I do quite well, thank you. And, I'm Alex's paramour."

Another lift of Lorna's eyebrows set Julia's teeth on edge. Casually, she strolled over to the table and poured herself a cup of coffee, taking her time. "If you'll excuse me, I'll—"

She felt Alex grip her elbow, pulling her close to his side. Was that a twinkle she saw in his eyes? She fervently hoped so.

"Excuse both of us, Mother, while we dress." He filled the second cup and handed it to Lorna. "The parlor is to your right. We'll join you shortly." The twinkle became more pronounced as he selected two Pop Tarts and slipped them into his pocket and led Julia up the stairs.

At the landing, he whispered out of the side of his mouth. *"My paramour?* From what dusty old trunk did you dig up that word?"

"Well, it was perfectly obvious that I'm not the scullery maid," she whispered back.

Alex closed his bedroom door and shook his head. "Julia, during the century in which that particular word was coined, it was quite normal to find the scullery maid in the master's bed.'' He bit into his pastry and raised her hand so he could drink from her cup. "I can't believe you said that."

"Neither can I," she said under her breath as she swept into the bathroom. With the internal radar that always picked up on Alex's every move, she knew he was following her. A quick glance found him in the doorway, his shoulder propped against the side. She met his gaze. "Alex, I'm going home. You can call me later... or whatever."

He nodded absently, his thoughts at a level she couldn't reach. "It won't take long, Julia, an hour or two at most."

An hour or two at most. He made his impending visit with his mother sound like a root canal. Swallowing, Julia bent over the sink to wash her face.

"Do you require privacy, or may I use the other sink?"

It hadn't occurred to her to be self-conscious when she agreed, not after the intimacies they had shared. The reality was different. He was leaving her, withdrawing by the second, becoming a man she didn't know, becoming the man, she suspected, who survived in the business world and among the jet set by not really *being there*.

Suddenly, brushing her teeth, washing her face side by side with him seemed more intimate than making love—a little too intimate under the circumstances. Belatedly, she was mortified by the circumstances. She had met Alex's perfectly coiffed, perfumed and bejeweled mother while wearing his robe, for heaven's sake.

She was dressed by the time he'd finished shaving. Not another word had been said, and for the first time since meeting him, their silence was uncomfortable, strained. Sitting on the bed to fasten her sandals, she watched him walk to the closet with that easy grace of his, totally unconcerned that he wore only his shorts.

It was killing her—not knowing what to say, yet wanting to ask so much. Downstairs she'd witnessed the aftermath of tragedy and somehow, she knew that the emptiness she'd seen in his eyes had been a part of him that had died. Painfully. She knew Lorna Sinclair, not personally, but it didn't matter. She knew the type. Such women had about as much depth as a mud puddle. How had Alex managed to survive Lorna's coldness with his humanity intact?

The silence was making her crazy. She hated it—this distance that Alex's mother had wedged between them. Alex wasn't being Alex—open, sensitive, even arrogant. She felt as if he'd left her and she wanted him back.

Impulsively, she cupped her chin in her hands and gave him a slow, dreamy once-over. "Nice buns," she commented, her voice scratchy, ruining the lightness she'd wanted to achieve.

Alex paused in the act of opening a drawer and sighed heavily, touched by her attempt to ease the strain. All he could manage in return was a stiff smile tossed over his shoulder. He hated it: the tension he couldn't control over a situation that was forcing Julia to leave him and the relief he felt that she was leaving. His mother was here to talk about Nicholas, and Alex couldn't risk Julia hearing the truth about himself, or the Veil of Tears. Not this way, and not from his mother who would freeze-dry the facts and to hell with the packaging.

Most of all, he hated the comprehension he'd seen flicker in Julia's eyes. It had hurt, that look of instant knowledge of what kind of childhood he'd had—cold, desolate, bewildering. For one agonizing moment, Julia had seen all the dark, untidy corners of his life. He wanted to share so much with her, but not that. Julia deserved honesty. His mother's intrusion reminded him too forcefully of all the secrets between them, those he didn't want her to know, as well as those he'd sworn not to share. For Julia, he wanted to be strong, invincible, ideal.

He straightened, but still kept his back to her, afraid of what else she might see, afraid that his secrets were too close to the surface, afraid, too, that she would see vulnerabilities even he didn't understand.

He lifted his gaze, caught hers reflected in the mirrored closet door. "I'll call you." He winced at the flatness of his voice, the sight of his grim smile. He'd sounded as if he were delivering a generic promise to a woman he couldn't wait to be rid of. The hell of it was that it was true.

"All right," she said. Unable to look anywhere but down, Julia smoothed out her skirt, adjusted her belt, picked up her purse. Her chest ached. As she walked toward the door, she caught movement out of the corner of her eye and turned to look at him.

His hands were in his pockets, and he was staring at his feet. "Julia, get out of here," Alex said, his voice strained, harsh.

Her eyes burned at his brutal dismissal. The ache in her chest became pain, sharp and twisting. She wanted to run, down the stairs, out of the door...away. Pride saved her from breaking into tears. Memories kept her from jumping to the wrong conclusions, memories of what they'd shared the day before and throughout the night, of the bleakness now in Alex's eyes, the suffering. The woman downstairs had the power to hurt him. His sudden stiffness wasn't a rejection of her, but rather a concentration of will not to let the pain show. Alex, too, had his share of pride.

Lifting her chin, she continued to stare at him. "You have an enviable talent for shutting yourself off like the proverbial faucet, Alex." Shrugging, she gave a little laugh. "I've tried for years, but I just can't seem to get the knack of it."

"Julia . . ." He turned to face her, warning her off with a glare of blue ice.

She knew self-imposed exile when she saw it. Beneath the ice were signs of life, signs of the man who knew so much about her because he, too, had dark and empty places inside himself. She spoke in a soft, clear tone, finding it easier than she'd expected. "I love you, Alex."

He raked his hand though his hair. *Love.* There were only two women he'd ever wanted to hear say those words to him. One was downstairs, the other standing in the doorway to his bedroom, one an embodiment of the past, the other representing the present, both tearing him apart. Love and secrets didn't mix. His mother's secrets had deprived him of love. That same secret could very well cause Julia to take back her love and bury it so deep, he'd never find it again.

Abruptly, he turned his back on Julia, not knowing what to say to her. *I love you, too, Julia, but I've been lying to you.* He knew all too well that love and lies didn't mix.

Hearing the swoosh of the door rubbing against the carpet, he glanced over his shoulder just in time to see Julia walking out, then all he saw was her hand—just that—tighten on the knob before letting go and disappearing as the door shut.

"GOOD MORNING, MOTHER," Alex said, strolling into the parlor, a cup of coffee in his hand, acting as if the scene earlier had never taken place and he'd just been informed of her arrival. "How long has it been? Ten years? Fifteen?"

Lorna's eyes widened, and she stared at Alex as if he were a stranger. She'd never known how to deal with him, but he'd always made it easy for her by being respectful and indulgent. Disoriented, she frowned. "We've kept in touch, Alex," she chided.

"No, Mother, we've kept up appearances." His voice was dispassionate even though he felt anything but indifferent. His mother's visit resurrected hurts he'd thought resolved long ago: rejection, the knowledge that he didn't belong with the Sinclair family, the fear that he might not belong anywhere. He'd worked damn hard at emotional survival and here his mother stood with an expression that could make a statue weep, making him care in spite of himself.

"Is there a specific reason why you're here?" he asked.

Ignoring his comment, Lorna strolled around the room, touching things, as if she were absorbing whatever traces of Nicholas's life they might hold. "I didn't consciously think about Nikki when he was alive. Now, I can't seem to think of anything else."

His mouth tightened. "I see. A postmortem. Have you come to make sure old skeletons are properly buried?"

"If they were buried, Alex, I wouldn't be here and neither would you," she said calmly as she lingered at the French windows that opened onto the gardens. Her shoulders seemed to sag a little and her voice softened. "Nikki promised to build me a castle, fill my life with magic and beauty."

Alex gave a single mirthless laugh. "He was, it seems, a man of his word. You should have taken him up on it."

Before his eyes, Lorna changed, again becoming the stiff and formal woman who would never reveal her weaknesses to anyone. Weaknesses meant emotion, vulnerability, a link with the masses she'd always been so careful to avoid, with the exception of Nicholas.

"Well," she said, smoothing the front of her suit jacket. "I'm surprised that you claimed the estate. This can hardly compare to an entire island."

"Petrov's bait was irresistible."

"Yes, the Veil of Tears. I can't imagine why you would want it, Alex. The workmanship is primitive."

"Primitive or no, it is priceless, Mother," Alex said, giving her the only reason she would understand. Dreams and magic and beauty had no meaning to her. If she couldn't spend it, convert it into stock or use it to finance a building with the family name on the cornerstone, it simply wasn't worth consideration.

"I see. That certainly explains why Miss Devlin was here. I take it you haven't yet retrieved your priceless artifact." Lorna's expression was benevolent, approving. It was all right to mingle with the masses as long as the result was profitable.

Alex drank from his cup, set it on an end table, adjusted the crease in his trousers as he sat down. "Actually, I purchased it back from her father a few weeks ago."

"And you're still involved with her? Alex, she's not your usual type."

"Exactly," Alex said, his eyes narrowing, establishing ground rules without saying another word: *Keep Julia out of this.*

Lorna was shallow, not stupid. She changed the subject. "Have you read Nikki's diaries?"

"Did Petrov tell you about those as well?" Or, he wondered, had she been seeing Nicholas all these years? The thought tied a knot in his chest, made him feel betrayed.

"No..." She paused, let her gaze wander around the room, stared down at her wedding ring. "Nikki phoned from time to time. He told me about the room he'd built for you, and the journals he kept up so that you would know your father, that he loved you."

His jaw ached with the effort to contain a bitter laugh. "Conscience and guilt. Love requires involvement."

Lorna shook her head. "He wrote letters to me for a while. They were so full of emotion. I never knew how to respond."

"I can imagine." Impatient, Alex pulled forward in his chair, clasped his hands between his outspread knees. "Mother, where are we going with this?"

"The diaries, Alex. Have you read them?"

"No. Why?"

"I just wondered." She gave him her Madam-Chairman-of-the-next-charity-function smile. "It's just as well. I'm sure they wouldn't be kind to me."

"On the contrary," Alex said, "they probably read like a fairy tale with you as the princess." He glanced at the view outside the windows, the art scattered around the room, the furniture, which had been custom-built. "Look around you, Mother. Everything he did was for you. I doubt he had anything left for anyone else."

"Nikki wanted you, you know. I should have sent you to him."

"I'm surprised that you didn't," Alex said, his anger building upon itself, roiling like a storm with no place to go. "I'm sure Jeffrey would have preferred it."

A small sigh escaped her, another hint of color in an otherwise gray existence. Those hints kept Alex rooted, waiting for something he thought he'd given up on years ago—hope and need, though he felt he shouldn't need anything from his mother at this late stage. He thought of Julia, the relationship she'd had with her father and how much she hurt because it was gone. He should be able to identify with it. Instead, he felt as if his life were deformed, missing a vital part that others took for granted.

Lorna was up again, wandering around the room, studying its appointments without really seeing them or understanding why they were there. "I know, Jeffrey hasn't been kind to you. I suppose it was my fault."

"No, not your fault, Mother. Kindness was bred out of our family centuries ago."

An odd little smile touched Lorna's face as she looked at Alex. "You've always been kind, Alex."

"Ah, but I have bastard blood. It's a wonder you were forgiven for diluting the strain. Or does the family know the truth?"

"They know that you're not Jeffrey's."

"But they think you transgressed with one of your own class. Embarrassing, but acceptable."

"You can stop baiting me, Alex." Lorna met his gaze with a direct one of her own. "I know what I am—a shallow, selfish woman who has never had a passionate moment in her life. Not even with Nikki and I felt more for him than anyone before or since."

"More than *anyone,* Mother?" He heard himself ask the question, hating it, hating the need to ask. After all that had gone before, it still mattered.

Lorna began another sigh and abruptly swallowed it down. She looked away. "I don't know how to answer that."

His mouth twitched in a parody of a smile, a flicker of pain. "Then, why are you here?"

"I don't know that, either." Tentatively, she raised her hand, to touch the same crystal free-form sculpture that had attracted Alex his first day there. But, it was just that—a light touch and then a drawing away. Inside the crystal, a single rare gemstone was trapped. "I wonder why Nikki chose this piece."

In that moment, Alex had to fight an urge to open his arms and his heart to her, but he knew she would back away as she had from the sculpture. He sat back and stared broodingly at her. What he wouldn't have given to share this conversation sixteen or even ten years ago when he'd been drifting through life without the anchors of love and acceptance and belonging, without understanding *why*.

Suddenly, Lorna sat in the chair facing him. "I made a terrible mistake, Alex. You were the result—"

"And the penance?" he asked softly, finally comprehending, as her mouth tightened and she avoided looking at him. His mother wasn't here to right wrongs or to try again; she was here to wipe away the stains from her past. A stray memory caught his attention: Lorna telling her maid to make sure a garment had been cleaned before it was packed in a box destined for charity. She wanted to wipe her past clean before discarding it like last year's fashions.

"It's all right, Mother," he said simply, offering the only thing he could in the only way she would accept. He rose from the sofa and held out his hand to help her up. "You should go home. You don't belong here any more than I belong in Philadelphia. I doubt our paths will cross again."

"You're right, of course." Lorna's expression cleared and she looked almost grateful to him for letting her off the hook without recriminations and bitterness.

Impulsively, Alex placed his hand over hers where it rested on his arm. She felt soft, approachable, human. He walked her to the door in silence, feeling as if he were split in two with one part watching the other from a distance, as if this had happened before and he were simply remembering it with the chasm of years giving him added perspective.

Alex watched his mother descend the front steps, pause, lower her head just a little. "Alex...I intended to be a good mother—"

His voice brusque, Alex cut her off. "Yes, well, you know what they say about good intentions." He didn't want to hear it, not now when he was letting go once and for all, and not from her when he was just beginning to see her as more than he'd thought she was. Not now, when the anger of his youth was pummeling him from the inside, wreaking havoc.

Lorna drew a breath, turned her head, but not completely, not enough to see her son. "It's true, you know. My intentions led me straight to hell. I do regret that I took you with me." Her body jerked, straightened, all trace of softness gone, as if she had wandered from the straight and narrow, and a leash had snapped her back into place. "I believe you're right, Alex. Kindness was bred out of us a long time ago."

With his hands in his pockets, Alex watched her climb into a limousine, pull the curtains over the window, and he winced as the chauffeur shut the door. He couldn't see her anymore and it was as if a part of his soul had been caught in that door, ripped away and dragged along as the car disappeared down the road.

ALEX WANDERED AROUND THE HOUSE, pausing here and there to stare out a window, smooth his fingers over a texture, adjusting to the presence of hopelessness. Something inside himself was growing, too many revelations, too much insight, too fast. He couldn't adjust quickly enough, couldn't slow it down enough to ease the pressure, contain it.

A locked door beckoned him in the upstairs hallway and he stood in front of the one room he'd avoided since coming here. The key protruded from the lock like a dare, mocking him when he didn't immediately take the challenge. A part of his life was in that room. A part he'd never had. He wasn't sure he wanted to be confronted with physical evidence of what was forever lost to him.

He reached out, his fingers grasping the key, turning it, working independently of his will. The door swung inward with a creaking complaint, berating him for not coming sooner. One step, then two before he pushed the door closed, again isolating the room from the outside world, not wanting reality to intrude upon the remnants of his dream, Nicholas's dream.

He stared at the contents, drawn in by them, compelled to examine each one. All the photographs taken of him over the years, yet never seen in the Sinclair house, were in albums and on the wall. Toys and model kits, posters and stereo equipment were stacked on shelves, unused, free of dust and memories, waiting for a boy who had never come. They were symbols of hope and love kept for a boy who had never been. All this, wasted because Lorna had feared disgrace more than she had cared for her son, meaningless because the love it represented had died with Nicholas Alexander.

A journal lay open on the desk as if someone had just left it there. He walked around the desk, looked down, reading the pages, turning them slowly.

I have made so many mistakes, loving the wrong woman, not fighting for my son. I believed in Lorna—at first that she loved me and would find the courage to come to me. When that hope was gone, I believed she would listen to me. But she told me that Alex was fine and happy, that Jeffrey was a good father, proud of his son. His son! Never! I know that now when it is too late. Petrov and I stood at the airport, behind a pillar, like spies, observing him while he waited for his flight to London. It was such an important time in his life, leaving home for the first time to accept the honor of a Rhodes Scholarship.

I exploded with pride in him from the day he was born. I wept watching him, knowing he would be so far away and that he was now a man. Though his cheeks were fuzzy, his body still awkward from growing a part at a time, still he was a man. In his eyes I saw a year for every minute that he has lived without love. The blame is mine alone. And now I know that the suffering was Alex's alone. He was alone at the airport with no one to embrace him, to cry over the coming months without him, to straighten his collar and express pride in his accomplishments and the strength I can sense building in him. I do not count. My tears are too late.

I want to go to him and show him these things that are in my heart, but the anger I see in his eyes is like a fence between us and his coldness is too much like death. I did this to him. I did nothing and now am I to go and offer him crumbs? My little son is gone and a man stands in his place. I do not know either one. Too late.

Alex closed the book and stared at the cover, unblinking, expressionless. Then, he wandered around the room, bent over to study the train set mounted on a table. He picked up the engine, turned it over in his hands, examining the detail. Pressure built in his chest and behind his eyes as he looked at the set of Doc Savage books, the posters of the Grateful Dead and the Starship Enterprise, the bedspread printed to look like a car—all things he'd never had as a boy. Every stage of childhood was represented. *Too late.*

With a single violent motion, Alex hurled the toy engine through the window and strode out of the room before the last echo of breaking glass had faded.

Chapter Thirteen

"Impossible! He *can't* be deceased," the man screeched into the phone. "We have business to finish!"

Julia held the receiver away from her ear. The strange man on the other end of the line was straining her hearing and her patience. "I'm sorry, Mr...?"

"Do *you* know where it is?" The voice reached a hopeful note.

"Where what is?"

"Oh dear. Your father didn't tell you, did he? How can I buy it if you don't know where it is?"

"Can you give me a clue?"

"No, of course I can't," he snapped. "You don't suppose he told someone else, do you?"

"Told someone else *what?*" Julia glanced at the clock, her mind wandering to thoughts of Alex. Where was he? It had been hours since she'd left him.

"Look, miss, you're not cooperating. Your father wrote to *me*. I wrote back. Then nothing. He should have answered my letter!"

"When did you write back?" Julia asked.

"Well last week, of course."

"Of course—" Hearing the beep on her call-waiting, she smiled. It had to be Alex. "Will you hold for a moment, please?"

"Is it necessary?"

"Absolutely crucial," she said and hit the button to switch lines. "Hello? Alex?" There was a pause and her heart sank to her knees when she heard a metallic clicking. As she listened to a recorded voice inform her of the special price on cruises to Bermuda, she idly leafed through the day's mail. A heavy vellum enveloped addressed to her father caught her eye.

She ripped it open and scanned the letter as she cut off the travelogue and returned to her hysterical caller. "Hello? Sir, are you by any chance 'P'?"

"Who else would I be?"

"According to your letter, you are interested in acquiring something that my father had offered for sale." She reread the letter. "And you insist on absolute secrecy."

"Yes! Now we're getting somewhere."

"No, sir, we are not. I still have no idea what this is about. My father had nothing of value, unless you mean the antique music box and he would never—"

"What would I want with that? Young lady, my time is valuable—"

"So is mine, Mr. P. Unless you are more specific, I see no reason to continue this conversation."

"I'll double my offer—triple it—anything! I must have it!"

Anything? Julia frowned as a vague sense of unease settled in the pit of her stomach. "I'm sorry, Mr. P., but I don't know what you're talking about, and frankly, I don't want to know."

"Are you sure?" he said, his voice a whisper of disappointment.

"Yes, I'm sure."

"I'll call again, just in case. I really *must* have the Veil."

Before Julia could tell him not to bother, he had hung up on her without so much as a goodbye, or a thank-you. She dropped the receiver into the cradle and, letter in hand, walked to the doorway of her father's room.

Discretion and a direct transfer of cash were the terms of this mysterious transaction, terms with an ominous ring and less than ethical undertones. What could be so secret that the purchaser wouldn't even sign his name? She remembered her father's words the night he died: *My secret...can't die now...* Another theft? But, that didn't make sense, either. Everything he'd stolen from Nicholas had been recovered. He certainly couldn't have robbed anyone else. Could he?

Julia's thoughts were taking her in directions she didn't want to go, showing her possibilities she'd rather not consider. And, she wouldn't, she decided. Whatever her father had or hadn't done was of no importance now. All he had left behind were a few family treasures, richer in memories than monetary value. She hoped.

Ostrich, she chided herself. But what could it hurt? She had her memories, thank you very much, and she didn't want anything or anyone corrupting them. The letter in her hand felt as if it were gaining weight by the second. With a firm shake of her head, she crumpled it into a ball and pitched it into the wastebasket.

A light film of dust covered the polished wood surfaces of furniture. Already, the room had a musty, unused smell. Gone were the scents of pipe tobacco and after-shave, and the comfortable clutter of books and shoes and an old plaid flannel robe laying over the pillow on the bed. Julia's mouth trembled at the complete absence in the room, no clear images of the man it had belonged to. So quickly he had come and gone through her life, like the morning fog. All that was left remained hidden behind the closet door and tucked away in drawers. Perhaps it was time to go through the remainders of his life and go on with hers. She had mourned for fifteen years. It was time she did something about tomorrow.

The grandfather clock chimed the half hour. She looked up, checked it against her wristwatch. It was two-thirty, five hours since she had left Alex. She couldn't imagine the cold Lorna Sinclair maintaining a conversation for that long. And she couldn't forget the look on Alex's face, empty, distant, as if he'd sent his emotions out of harm's way. Worry had been nagging her like the brush of a feather, subtle, persistent, underlying her every thought. She kept having the feeling that he needed her.

She jumped as the telephone rang. Holding her hand over her chest, she dashed back to the living room and snatched up the receiver. "Alex?"

"It is Gregori Petrov, Julia. I'm sorry."

Julia sank onto the sofa as apprehension slammed into her. "Is he all right? What's wrong?"

"Alex is well and nothing is wrong, except—"

"What, Mr. Petrov?"

"I must go out this evening, and the housekeeper is away for the weekend."

For the second time in an hour, Julia stared at the telephone as if it were responsible for the craziness she heard. "I hope you enjoy yourself, but, what has that to do with—"

A heavy sigh transmitted itself through the wire. "Alex cannot cook, Julia. I thought perhaps you might come here and—"

"Baby-sit?" Julia asked, amused by the idea.

"Hmmph. Ah...no...you see..." Another sigh. "Julia, there are times when one should not think too much. It is better to talk, to be given reassurance that..." His voice trailed off and Julia could picture him shaking his head. "I am meddling, I know."

Julia smiled. "You know, Aunt Chloe meddles and I'm always grateful that she does."

"Then perhaps I will be forgiven."

"Tell me, Gregori—was it awful?"

"I do not know what happened. Alex threw something through a window and he has been sitting on the cliff above the beach ever since."

He threw something? Alex? "His mother was here."

"Ah. Now it makes sense."

"I told her that I was Alex's paramour," Julia confessed.

Petrov gave a great shout of laughter. "That is good, Julia. *Very* good! Lorna needs to think more."

"Gregori, when she walked into the room and Alex saw her . . . he changed. He wasn't Alex anymore."

"Yes."

That simple response confirmed her worst fears about Alex's childhood, that it had been without love and warmth. She leaned back against the table and closed her eyes. She didn't want to think of Alex being unhappy, or hurt. And, Alex, who was always so full of restless energy, had been sitting in one place all afternoon, staring at the sea. "Are you sure he's all right?"

"He will be if you feed him, Julia—food and companionship. He does not need more loneliness. Will you come?"

"Maybe he wants to be alone, Gregori."

"No," Petrov said softly. "He does not know how to ask. He does not even think to ask."

SHE WAS LATE, but the delay was worth it, Julia thought as she buzzed at the gate. A bag of groceries tilted on the floor of her car when she turned into the circular driveway. The covered basket on the seat lurched as she stopped in front of the house. Gregori stood on the front steps and she favored him with a bright smile.

She had a good feeling about what she'd done.

Gregori opened the passenger door and reached for the basket.

"No. I'll get that, Gregori." She pulled the basket out with her. "Is everything ready?"

"We do have food here, Julia," he chided.

"I needed certain ingredients. Your pantry is full of junk food and specialty items." She stopped at the patio doors. Outside, Gregori had everything she'd requested stacked and ready to roll. "A little red wagon? Wherever did you get it?"

"You do not remember? Nikki kept it in the shed for you."

The memory popped up like a child waking suddenly on Christmas morning. She smiled. "Yes. He said I would need it to carry the gold I'd find at the end of the rainbow." She followed him out and moved some items to make room for the groceries. Tilting her head, she looked up at him. "How is it that you know Alex's family?"

Petrov's head jerked up. "Ah...we have met before...in the East when Nikki designed some buildings there."

"Oh," Julia said as she bent over the wagon again to rearrange the load. "It's quite a coincidence that he bought the estate."

"No coincidence, Julia. I am the one who told Alex about it."

"You stayed on. Why?"

Petrov looked a little frayed around the edges. His hands gestured expansively. "Ah, I am a fixture here. It is my home. I will watch over things when Alex is away."

Julia's heart did a nosedive at the reminder that Alex had other homes, other galleries. The new one was almost finished. What then? Last night she had made a commitment, but had he done the same? Uncertainty gnawed at her, the hunger of not knowing and not being able to ask.

"I must go. Chloe is waiting for me," Petrov said.

She smiled again, too brightly this time. "Aunt Chloe, hmm? Where is it tonight, the ballet or the Roller Derby?" His face turned red, shocking her. *Why, he's in love with her,* she thought.

"Ah, that woman. Her tastes in entertainment are barbaric." Petrov shook his head. "I am surprising her. She believes we are going to a comedy club, but I am taking her out on Alex's yacht."

"A yacht?" Another thing she didn't know about Alex, though she should have. A man who lived on an island part of the year would naturally own a boat.

Petrov shrugged. "It is small, but quite luxurious."

"I'll bet." Straightening, she stared toward the bluff. "Where is Alex?"

"He is there, leaning against that tree." Petrov pointed to the highest point on the bluff.

She pulled the little wagon behind her as she walked toward Alex at a steady chip, the basket gripped firmly in her left hand.

Alex's head snapped around at the creaky sound of wheels turning. Bemused, he watched her wrestle the wagon over the rise and stop suddenly as she caught sight of him.

Julia paused uncertainly. "Hi," she whispered, her gaze looking him over, checking for damages. He looked wonderful, in spite of his blank expression.

"I'm not good company tonight, Julia," he said, wishing it wasn't true. He'd hurt her this morning, and in his present mood, he was afraid he'd hurt her again. He didn't know how much longer he could contain the solid, choking anger that made him want to lash out, diminish it any way he could. But not at Julia, who was already a victim of their respective parents' schemes and mistakes. "I'd rather be alone."

"Nonsense. Misery loves company." A few feet away from him, she began unloading the wagon. One-handed, she carried items to a point clear of the tree branches, while keeping hold of a covered basket. She set up a hibachi and arranged a bag of charcoal, a bottle of lighter fluid, utensils and a thermos to one side. Foodstuffs followed: tenderloin steaks, potatoes and ears of corn, a container of sour cream, a stick of butter, and condiments. It took him a minute to realize that she was chattering like a magpie.

"I've kept it to basics this time, Alex. A simple barbecue, nothing fancy. You'll be able to do it with your eyes closed—" She surveyed the small outdoor kitchen she'd assembled. "I can't believe you don't know how to cook." She didn't want to look at him. One glance had been enough to warn her off. But, it was too late now. She was here, the basket was bumping against her leg and there was no way to make a graceful exit.

"A man should be allowed to wallow in solitude, Julia."

"Really? Is that an unwritten rule in the *Manly Man Handbook*?"

It just seemed to happen—a muscle twitch in his cheek, then the lift of one corner of his mouth, followed by another. That tartly voiced question was like a painkiller. He'd been in a trance for hours, fighting the pain, trying to work his way through it. Yet, Julia came along, and with a few words, established his feelings as normal, acceptable, like changes in the weather.

"Well!" she said, rubbing her hands together. "We'd better get started if we're going to be on time. If we're lucky, we'll be able to watch the sunset and eat at the same time...here." She tossed a packaged towelette at him. "Clean your hands and get over here. We do have one immediate problem, though." She put down the basket, and lifted the lid. Reaching in with both hands, she grinned up at him as she pulled out a limp, brown mass of...something.

Alex wasn't sure exactly what she was holding like a football as she attached a leash to a collar hidden by folds of skin.

Julia walked a few feet away before bending over again to set it on the ground. Four legs emerged, then a head with eyes and ears attached and a tongue that hung out of its mouth. No sooner had its hind legs touched down than the creature answered a call of nature. With raised eyebrows, she looked up at Alex. "This is Pansy," she said and kneeled in the grass to rub the area behind Pansy's long floppy ears.

"And what a good girl, you are, Pansy. I'm so glad you waited till now. Good girl!" Julia produced a bone-shaped cracker from the pocket of her softly draping knit pants. "Here you are, sweetie." Pansy delicately picked the treat with her teeth, took two steps, and dropped it on the ground before lying down and placing her front paws on either side of her treasure.

"A new member of your family?" Alex assumed the animal was a dog—the most bizarre looking dog he'd ever seen. It had to be a puppy, but it gazed at the world with hundred-year-old eyes.

"No. Pansy is a new member of *your* family," Julia said as she rose to her feet and frowned at the dog. "Look at her, Alex. She's afraid of everything. Her former owners tried to drown her—"

"Mine? Julia, the last thing I need is a dog."

"Well, she needs a home, poor thing. And, you have all this land. It's perfect. She can run and—"

"Julia, if that dog ran, she'd trip over her own skin."

"I know. Can you imagine having so much skin you could crawl into it whenever you needed a place to hide?"

The question caught him off guard, toppled him from the fine edge he'd been balancing on all day. He blinked, then stared at the dog. He'd never had a pet, never even thought of having one. How unnatural, he thought, that he had not had such a normal dream as a child. The realization made him feel like a freak.

Pansy inched her way toward him, still on her belly. He couldn't take his eyes off her. "A dog," he murmured.

"What else do you give the man who has everything?" Julia asked. "You have so many beautiful things."

"Pansy certainly doesn't fall into that category." His tone was absent as he held out his hand. That was all it took. The dog crawled over his leg and curled up in his lap, the treat forgotten at Julia's feet. He closed his eyes and swallowed. *Julia, what are you doing to me?* "Why, Julia?" he whispered.

"Just because," she said as she arranged charcoal on the hibachi and doused it with lighter fluid, her movements stiff, hesitant. She stared out at the ocean and shrugged, a small defensive gesture that spoke volumes. "Pansy is hard to resist."

Meaning, Alex thought, that because Julia hadn't been sure that she would be welcome after the cold dismissal he'd given her that morning, so she brought an irresistible force to pit against the immovable object—himself. Sighing, Alex stared down at the dog, his mouth twisting into a bittersweet smile, his hand idly stroking Pansy's velvety fur. "I think I'm in love."

Julia lifted the dog's muzzle with the tips of her fingers. "You hear that, Pansy? You're in. I told you he was a pushover."

"The *pushover* thanks you, Julia."

"Thank the woman at the pound who didn't have the heart to put her down yesterday." She frowned at the potatoes. "We're going to cheat a little tonight, Alex. I nuked the potatoes in the microwave to get them halfway done, but by the time you finish cooking them in here, we'll never know the difference. I cheated on the corn, too. It's the precooked frozen kind."

"You're joking..." He looked from the potatoes to the dog to the corn and then, completely confused, made the circuit again.

"'Fraid not, but the potatoes and corn will be just fine. I promise." Julia stared at the horizon, a barely discernible line separating ocean from sky. The sun hung a quarter of the way up, still blazing. "We might miss the sunset. You're a sailor, Alex—what do you think?"

"Not the food, Julia—Pansy. Why would they put her down?" His thoughts had polarized on the dog, the problem he shared with her. All he had to do was look at Pansy to know she was a misfit.

"A neighbor of the owners turned her in to the pound. Her mother was a registered Shar Pei and her father was a Basset Hound with terrier mixed in. She was too ugly, not lively enough, and she cowers all the time. Cowering isn't 'cute.' It makes people feel guilty and—"

"Culpable," Alex finished for her as he reached over to capture the single tear rolling down Julia's cheek on his finger. "Pushover," he accused softly. "It takes one to know one."

"Be quiet, Alex. You have work to do and there's not much time before we have to leave."

"Where are we going?" He analyzed her clothes, looking for a clue. Her soft cotton knit ensemble of taupe pants, peach-colored T-shirt and trapeze jacket ruled out a formal affair. It was also more than was practical for a cookout.

His eyes narrowed as all the bits and pieces of her disjointed chatter caught up with him. "What do you mean by the time *I* cook? Julia, I don't know how to cook."

"You will."

LEANING BACK AGAINST THE TREE, Alex watched the sunset as he stroked Pansy with one hand. Contentment, he thought, was not only a warm puppy, but a friend willing to share silence when words were not adequate to express pain and love.

Soft whuffles came from the basket where Pansy slept on an old blanket donated by her rescuer at the pound. Alex breathed deeply, enjoying the mixed scents of the charcoal and hickory chips still smoldering in the hibachi. Contentment had come in many forms tonight: the feel of warm butter oozing between his fingers as he'd coated the potatoes before wrapping them in foil; eating corn on the cob without having to worry about melted butter dripping down chins, and juice spurting with every bite; having Julia near, trying so damned hard to keep him busy and smiling. And it was the single, gratifying twitch of Pansy's tail when she'd taken her treat from his hand and eaten it, a sign that she had not lost faith in the human race. A sign of trust.

So simple, these pleasures he'd never known. So profound.

Julia watched Alex on the sly, wondering what thoughts held him so completely. His containment unnerved her, made her want to peel away the image he wore, take the lid off his emotions. His pain had been like a silent companion all evening, underlying every smile, every expression, every word. *Get rid of it, Alex,* she wanted to say. *Do for yourself what you did for me.* She didn't care about the whys and wherefores, or a blow-by-blow account of what was tormenting him. It only mattered that he express it. *Cry. Scream. Anything.*

He stretched out on the grass, crossing his legs at the ankles, his upper body supported by his elbows. Pansy stood up in the basket and stretched, her head sticking out from one end, her tail from the other. Her mouth opened, just a little, as if she were smiling at him, and—yes—her tail was actually wagging. It seemed of paramount importance to him, that further sign of Pansy's hope that all humans weren't beasts.

"It's damned demoralizing," he said as he scratched between her ears, "to be outdone by a dog."

He felt Julia's gaze, saw the question in that telltale tilt of her head.

"I've been wondering how long it will take me to catch up with myself." He smiled at Julia's frown of concentration. "How old is Pansy? Six months?"

"Five," Julia whispered.

"Five months," he repeated. "I'm thirty-six, supposedly an adult. Yet, all it takes is a reminder of my childhood and I revert to feeling all the insecurity, the rejection, the guilt, as if I were solely responsible for my parents' shortcomings and unhappiness. I should know better. When I'm rational, I *do* know better, yet I'm still trying to figure out what *I* did wrong. It's insane."

Julia leaned back on her elbows, mirroring Alex's position. "Rationality has nothing to do with it. We're all products of our pasts. We're affected most by the bad experiences, so we build early warning systems because we're afraid that history will repeat itself." Her gaze skittered away from him.

She'd been feeling that fear in ever-increasing waves all evening. All of a sudden, things didn't seem quite right between them. Alex had been talking to her, but the conversation had the quality of a philosophical discussion rather than intimacy, sharing, *trusting*. She remembered the day she'd told him about her father, confiding in him, sharing her fears, coping with the situation rather than copping out. Admittedly, she hadn't been trusting Alex then as much as she'd been trusting the moment, the feelings, the needs. Needs Alex had awakened in her so abruptly that they'd been crowding her, screaming like cranky children demanding attention.

It bothered her that while Alex had said quite a lot this evening, he hadn't really told her a single thing about himself, as if there was something he didn't want her to know. Maybe, while she had been trusting moments and emotions to build upon themselves, he had simply been seizing them for the moment and nothing more—history repeating itself.

She glanced around restlessly, making sure everything had been put away. She'd been wrong before. She did want to know the whys and wherefores, not because she was curious—which she was—but because she needed a sign that they were more than two people caught in a moment of passion. Frustrated, she wanted to plant her fist in the trunk of the tree, yell at Alex, run as fast as she could to the nearest exit.

Instead, she lunged to her feet and dusted off the seat of her pants. She'd done enough running for one lifetime, and Alex had been right when he'd said they couldn't just have a beginning and an end. If she ran now, she'd always wonder what she had given up. "If we don't leave now, we'll be late."

"For what?" Alex asked, his gaze searching hers as he sensed a hastily erected barrier going up between them. His mouth tightened. Damn Patrick and his secrets that kept him from confiding in Julia for fear of revealing too much. And damn his own misguided sense of honor that prevented him from telling her the truth.

Rising to his feet, he picked up Pansy's basket and removed the handle of the wagon from Julia's grip. Suddenly, going out seemed like a good idea. "Exactly what have you planned?"

Julia's stride was determined, her smile grim as she led the way to the house. "We're going to indulge in a little vicarious brawling," she said, looking as if she'd prefer the real thing.

Alex almost smiled, feeling a measure of satisfaction in the pugnacious jut of her chin, the make-my-day challenge in her tone of voice. She wanted him to argue with her. And, she was willing to stand and fight rather than run away.

Chapter Fourteen

The seductive strains of the *Concierto de Aranjuez* blared out of loudspeakers strategically placed around the coliseum. Don Juan the Destroyer, a monolith in his own right, strutted down the aisle, saluting the onlookers like a matador, his cape a flashing mass of black sequins, his high black boots heavily embroidered and tooled and dyed in vivid primary colors. Shouts of "Olé" vied with feminine shrieks of "Kiss me! Kiss me!"

Don Juan paused often to accept the invitations being hurled at him, dramatically sweeping his cape over himself and whatever woman caught his attention. Finally reaching the ring, he climbed over the ropes and threw his cape aside. His opponent, already in the ring, glowered from his corner and made obscene gestures at the audience as he doffed his tuxedo jacket and top hat. Gentleman Jock never lived up to his name.

Alex felt like a seventy-pound weakling. Even Don Juan's muscles had muscles and he had to be at least seven feet tall. Standing beside Alex, Julia was cheering and throwing rose petals with the rowdiest of Don Juan's fans.

Silence fell like a lead balloon. Don Juan stilled, his gaze fastened with melodramatic intensity on one of the entrances. A shadow emerged and gained substance. With Grace Kelly elegance, one of the most beautiful women Alex had ever seen took form, wearing a simple black dress and a string of opera-length pearls. Languidly dragging a sable coat behind her, she looked neither right nor left, but kept her gaze fastened on Don Juan with a matching flair for theatrical expression. Don swept off his fringed gaucho hat, bowed and tossed it to the woman with a flourish. Without seeming to move at all, she reached up and caught it, placed a single rose inside the crown and tossed it back before taking her seat.

"How long did they practice *that?*" Alex asked.

"Not long," she said, sitting down again. "Sharon is on a touch football team."

Alex covered his mouth with his hand.

The fray began and rapidly deteriorated into a vaudevillian free-for-all. The referee was draped over the ropes where Gentleman Jock had pitched him and the announcer had caught a blow on his chin when he'd come too close to the combatants. Julia sat on the edge of her seat, cheering everybody on.

"Do you do this often?" Alex asked.

"Oh no! Don is going to get it." She stood up, her hands clenched at her sides. "Did you see that? That turkey pulled Don's mustache!"

Alex failed to see why Don Juan's facial hair was more important than his legs, which Jock was unmercifully twisting.

Jock's roar split the air as he lifted Don, swung him in a circle and hurled him through the air.

The earth moved. A collective roar of outrage filled the air. Instinctively, Alex grabbed Julia and pulled her behind him as Don landed flat on his back at their feet.

Shaking his head, the wrestler raised up on his elbows and squinted at the face peering at him over Alex's shoulder. "Hi, Ms. Devlin. Glad you could make it." He shook his head again, snarled in his opponent's direction, then gave Julia a beatific smile. "Isn't Sharon great?"

"Terrific!" Julia shouted between her cupped palms. "You did good!"

"The natives are getting restless," Alex warned as he saw Jock climbing the ropes. The referee had recovered and like a bulldog was holding on to Jock's lower leg. Alex searched the higher portions of the coliseum for safer seating. It was a full house.

"Who's the dude?" Don asked, unconcerned about the monster bearing down on them.

Julia sat down and leaned over. "Alex St. Ives . . . Don, look out!"

Don grabbed Alex's hand and gave it a fast shake before climbing Jock's back as if he were King Kong scaling the Empire State Building. "Better get him a beer, Ms. Devlin. He looks nervous," Jock yelled over his shoulder.

"Good idea!" she yelled back. Turning in her seat, she looked around for a vendor.

Alex spotted one and raised his hand. The vendor ignored him.

"Alex, this isn't a five-star restaurant." Julia put her thumb and forefinger between her lips and whistled.

Alex wondered if she was part of the act. And then the truth hit him from behind. This was the real Julia—the earthy woman who served beer at festivals, blurted out the most refreshingly honest observations about herself and had feathers painted on her cheek, a woman whose strength lay in her ability to admit her fears.

Within seconds, they each had a beer and hot dog loaded with the works. Julia stopped him from taking out his wallet. "My treat," she said, daring him to argue.

He chuckled at her defiant expression and sat back to watch the show—Julia, not the wrestlers. She was ferocious as she called Jock a creep and stomped her foot when he briefly pinned Don Juan. She cursed with words like "phooey", and encouraged her client by yelling for him to "knock the bejeebers out of that amoeba brain." Excitement took on a whole new meaning as he watched her two-fisted, yet dainty consumption of her food, the way she licked mustard from the corner of her mouth and ignored the dollop that landed on her chest. He couldn't resist leaning over to scoop it up, then lick it off his finger.

Julia's breath stalled as she looked down and followed the progress of his finger from her jacket to his mouth. The electricity that always arced between them was different this time, flowing like a low, steady current that was eternal and unrelenting. His gaze probed and revealed all at once, saying things she had yet to hear in plain English. Could she believe the message in his eyes? It spoke of desire certainly, but she had learned that want and need were two different things. Desire alone could only enhance a relationship, not sustain it.

"Thank you, Julia," Alex said distinctly, his mouth angled in a fraction of a smile that reeled her in, made her believe that this time, she'd met a man for whom it was worth taking any risk.

The crowd roared around them as Don Juan the Destroyer pinned Gentleman Jock's shoulders to the mat for the count of three.

"THE EXPERIENCE GIVES a whole new meaning to the term 'passive aggression,'" Alex said as he helped Julia into the driver's seat of her car. She'd insisted on driving, claiming equal rights in the dating department. Except that he'd had the feeling ever since they'd left the house that this wasn't a date as much as it was a test. And he knew that the only way he could pass was to cheat on his promise to a dying man.

She fastened her seat belt and grinned. "Yeah. Isn't it great?"

"Yes."

Julia's hands clenched the wheel at the pure seduction of Alex's voice. She felt his regard, steady, burning, provoking a response. But their isolation and the silence after several hours of high-decibel chaos had shocked her into recognizing how far she and Alex had yet to go. He had gone a lot farther with her than she had with him. *When in doubt, proceed with caution.* It had always seemed a good rule to follow, especially for reformed cowards who might be inclined to dive head first into a swimming pool before finding out how much water it held.

"If I had not already done so, Julia," he said, "I would have fallen in love with you tonight."

The simple declaration caught her by surprise, like one of Don Juan's body slams. Her mouth opened, but she didn't

know what to say. In a way it was anti-climactic, and less of
an issue than the accessories to love, like trust and sharing
the two-way emotional intimacy. She was selfish about love.
Giving wasn't enough. She had to receive, too, had to know
that what was vital to her was equally important to him.
When in doubt, punt, Julia.

"Screaming banshees turn you on, huh?" she asked
lightly, punting for all she was worth. "You like primitive?"

"I like freedom, Julia. Tonight, you were free."

Another body slam. Blinking, she whipped around another car and drove out of the parking lot. "No, not free,
Alex. I was angry," she said, opting for honesty. "I've been
furious all day."

"My mother," he said, resigned to the inevitable.

"Mmm . . . partly. Is she like that all the time?" *Was she
always like that with you?*

"Often she's worse. Lorna has only felt one honest emotion in her life."

Now that was an opening if she'd ever heard one, Julia
thought dryly. In her present mood, she wasn't above taking what she could get. "Yes?"

"She loved my father."

The starkness of his pronouncement alerted Julia to
something not quite right about an otherwise normal condition. There seemed to be a question she should ask, but
she didn't know what it was. "What's wrong with this picture?" she mused out loud.

"He wasn't her husband or her fiancé." Alex gave a
mirthless laugh. "She was engaged to Jeffrey Sinclair at the
time."

"And she married Jeffrey anyway." A swallow caught in
Julia's throat. "That certainty fills in all the blanks."

"Not all of them." Alex hesitated only a moment, resolving to offer as much honesty as he could. A *C* on the test
was better than failing altogether. "I didn't buy the estate,
Julia. I inherited it. Nicholas Alexander was my father."

A stoplight gave Julia the opportunity to catch her breath,
pull her scattered thoughts together. She glanced at Alex. He

was staring straight ahead, unmoving, like a statue carved from stone.

"You didn't know?"

"Not until three months after he died."

"That stinks!"

He smiled at her vehemence, relieved that she hadn't expressed sympathy. He'd been drowning himself in self-pity all day. He couldn't have stood her pity on top of that.

"And just what in the hell is your mother's problem? You're still her son." The car shot forward as she stomped a little too forcefully on the gas. "Never mind. I can guess." She eased back on the pedal, returning to a legal speed. "Damn it! Why do parents have to be so imperfect? Why do they let other things come between themselves and their children?"

Alex's eyebrows rose at her use of two expletives in less than a minute—the first ones he'd heard her use since they'd met. He reached over and wrapped his fingers around the back of her neck, massaging and soothing her and just plain touching her because she was the only person he'd ever needed to touch in his adult life.

"Julia—" he began.

"No, Alex. I really hate this. We had the same problem in childhood, always being expected to obey the rule, Do as I say, not as I do. Don't steal, Julia, but forgive me if I do. Alex, live up to the Sinclair name even though you're not good enough to use it. Aside from that, I can't imagine a mother not loving you. You had to be a wonderful child."

Alex gave her a second to wind down from her tirade. She had the situation pegged. But then, she'd grown up around people like Lorna and Jeffrey, and now she had them as clients, two-dimensional cardboard people with nothing but air and filler inside. All the glitter was on the surface.

"Not such a wonderful child. I decked Jeffrey."

"You what?"

Alex nodded. "Right on his . . . porch."

"Did it make you feel better?"

"Immensely."

Julia's sigh filled the car. "I gave Da' a really hard time when he came home . . . said some awful things to him."

"You didn't feel better?"

"No. I felt like a creep. But that's different."

"Is it? Why?"

Julia pulled the car as near to the pillar of Alex's gates as possible so he could punch in the security code to open them. Resting her forearm across the steering wheel, she looked at him. "Was Jeffrey good to you?"

"No."

"He was cruel," she stated and saw his jaw clench. "It was different for me. Da' loved me. He tried, even if it wasn't enough."

The gates swung open and she drove through. The tires squealed as she hit the brake in front of the house. "Well! I feel a heck of a lot better. How about you?"

"Hmm. Julia Devlin in a high dudgeon is a sight to behold."

Julia choked on a laugh. "Dudgeon? That word must have come from the same century as *paramour*."

"Come here, Julia," Alex ordered softly.

Suddenly, that slow, steady charge of excitement she'd felt earlier became a major power surge, blowing circuits, making her nerves vibrate and stand on end. Everything drained out of her—anger, doubt, insecurity, cowardice. Alex had a certain way of looking at her that encouraged confidence and brought out her most primal instincts. "Do you have a car fetish or something?"

"Or something," he murmured. "Come here."

Camouflaged by arrogance or not, she knew need when she heard it. At the moment she was feeling pretty needy herself—for closeness, warmth, the silent expressions of love. She slid over the console dividing the bucket seats and settled her bottom in his lap with a provocative wiggle, wrapped her arms around his neck, ran her tongue over his lips.

Angling his head to capture her mouth, Alex slipped his hand under her top.

She drew back, a wicked smile on her face. She'd initiated this date, orchestrated it, played aggressor to the hilt and Alex had loved every minute of it. Why stop now? Her jacket was off in a flash and she tossed it onto the steering wheel. The top came next, mussing her hair as she pulled it over her head. A rush of heat shot through her at the way Alex simply sat back, his gaze touching nothing but her face. Crossing her arms over her chest, she slowly slid the straps of her bra down her arms and hung it over the gearshift.

She sat straight in his lap, anticipation growing, a pleasure in itself. The look in Alex's eyes made her feel like liquid light, iridescent, magic. It didn't matter what she saw in the mirror. Alex's smoldering gaze, the slight tremble of his hands as he cupped her breast, repeated every poem ever written about beauty.

He moved his hand away then, and let his gaze wander over every exposed inch of her, acutely aware of the magnitude of her gesture. "Julia, you trust me this much?" he asked.

She swallowed hard against the sudden pain of his question. "I . . . trust you with my body."

"I see." Tension etched his face in harsh relief, betraying cracks in his composure, his ever-present calm.

"I love you, Alex."

"Right. It's *my* feelings you can't trust."

Her head jerked back at the flat statement. The shock of it was immediate, paralyzing. He had just taken the hang-ups of one Julia Devlin and lined them up in a neat row, as if he planned to shoot them at dawn. She felt the impact of what was happening between them, aware that Alex was as vulnerable as she, maybe more. She suddenly realized the enormity of what was happening between them. "I'm not a gambler, Alex," she said, her gaze darting out of reach, her fingers plucking at his collar. "I *can't* trust so easily, or so quickly. I've forgotten how."

He flicked her bra with his hand. "So, what is this called, Julia? Uncontrollable lust? Self-indulgence? *Charity?*"

Her gaze snapped to his. "It's called taking one step at a time." Her face felt stiff, aching with the effort not to let her mouth tremble. She knew that she was hurting him. He must have fought some horrible battles with himself to become the man he was now—open, giving, trusting. He deserved to be given all of that and more, yet it just wasn't there, not completely, not without a measure of doubt and fear. In the past, her own personal battles had always ended in a draw.

"I need time to remember how to trust, Alex."

He was angry, his expression as uncompromising as a bomb-proof security door. He reached out for her clothes.

She was faster and caught his hand, holding it between them. "Alex, I've swallowed a lot of pride since you walked into my office and I've taken a lot of giant steps toward you, not away from you. Nothing has ever been as important to me as taking those steps. Don't you dare go macho and dismiss me just because you're impatient and—"

"Greedy," he finished for her. "I'm a very greedy man, Julia." Her hand felt cold, clammy; she was controlling her breaths, as if she were panic-stricken. Tenderness replaced anger and damaged pride as he raised her hand, kissed it, held it to his cheek. Guilt sat on his shoulder like a demon taunting his actions and his lack of them. "It occurs to me that the person you really can't trust is yourself."

Her fingers wrapped around his, holding tight. "I've made some pretty bad mistakes, Alex. The price has been high."

"Then all that's left is for me to give you time to recoup your losses." His mouth twitched once, quickly, as if he'd just experienced a sudden sharp pain deep inside. Just as quickly, his face smoothed out and his eyes twinkled devilishly. "While you're at it, remember that even I make mistakes, Julia. Bad ones."

She rolled her eyes and clicked her tongue. "My hero, in all his arrogant glory—" And then she sobered. "I can do that, Alex," she said, wondering what mistakes he'd made and what the cost had been. Glancing down, her gaze went from her nakedness to the clothing he still wore. "The rest will come."

The wicked grin slashed across his face again. His forefinger trailed up her neck. "It certainly will," he said, accepting what she offered. It would have to be enough for now.

His eyes were glow-in-the-dark silver as he whispered, "Julia."

"What?"

"Simon says, come here."

In one swift movement, she scooted forward in his lap, pressing against him. Her neck arched and her head fell back in blatant invitation.

His mouth found the steady pulse there, the hollow of her throat, her breasts thrust so provocatively forward and her body responded, becoming liquid and hot. A hum seemed to begin in her chest and sing through her veins, making her tingle from the inside out. She didn't try to fight it. She needed closeness. So did Alex. They each had so many years to make up for.

Alex watched her as he caressed her bare skin, enjoying her lack of inhibition, knowing he was responsible, and that she was this way only for him. Her passion and pride were for him—gifts that meant far more to him than the gifts of her body. And as she continued to remove the rest of her clothing while he remained fully dressed, he experienced a poignant emotion that transcended any he'd ever known. It felt like hope.

He bent his head to her breast and circled kisses ever closer to the center.

"Alex...stop teasing," she said breathlessly. She shivered with excitement as his fingers stroked her sides, then lifted her breasts to his mouth. His teeth scraped the sensitive aureola and she grasped the back of his head, urging him closer. He took the hint and his lips closed over her, drawing her deeper into his mouth. Pleasure shot through her.

Her hand found his belt, his zipper...him. Urgency ruled. She lifted herself and fitted her body to his, moving rapidly, demanding, giving, feeling more than she had ever thought possible.

"Julia," Alex said between breaths, grimacing.

She stilled, then gripped her thigh and whimpered. "Oh no." Lowering her head, she rested her forehead against his. "Alex, I have a charley horse."

"Yes," he said, wincing and rubbing his seat. "I know."

Her fingers kneaded her thigh as she looked up at him. "You too?" At his nod, she moved her hand from her charley horse to massage his.

Passion was gone, but love remained.

"This is incredibly decadent," Julia said as she nestled deeper into Alex's embrace. The hammock swayed gently with their movements, the swish of the trees supporting it in counterpoint to the distant sound of waves ebbing and flowing on the narrow beach far below. Moonbeams streamed in silvery ribbons of light onto their skin even as the darkness shielded them like a curtain separating truth from lies.

"Decadence is nice." Alex held Julia close and wrapped himself around her. They'd abandoned the car for the hammock after a brief and awkward struggle to disengage themselves. Passion had made an amazing comeback, more acute than before. And later, as they'd rested, he'd told her more about Lorna, Jeffrey and his father, omitting the salient details, the promise he'd made to Patrick forbidding him to return the honesty Julia had given him. He cursed his stupidity in making such a vow. For the first time in his life, he didn't know what was right or what was wrong. He didn't know what to do and was afraid to find out. For the first time in his life, he had something to lose.

Julia sighed. "It's true."

"What is true?"

"Broken hearts mend. Untouched hearts wither and die."

"That sounds like something Chloe would say." His lethargy was disappearing fast under the casual stroking of Julia's hand.

"Yes. And Aunt Chloe should certainly know." She shuddered at the feel of his teeth nibbling on her ear.

"Is that why you listened to her?" He swept her hair upward, baring the back of her neck.

"That and because she said what I wanted to hear. You touched me from the first—" She felt his tongue explore the tiny hollow at the base of her neck.

Alex placed his fingers over her mouth. "And I'm going to touch you even more."

Chapter Fifteen

"It's hard to believe," Julia said the next morning as she looked at the things Nicholas had so painstakingly collected for his son. "You were so real to him, yet you lived only in his imagination."

"He's still not real to me, Julia."

She glanced at the broken window. "I think he's more real to you than you're ready to admit."

With his hands in his pockets, Alex followed her into the hall. "Maybe."

"Aren't you going to shut the door?"

"No. For over thirty years, that room has been a memorial to a life never lived. I'm going to clean it out, give those toys to children who do exist."

"Children who also need to know that someone cares."

Alex kissed her. "Are you sure you won't spend the day?"

Shaking her head, she smiled. "I have to go through Da's things and with the gallery opening scheduled for next week, this is the only time I'll have. You can come keep me company, though."

"You haven't gone through Patrick's things yet?" Unease prickled his scalp as they walked down the stairs.

"No. A case of pretend-it-isn't-there-and-it-won't-be." She stopped at the front door. "But, someone called for Da' yesterday and I realized that he had mail to be answered and maybe some unfinished business I should attend to."

"Have there been many calls?"

"Only one." A shadow seemed to come between them as Julia remembered the call, the questions it had raised. Maybe she would find nothing else to support her suspicions. "Why don't you come over tonight? I'll toss a salad and open a can of soup."

"I'll bring dinner," he offered. "I've been having a Big Mac attack."

"Junk food. Hasn't anyone told you it's bad for you?"

"Julia, I was raised on a gourmet diet. I have a lot of unexplored youthful excesses to enjoy." He tilted her chin up to meet his kiss. His resident demon had a stranglehold on his thoughts. What would Julia find among her father's possessions? A trail of questions, leading her to the truth? Sighing, he pulled her into his arms and held her tightly, not wanting to let her go.

'AH, ALEX. It is a fine day, is it not?" Petrov looked up as Alex walked out the front door an hour later. He was waxing his own car in the front driveway.

Alex picked up another chamois and began polishing a fender. "I didn't expect to see you until tomorrow morning."

"I won't be here long. Chloe and I have plans." Petrov increased his speed, threatening to rub a hole in the hood of the Crown Victoria. "And what of your day?"

If Alex didn't know better, he'd think Petrov was nervous, but it couldn't be. Gregori was unshakable in all things. "No plans, except to enjoy a day at home."

Petrov's head jerked up. "*Home,* Alex?" His accent was especially thick, his eyes searching.

Alex met Petrov's gaze. *Home.* When had he begun to think of the estate as such? When he had seen the diaries and the room furnished with such love and hope? Or even before that, when he had seen the house and grounds that reflected a dreamer's soul so much like his own—mute testimony that he was Nicholas's heir in more than tangible ways? It had crept up on him—the acceptance of the man he'd never been allowed to know or love as his father, the home Nicholas had built as much for him as for Lorna. The

past was irreversible, times and events that had made him
what he was today.

"Alex? Everything is all right?"

Alex sighed, a short burst of relief that a battle was ended.
"It will take getting used to—being a man's son."

OH DA' WHAT HAVE YOU DONE?

She should have stopped after boxing up her father's
clothes, Julia thought as she sat in Patrick's rocker with the
family Bible in her lap. She should have thrown away every
scrap of paper. Her hands clenched around the papers she'd
found tucked between the pages of Proverbs. A verse was
marked with yellow highlighter:

An heart that deviseth wicked imaginations, feet that
be swift in running into mischief.

Prov. 6:18

She reread the letter she'd found.

P—

I know we had a deal, but I've accepted another offer from a man who has a prior claim on the merchan-
dise. I will tell him of your interest in case he decides to
sell. This decision was not made lightly. I have an interest to protect.

By the time you receive this, the transaction will be
complete.

With regret, Patrick Devlin

Patrick's scrawl appeared shaky and splotched with ink.
Had he been writing it the night he died? He must have been
since it hadn't been mailed.

In her other hand, Julia held a single, rectangular piece of
paper—a check made out to Patrick Devlin and signed by
Alexander St. Ives. She'd found it in an open envelope with
a note attached.

Alex—

I told you I had other plans for this. What am I going to do with so much money? Julie won't have it, yet I feel it should benefit her. So, I return it to you as further insurance that your interest remains in her and not what she might have. Destroy this check and our secret at the same time. I pray she will never know that I kept the Veil.

Patrick

The telephone rang and she ignored it the first time. A few minutes later, it rang again. She rose from the chair and moving like a stick figure, she picked up the extension. "Hello."

"Julia? Is everything all right?"

She lowered her head, rubbed the spot at the bridge of her nose. "Yes, fine, Alex. It's difficult sorting through Da's life and packing it away."

"Yes, I imagine it is." He paused. "It's time for a break. Petrov told me about an old-fashioned diner that serves real hamburgers and milk shakes so thick you have to eat them with a spoon."

"Melvin's Diner? It's so popular that you have to have reservations to get in."

"Already done. I'll pick you up in forty minutes."

"I have an errand to run. I'll meet you there," she said quickly. She didn't want Alex here, not tonight, not here where memories crept out of every corner—memories of Alex picking her up for Chloe's party and Alex supervising Patrick's wake, and Alex holding her on the sofa. "I'm on my way out now."

"Julia—"

Forcing herself to put a smile in her voice was difficult, but she managed it. "Everything is *fine,* Alex. I'll see you in forty minutes at Melvin's." Very gently, she hung up the phone.

With determined steps, she walked back to the rocker and picked up the check and accompanying note, sealed the envelope and slipped them into her purse. Another verse in

Proverbs caught her eye before she closed the Bible:

The wise shall inherit glory: but shame shall be the promotion of fools.

Prov. 3:45

PARKING SPACES IN the large lot at Melvin's were almost as scarce as empty tables on short notice. Julia pulled into the row farthest away from the building and wondered how Alex had managed it. But then, she reflected, he was used to getting his own way.

She was about to make his day.

The tables were laminated with yellow Formica, chrome-rimmed and flanked by booths upholstered in red vinyl. A jukebox selector was mounted on the wall inside each booth. Alex flipped through the selections, reading them with interest. A record by Ed "Kookie" Byrnes was winding up the story of his famous comb.

Julia watched him from the doorway, enjoying, in spite of herself, the way he fed quarters into the machine. The song ended and Nancy Sinatra took over with the promise that her boots were going to walk all over a faithless lover.

It was definitely her cue.

With the uncanny internal radar he'd developed upon meeting Julia, Alex felt her presence before he raised his head. She looked exhausted as she weaved her way through dancing couples toward the dining area in the back. Her lips were free of gloss, as if she'd chewed it off and her smile was pasted on like glitter.

"Hi. Sorry I'm late. Lots of Sunday drivers out there today." Julia waved him down and slid into the booth when he would have risen to seat her. A waitress was hot on her heels, whipping menus out from under her arm, her order pad ready.

"A cheeseburger, fries and chocolate malt, please," Julia ordered briskly. "And lots of onion on the burger."

"I'll have the same," he said.

"Double onions...no big plans tonight, huh?" The waitress popped her double wad of bubble gum and sauntered away.

"Did you finish your errand?"

Julia shook her head. "No. That man called again."

"What man?"

"You know, the one I told you about that wanted to speak to my father." Lifting her chin, she looked at Alex, searching for the man she'd fallen in love with. Why couldn't he look different, uglier, less genuine?

On a threat, Nancy ended her song and Peter, Paul and Mary took over with "Leaving on a Jet Plane". "This seems to be a night for goodbyes," Julia remarked. "Don't they have anything more cheerful on this thing?

"Anyway," she said after making a selection with one of the quarters Alex had on the table. "Da' had arranged to sell something to this Mr. P and he won't believe that I don't know where it is. It's very mysterious. All I know is that it's something to do with art. Do you know a collector named *P*?" she asked. "He has a high squeaky voice and he's—"

"Nervous," Alex finished for her. He'd known immediately who "P" was. Irving Penn—one of his clients and eccentric as they come. He had a streak of paranoia a mile wide and always insisted on employing cloak-and-dagger methods in his transactions. Patrick couldn't have picked a better person to approach about the Veil.

"That's him," Julia said. "He won't tell me exactly what it is Da' was supposed to have sold him, though."

"No clues at all?"

"No, except once he did mention—"

The waitress announced the arrival of their meal with another pop of her gum, slid food-filled baskets toward them and tossed cutlery and straws onto the middle of the table. Tomatoes, onion, lettuce, thick melted cheese and grilled hamburger tantalized with an irresistible aroma. French fries steamed in the basket.

It surprised Julia that she was hungry and she dug into her food as if she hadn't eaten all day—which she hadn't. "What did he mention?" Alex stared at his burger, but made no move to eat it. Idly, he jabbed the straw in and out of his chocolate malt.

"He said something about a veil." A memory clicked into place and Julia paused in dipping a fry into a pool of ketchup. She dismissed the memory, afraid to face too much at once, afraid she might buckle under it all. Her taste buds became as numb as the rest of her, but she kept on eating as if it were her last meal, giving nothing away. "It must be a painting."

Though there was nothing overt in her manner, Alex sensed that Julia wasn't chatting just for the hell of it. Either she was methodically giving him enough rope with which to hang himself or his conscience was trying to tell him something. He was more than ready to listen. "It's not a painting, Julia."

Her gaze snapped to his, then she tilted her head. "No?"

He pushed his basket aside. "Shall we go?"

Her spoon clattered on the table as she dropped it from nerveless fingers. "No way, Alex. I'm not finished yet." She reached for her malt, ignoring the spoon.

"Neither are we, Julia. We have unfinished business to discuss."

"I'm not going to like it, am I?"

"No."

Suddenly she was frightened. The truth could hurt so much. Maybe she should forget the whole thing, live with her suspicions rather than live without Alex. "No," she echoed tonelessly.

That simple word fell between them like a stone, telling him more than he wanted to know. Time had grown short, too short for him to find the words with which to admit deceit, to make her understand. She'd had such high walls around her when they'd met and in the course of a few weeks, he'd seen them turn to rubble. How long would it take her to rebuild them when she learned the extent of his folly? A few minutes? An hour?

"Where do you want to start?" Julia asked, impatient now to get it over with.

"Your father and mine—"

"Oh . . . speaking of my father—he left something for you." After wiping her hands on her napkin, she opened her purse and pulled out the envelope, sliding it across the table with one finger. "Go ahead, open it. I've already seen it."

Alex felt her coolness, her unnatural calm—not exhaustion at all. He'd waited too long, dropped the noose around his own neck, tightened it. His hesitation in opening the envelope was the same as dangling over the trapdoor in the gallows floor.

His expression when he saw the check and read the note showed Julia the truth as clearly as graffiti on a bathroom wall. How far had she sunk that she could wish for his lies rather than his honesty?

Alex crumpled the letter and check in his hand, his expression calm, remote, his movements slow, restrained. "Do you know what this is about, or are you guessing?"

She twisted the napkin in her lap around her fingers. "I'm guessing that Da' had something that you wanted, the same thing Mr. P. was supposed to buy." One of her hands emerged from under the table, reached for her glass. "You used me to get to Da' and now poor Mr. P. is out of luck."

"That was the original plan." Knowing that she was ready to bolt, Alex reached across the table for her hand, needing to keep her there until she understood that he'd made his promise to Patrick with the best of intentions, forgetting in which direction that particular road led.

She jerked her hand away, feeling as mangled as the napkin she tossed into her basket of half-eaten food. "I'm also guessing—" she said as if she hadn't heard him "—that you didn't get what you wanted. You must think I know where it is."

"I don't give a damn about the Veil!" he said savagely.

"Oh Alex, I'm so glad." Tenderness gushed from her voice, her eyes. "I'm sorry that your plan backfired, though. You ought to have something to show for all your trouble."

Her smile was fleeting, painful to watch as she grabbed her purse and slid out of the booth. "At least you have your check back, so I guess we're even." Without another word, she walked quickly out of the diner.

Cursing under his breath, Alex caught up with their waitress and stuffed enough money into her hand to pay several bills, before running out to the parking lot.

Julia stood in the middle of a row, looking around helplessly, frantically. The numbness was wearing off. She sensed Alex's presence behind her, a magnetic force drawing her toward him. But she couldn't talk anymore, knowing that she'd fall apart if more was said. Lies would almost have been preferable. At least then she could have tested the theory that ignorance was bliss. "Damn it, where is my car?" she said, panicked.

Alex took her arm in an unrelenting grip and steered her toward his Rolls Royce. Julia tried to pull away, but he held firm. "No, Julia. No going to ground until we've talked this out." Without letting go, he seated her and slid in next to her, automatically hitting the switch to lock the doors.

"Am I supposed to listen to you tell whatever lies are required to get the job done?" Detachment took over then, relief from betrayal, misery, rage. She sat back, angling her body so she could look straight at him. It was important that she meet this squarely. She couldn't go to ground or hide from her memories. She knew better than most how impossible it was.

"No lies, Julia."

"All right." She braced her back against the door, knowing that the truth would hurt. Not ready to know the full extent of her naïveté, she decided to start with something nonthreatening. "Tell me about the Veil. What is it exactly?"

"The Veil of Tears—a headdress made of gold mesh and pearls, and very old."

An enchanted veil . . . gold mesh, studded with pearls to reflect the glow and heat of a woman's skin . . . a crown and veil in one . . . a headdress for a queen, barbaric and incredibly beautiful. The memory materialized in Julia's mind, word for word, sensation for sensation: Aunt Chloe's patio; Alex's arms around her as they danced, his voice seductive, weaving magic around her. "It would suit me," she quoted.

Angry now, Alex didn't bother to contain it. The memory was too vivid, too real, like the dreams he'd had of the future. He had to reach Julia, but he didn't know how, so he lashed out. "No. The Veil was made for a woman sure of her power." He saw her blanch and press herself harder against the door. "There are similarities, though, between you and the young woman in the legend."

Idly, he draped his arm over the steering wheel as he recited the story. "She was loved all her life by everyone around her. On her wedding day, she was betrayed by the man she loved. His father's army stormed her castle and killed her family." He slashed the air with his hand when Julia opened her mouth to interrupt. "She gave up rather than fight back, hid in her walled garden and turned to stone. Some believed that her betrothed was also betrayed. It's possible that his father used him, a lesser son, to catch his victims off guard. The shame of it is that she believed in his guilt and disappeared without knowing for sure whether he actually had betrayed her."

We'd always wonder what we missed. Subconscious thoughts kept intruding, resurrecting memories one by one, stimulating doubt and second thoughts. Yet there was nothing to doubt by Alex's own admission. He'd used her. Period.

"Why didn't you tell me that first day?" She had to work hard to keep her voice even, unemotional. "Why the games? I would have talked to Da' and convinced him to give it back to you."

The resignation he saw in her eyes infuriated him. "How should I answer that? You're not prepared to believe me. Either way, you're going to walk away without giving me a chance."

Julia ignored the crumbs of hope he tossed out to her. She couldn't understand why he was drawing it out, keeping her there...unless it mattered to him. And that was a possibility she couldn't afford to consider. "You're right, Alex. Either way, you lied—"

"By omission, Julia. Obviously, my reasons were well-founded." His mouth tightened; pride asserted itself, a last stand against pain. "You can't trust yourself enough to believe in me."

"Let me go, Alex," she said wearily. "We aren't going anywhere with this but in circles."

Without a word, Alex flipped the switch to unlock the doors.

Without a word, Julia opened her door, swung her legs out of the car. Her back to him, she spoke in a whisper, to herself more than to him. "I almost made it, you know—almost forgot that trust is just another word for stupidity."

Chapter Sixteen

"I know the signs, Julie. You're on the run," Chloe said. "I'm not leaving until you tell me what's going on."

Insulted, Julia rifled through a drawer in her desk. She could have sworn that she wasn't on the run. In fact, she was positive that she was hanging in there with admirable strength. She hadn't quit working on the gallery or tried to avoid Alex and she hadn't even considered joining a nunnery. It wasn't her fault that Alex hadn't been around for her to avoid. It was a blessing. Out of sight meant whole minutes of not thinking about him, not hurting, not wishing she could take it all back, pretend it had never happened.

"Of course, you're welcome to stay, Aunt Chloe, but I have to go to the gallery." Julia darted around her office, trying to look busy, accomplishing nothing.

"Sit!"

Julia sat and glanced at her watch. "Five minutes, Aunt Chloe, then I have to go."

"You'll stay put if I have to tie you down." Chloe remained in a low hover over Julia. "Greg and I planned to take Alex's yacht down to Mexico, but Alex has taken it out—without notice."

"It *is* his boat," Julia reminded her, feeling that familiar catch in her chest. *Just who's on the run here?*

"Never mind. I want to know why you won't stay in one place for five minutes and Alex is out there—alone."

"Because we want it that way?"

"Sure you do."

Ignoring Chloe's warning glare, Julia stood and planted both hands flat on the desk. "I love you, Aunt Chloe, but this is none of your business."

"Now you listen to me, young lady. Alex literally pulled me out of a bottle and walked me through the worst year of my life—"

Julia blinked. "Alex? No one told me who had stopped you from drinking."

"No one was supposed to tell you anything," Chloe snapped. "How did you hear?"

"The usual grapevine. Word was that you had a new lover and—"

"Lover? Alex? Not on your life. I couldn't give him what he wanted." Chloe noted her niece's relief with satisfaction. "Did you really think he was my lover?"

Her thoughts racing back, Julia realized that she had axed the idea a long time ago. "No, not after your party. It just didn't add up. You treated him as if... I don't know—"

"As if he was someone I respect even though he'd turned *me* down as a lover? He did, you know. Alex is a smart man. If we'd had that kind of relationship, we couldn't have been friends afterward." Before Julia could be diverted by such a cryptic statement, Chloe changed the subject again. "And for your information—Alex didn't make me stop drinking. He made me realize that I *wanted* to stop."

Chloe backed off and dropped into the chair behind her. "Damn the gossips for stealing my thunder! I was saving the tragic story of my downfall for a meaningful moment, when it might help you."

"No one can help me but myself, Aunt Chloe," Julia said gently. "Someday, after I've worked it all out, I'll tell you about *my* downfall. Not now, though. I can't."

"That bad, huh?"

Julia shrugged. "Just the same old story. I'll get over it."

"You'll have to be brain-dead to get over Alex."

"I really do have to go to the gallery, Aunt Chloe." Julia snatched her purse out of a drawer and headed for the door.

Chloe turned in the chair, her frown saying many things, none of which Julia was willing to hear. "Julie," she said, her gentle tone pulling Julia up short. That tone always meant vital revelations, which she needed to hear whether she wanted to or not. "I was worried about you and Alex at first, but I was wrong."

After such a statement, Julia couldn't have walked out the door if her life had depended on it. She stood like a statue, feeling chills race up her spine, over her skin.

"Julie, Alex has had one hell of a life and he's learned a lot from it. No one knows what he needs better than Alex. You're it, honey. He knew it the minute he set eyes on you. And there's not a man on this earth that can understand you and love you as Alex does. You know he's special. Don't tell me that he hasn't shown you how special you are to him."

"Not special enough," Julia said, refusing to be influenced. "Loyalty is your middle name, Aunt Chloe. That's why I'm not going to let this discussion go any further." She opened the door, glanced back. "Alex has been—is—a good friend to you. I can see that. What's between me and him has nothing to do with your friendship."

"What's between you and Alex is enchantment," Chloe snapped.

"Enchantment?" There it was again—a sputter in her heartbeat, a stall in her breath, acute symptoms of unrequited love. She hoped that it was something she could outgrow, like childhood allergies.

"That's what Alex said." Chloe examined her nails.

"Enchantment is good," Julia said. "Spells can be broken. It's real life you have to watch out for."

REAL LIFE WAS A WAR ZONE and after an hour of dodging obstacles at the gallery, Julia was ready for R & R in neutral territory.

As with all projects nearing completion, the mansion was a hotbed of confusion and disorganization. Workmen were everywhere, milling around like drunken ants, arguing about whose job took precedence over whose. If she wasn't soothing egos, she was approving overtime for the carpet layers so they could leave the drapers in peace and return Saturday. All she could think about was how soon her obligation to Alex would be over. If only she could decide whether she was as relieved as she ought to be or as miserable as she felt.

Except when she was thinking about enchantment. The word hit home, reminding her of Sleeping Beauty being out of it for a century. And then there was Rip Van Winkle and his twenty-year nap. She'd never make it that long. One way or the other, she vowed, she would get over Alex.

Home was a welcome respite from the insanity of the past week. The opening on Tuesday night was the goal she had to reach. If she went to bed early, she could sleep away that many more hours of abject misery. Too bad she couldn't sleep. All she could do was think—of Alex and where he might be. Had he gone to Sandcastle to walk along his beach, staring out to sea and dreaming, alone, as he'd always been alone, an island in the middle of nowhere?

She was doing a lousy job of boarding up her feelings for Alex.

Kicking off the covers, she grabbed her robe and made a beeline for the kitchen. Hot milk and a B-movie ought to do the trick. Maybe *Attack of the Killer Tomatoes* was on the *Friday Night Frights*. It was eight o'clock. The *Frights* were scheduled for ten-thirty. So what was two hours to a fledgling insomniac?

Cup in hand, Julia sipped the warm milk and checked out the titles in the bookcase. Her father's book of old legends caught her eye and she pulled it out, curling up on the nearest chair to skim the table of contents. Nothing. Five books later, she found the legend of the Veil of Tears in an old volume on the relationship between archaeology and myth.

She read every word, studied every picture. One was of an ancient statue in the United Kingdom, old, yet whole, surrounded by the crumbling walls of a barren garden. Another was a sketch of the Veil, which didn't look like much in black-and-white. Julia re-read the story, her attention riveted each time to one particular sentence: *...her spirit fled to the sanctuary of Lyonnesse to await a better time to live* *and love*. She dropped the book onto the ottoman and wandered to her father's room, trying to relate what she had read to her father's crime, his secret, Alex's deception. Was the Veil of Tears special enough to be worth more than love?

Why Julie darlin', I have it on good authority that the little people buried gold here. It was as if Patrick had spoken. She could almost see him kneeling on the floor—

Julia ran to the kitchen where she kept a drawer full of tools for household emergencies. Back in Patrick's room, she moved the bed and found that the carpet had already been loosened. Rolling it out of the way, she pressed the floorboards. A nail was sticking up a little, its head bent. Her hands shook as she pried it up.

Two boards were loose before she resolutely lifted them up and out. Beneath the flooring was a metal plate and beneath that a metal-lined compartment. Empty. Had her father moved the Veil the day she'd caught him crawling around on the floor? She sat back on her heels and glanced around the room. Uncertainty was gone. She had to see it, had to know what the great attraction was.

Don't forget . . . a rose . . . Elise. Her father's last words—had they been a request or a clue? Suddenly, it all fell into place. *My secret can't die now . . . Too late.* He'd known that she would find the check and the letters he hadn't had enough time to mail. There had never been enough time. Not enough for his secret to die. Not enough for her to know the truth about the reason for Alex's interest in her before she'd fallen in love with him. Too late.

She wiped the tears from her cheeks and looked around the room, forcing herself to remember more.

Her gaze flew to the window. There were roses in the garden. Elise—her mother's name. Elise—the name of her father's prizewinning rose. Another memory drew her attention to the old music box with a single rose carved on the domed lid. And she remembered the tune it had played before it had stopped working—fifteen years ago. *Elise*—a composition by Beethoven. The music box—her mother's most prized possession. *Oh, Da', you did everything but paint arrows on the floor.*

The box was empty. She closed her eyes and rocked back and forth, her arms wrapped around her middle as if she'd been stabbed. Empty. Dear God, had it all been for nothing? Had her father already given the Veil to Alex? *She believed in his guilt and disappeared without knowing for sure whether he actually had betrayed her.* Guilt twisted inside, deep and sharp. And disgust—for herself and her actions. If Alex did have the Veil, then she had been wrong and horribly cruel to both of them. He'd lied to her, but in this context, it took on a different meaning. There would have been a good chance that he hadn't been using her at the end, that he did want her, and Aunt Chloe had been right after all.

Methodically, Julia reviewed all that had happened, unable to deny her own complicity. Her attitude had contributed to her father's and Alex's belief that she wasn't secure or confident enough to hear the truth without being suspicious of their motives. Still, she would have liked to have had the opportunity to prove them wrong. If she'd failed, the blame would have been on her head and no one else's. Slowly, as if she hurt in a dozen places, Julia pulled herself up, turned away from the music box, walked stiffly toward the mess she'd made on the floor, the empty compartment . . .

She stared at the metal-lined hollow in the floor, then back at the music box. It hadn't worked in fifteen years—since her father had robbed Nicholas. She carried the tools across the room, kneeling again, pausing, thinking. Did she want to do this? How much easier it would be to live with her own guilt than to be disillusioned with Alex. More than she wanted to be right, she wanted to believe that Alex was all that she thought him to be.

Her decision was the most difficult she'd ever made, but she had to know one way or the other.

She worked slowly, careful not to damage the wood, delaying the moment when she would know. The bottom of the box gave, and she lifted it out to expose the works. Wedged inside was a chamois pouch. Inside that she felt metal, cold and heavy, yet feeling liquid in her hand, spilling over her fingers as she pulled it out. Rich gold and creamy pearls with a hint of pink. Delicate links joined in a weblike mesh. Irregular round medallions inscribed in a mixture of pictographs and hieroglyphics. She wanted to be sick. It was beautiful. And it warmed in her hands, glowed in the light, as if it possessed its own energy. This was what so many had sought for centuries. This is what brought two men to freedom and one of them to a love so strong, he had given up his son. Gold and pearls and the near magical skill of a man so far in the past there was no record of his existence. Gold and pearls, paid for with her father's life. Beauty, paid for with her heart. A diadem made for a queen who wore her crown only long enough to have her dreams destroyed by a man who wanted everything but her.

Her finger skimmed over the pearls, perfect drops like tears too bitter to simply disappear. She held it up, spreading it between her hands. A headdress for a queen. A wedding veil. A veil of tears. She felt a strange kinship with that other woman who had lived so long ago.

And she felt anger, overwhelming, unreasoning. Not once since she'd discovered Alex's deception had she been angry. It hadn't been natural, she realized, not to feel anger, not to show it. Now, her head ached with anger, her blood churned in her veins threatening to overflow and drown her in it. She clutched the Veil tightly, felt it dig into her palms, and screamed inside where no one could hear but herself.

The story of Julia Devlin and Alexander St. Ives had its beginning and middle. Nothing was left but the end.

Chapter Seventeen

On Tuesday night, the elegant old mansion came alive, glowing with modern lighting, warm with antique furniture and plush carpeting. It looked like the grand home it had once been, a place of comfort and richness, displaying objets d'art of every form and composition in compatible settings. Security guards wearing tuxedos blended unobtrusively with the guests. Jewels glittered on richly gowned women as they strolled on the arms of men in sedate formal wear, their hushed conversations like a heartbeat restored. It was beautiful, Julia thought as she stood in the threshold listening to the chamber music provided by a quartet set up in the entrance hall.

Seeing the look on Alex's face as she walked into the grand salon was even more satisfying. He stopped his conversation in midsentence to stare at her. She felt that old bell-ringer excitement as his gaze wandered over her, admiring her gown, the wide gold bracelet cuffed around her upper arm in lieu of the traditional evening gloves. And then she felt sick as his eyes widened in surprise, then narrowed in anger. Maybe he hadn't expected or wanted her to be there. Maybe it was the Veil.

She hadn't consciously set out to wear the Veil, but when she'd searched her jewelry box for accessories, nothing had seemed quite right. The Veil was ideal, draping over her chest and shoulders, its length covering the skin exposed by the low back of her gown. Something had compelled her to wear it, just this once. Only this once would she have the right.

Alex stared at Julia, aware of nothing but that she was there. He'd docked yesterday, macho tendencies blazing, resolving to track her down, tie her to the hammock or lock her into the back seat of the Rolls, whatever was necessary to straighten things out between them. He'd tempered those urges by the time he'd arrived at the gallery for a thorough inspection. He'd phoned her, but there had been no answer. And he'd gone to her house earlier to escort her to the opening—or drag her there—but she'd been gone. Her presence gave him hope that drastic measures would not be required to get the job done, especially since kidnapping was against the law.

He tossed back his champagne, his gaze riveted on Julia. She stood out like a rose among dandelions in her gown of rich, warm red that clung like another layer of skin to below her waist, then flared into a floor-length skirt of crystal pleats. Her arms were bare, except for a heavy, carved gold bracelet, and the neckline showed more than a little skin, dipping to a V from the tips of her shoulders. Whether Julia knew it or not, she was a total washout as a runaway from life's little glitches. Her presence at the opening was proof of that. Her clothing was the equivalent of full battle dress. Holding her gaze, he lifted his glass, saluting her, the pride in her carriage, the defiance sparking in her eyes.

Something was different about her. He squinted his eyes, looking at her more closely. The world seemed to stop rotating. The gallery, the people, the music, were a fade-out. Nothing existed except the woman standing in the threshold, a fall of gold and pearls flowing over her head, appearing so much a part of her that he hadn't noticed right away.

She is wearing the Veil.

How ironic, he thought, that his first sight of the Veil of Tears would be this way, with Julia's hair in silky waves beneath the links of gold. And how appropriate. The Veil had been made for a woman like her, not the delicate child bride of legend who had retreated so far into herself that in the end nothing was left but cold, lifeless stone. He was enthralled by the image of Julia transposed into that other time, that other place where legends were born and enchantment was an everyday word.

His blood ran cold as he saw several people stop to talk to her. One woman touched the Veil, then Julia pirouetted, showing it off. He slammed his glass onto the tray of a passing waiter. *Damn.* She was walking around with a king's ransom on her head as if it were just another hat.

Questions and answers ran rampant through his mind as he dodged guests and ignored greetings. She had the Veil. Had she always known where it was? *No!* Julia lied well only to Julia and that only because she wanted to believe whatever nonsense she told herself. She must have found it recently. Had she tried to contact him? The challenge in her expression, and the pride, said *no, not yet.* So, she'd decided to shock him. She'd certainly done that. Was she here to work things out? *Not on your life, Alex.*

People scattered and swirled around Alex like clouds in a storm as Julia watched him advance. His obvious fury calmed her. In the past, he'd been in control while she'd floundered around, reacting and responding to him. She'd been victimized by his deception and her own emotions. This time, they would meet on equal ground.

She felt his arm clamp around her waist, his thumb finding bare skin through the Veil. "Hello, Julia." His gaze swept over the crowd around her. "Would you excuse us?" Without waiting for assent, he steered her on a slow stroll around the perimeter of the room. "What do you think you're doing, wearing that thing in public? Do you know what it's worth?" he whispered savagely.

"This is the only place I could wear *this thing*," she said. "You have enough security here to guard Fort Knox."

Alex glared down at her. "Don't you know what lengths people will go to for such a piece?"

Her look cut into him like a cold wind. "Oh yes, Alex. I know exactly what lengths some men will go to for the Veil of Tears. Isn't that how it got its name?"

"Give it to me."

"No. Tonight, it's mine." With a brittle smile, she tried to break away from him, but he pulled her up short, shifting his hold to a tight grip on both her arms.

"Damn it! I'll put it in the safe. Tomorrow, you can take it to a bank for safekeeping."

Her smile grew, became bitter. "Safekeeping, Alex? I've been complimented numerous times tonight on my 'costume jewelry.' All these patrons of the arts think that I'm making a fashion statement by wearing something I bought at a movie auction. If it wasn't so funny, it would be tragic."

"Someone is bound to realize what it is."

"I don't think so, Alex. People see what they expect to see."

"Like you."

"No. If that were true, I would have seen you for what you really are." With a quick twist of her arms, Julia broke his grip and walked away.

"Julie!" Chloe and Petrov caught up with her a few feet away from Alex. "Good grief. You sure know how to make a fashion statement," Chloe remarked, her hands on her hips as she surveyed her niece. "You look wonderful."

Julia turned her head and raised her eyebrows at Alex.

"Where on earth did you find it?" Chloe walked a slow circle around Julie, then mumbled, "And, why didn't I find it first?"

Julia shrugged. "Tucked away in a little out-of-the-way place."

As soon as Julia moved away, Alex gestured to a security guard.

"Trouble, sir?"

More than you could know, Alex thought grimly. "Stay within arm's reach of Ms. Devlin . . . and don't let her leave until I say so."

A spot right between her shoulder blades tingled, as if someone was burning a hole through her. For the fourth time, she glanced around, but no one was there except the security guards wandering back and forth, pretending to admire the objets d'art strategically placed to look as if they were part of the decor. She could swear she was being watched. Shaking her head, she gave Chloe her full attention.

Petrov, on the other hand was staring at her, his expression a mixture of frustration and worry. "Julia, you do not know what you are doing," he said gently as Chloe was diverted by a passing acquaintance.

"It doesn't matter, Gregori."

"To you and Alex it matters very much."

"What matters?" Chloe turned, her hair a fiery cloud whirling around her head.

"We've already had this discussion, Aunt Chloe." Her jaw ached from the pasted-on smile she'd been wearing all evening. So did her head and neck. The Veil weighed a ton. "I'll see you later."

"Hold it, Julie."

"Chloe, let her be." Petrov warned.

"Cool it, Greg. I just want to tell her our news."

"Perhaps, my love, this is not a good time."

Greg? My love? Julia's grin was genuine as she looked from one to the other. "You're pregnant, Aunt Chloe?" she teased.

To Julia's amazement, Chloe's eyes grew soft, dreamy. Petrov blushed.

"Hah! You and Alex are all the children Greg and I can handle." Her expression was for Petrov alone. "Greg and I eloped to Las Vegas yesterday. We wanted you to be the first to know."

A lump grew in Julia's chest, heavy as stone. She bent forward to hug Chloe. "Oh, Aunt Chloe, I'm so happy for you." Over her aunt's shoulder, she winked at Petrov. "Gregori, you don't know what you've done."

Petrov beamed as he rocked back on his heels, his chest puffed out. "It will be interesting to learn."

"Believe me, Greg, you've already learned plenty." Chloe stepped into his embrace, fitting perfectly under his arm. "And you, Julie—"

Clearing his throat, Petrov said, "Chloe, you promised—"

"I can't just stand by while all the residential property in Oz is condemned."

"What are you talking about?" he asked.

Julia took the matter into her own hands by kissing Petrov's cheek. "Welcome to the family, Uncle Gregori. Aunt Chloe, I just saw Dina and Will. I'll see you later."

Chloe slipped her arm through Petrov's. "I'll talk to Dina. You go straighten things out with Alex."

"They are both over twenty-one, Chloe. Let them be." He led his bride away, but not before Julia heard her irrepressible relative. "Damn it, Greg, somebody had better do something. Julie's on her last dream."

"And Alex is on his only one, but we can do nothing."

Julia's eyes blinked away sudden tears as she pretended she hadn't heard, wishing it weren't true.

AN HOUR LATER, Julia tilted her head at the man sharing the elevator with her. "Are you following me?" she asked. He'd been nearby every time she'd turned around.

"Yes, ma'am."

"Why?"

"Mr. St. Ives ordered it."

The elevator stopped at the third and top floor of the mansion. "I see. Well, I'm going into his office."

"May I ask why, ma'am?"

"Of course." Her key turned easily in the lock. "I'm going to take off my girdle. Trust me, you don't want to watch. It's not a pretty sight." She slammed the door in his face and locked it again.

She sagged into a chair, feeling like an inflatable doll that had a slow leak. She wished she was wearing a girdle just so she could feel the relief of taking it off. Her shoes plopped onto the carpet as she kicked them off. She contemplated removing her panty hose, but decided that doing so would use up too much energy.

The evening had taken its toll on her. Pride always did. And she had more pride than sense. What, she wondered, had made her think that she could breeze through the evening as if nothing had changed in her life and she was the same old Julia? *Old* seemed to be the only word that applied. She felt as ancient as the Veil. Her neck was sore from holding her head up. Her heart thumped in her chest, battering the walls she'd built around it, refusing protection. Her heart didn't listen to anything but itself. All night, it had been listening for Alex.

Alex had treated her with impersonal courtesy the few times they'd found themselves in the same group, yet his eyes had spoken of barely controlled fury. She hadn't missed the way his gaze had been drawn to the Veil time and time again. It would have surprised her if he'd reacted differently. He was addicted to textures, colors, all things sensual. To one who knew the legend, the Veil was the ultimate fix, stimulating dreams and belief in magic. Hadn't she spent the weekend touching it, looking at it, sensing the shadows of the past that seemed to cling to it?

Alex had been right. Wearing the Veil had been a mistake. She reached up and tore it off, wincing as it yanked a strand of hair and snagged on her gown. Her hand stopped in midair at the rattle of the doorknob. Only four people had keys: Alex, the manager he'd hired, the security chief, and herself. Fatalistically, she watched it turn, knowing it was Alex, acknowledging that she had come to the office to wait for him.

Alex walked in, saw Julia, paused. She looked ravaged, her eyes huge and surrounded by shadows, her skin pale. Her mouth was tight with strain and her body was stiff, her hand clasped around the Veil in a white-knuckled grip. His gaze moved over her again, the gown of red silk, then caught on the Veil in her lap. Silence seemed to enshroud him as he stood there, unmoving, staring at it.

"Is this what you came for?" she asked, rising from the chair and holding the Veil out to him, its weight spilling over her hands.

Alex's gaze moved up to her face, but it seemed to waver, as if the Veil were a magnet, drawing him back. "Put it down, Julia. We have to talk and I don't want that between us."

With a shrug, she lowered her hand. "It's always been between us. Even now, you can't stop looking at it. You want to touch it so badly you can't stand it."

"Of course, I can't stop looking at it. You're damn right I want to touch it," he shouted. "One man spent his entire adult life making it. Those medallions tell the history of a people who are supposed to exist only in myths and movies." He untied his bow tie, unfastened the top stud on his pleated shirt, raked his fingers through his hair. "The composition and workmanship shouldn't have been possible when this was made. The pearls should have decomposed long ago. Everything associated with it speaks of magic and miracles." His voice lowered. "I'm a romantic, Julia, a dreamer. I've always believed in magic and miracles."

Julia laid the Veil on the desk. "Touch it all you like, Alex. The Veil of Tears is your dream, not mine."

"What it represents is my dream, Julia. The Veil itself is nothing but inert metal."

"No? You came to San Francisco just for the hell of it, right?"

"I came to claim the estate."

"Of which the Veil is a part." She held it up again.

"Only in the broadest technical terms." Alex leaned a shoulder against the wall, keeping himself in check.

"Of course you've been planning to open a gallery here for ages," Julia said. The calmer he was, the angrier she became, spoiling for a fight. "Choosing me to help you was a coincidence. From the beginning, everything you've done has been calculated."

"*At* the beginning, yes it was," Alex answered, his jaw tight. "But not everything, Julia, and not *from* the beginning."

"Sure, Alex," she snapped. "Our eyes met across my office and you were swept away by my beauty. It drove all thoughts of the Veil right out of your mind."

"Close," Alex said as he pushed away from the wall to stand directly in front of her, close enough to touch, close enough to see the tracks of her tears drying on her cheeks.

She stepped back, her calves bumping into the chair behind her. "Tell me, Alex, when did you forget about the Veil? When I dared to say no to you? Did your arrogance override your greed?" The lump in her throat developed instantly when he flinched, as if she'd hurt him. It was what she'd wanted when she'd been hurting and alone. But wanting it and seeing it were two entirely different things. In hurting Alex, she felt as if she had hurt herself. She backed up more, trying to push the chair away with her legs.

He grasped her arm to keep her from falling backward, then let go just as quickly, shoving his hands into his pockets. "No, Julia. I forgot about the Veil when I saw the combs in your hair."

"What?" She dropped to the chair. *"What?"*

"Lotus-eating dragons and butterflies," he explained. "I knew you then, Julia, a dreamer afraid to dream. And, I was searching for a dream. I thought I'd found it."

Her breath skipped in and out. This wasn't right, she thought. He'd used her and lied to her. Men like him didn't say such things—romantic things—in the middle of a fight. And angry as she was, knowing what she knew, she shouldn't want to believe him.

Dropping her gaze, she saw the Veil still clutched in her hand. She stood and thrust it out to him. "This belongs to you."

Alex stared at Julia. She was so easy to read and right now, her expression spelled out *hopeless*. He took the Veil from her, holding it as if it were refuse, then let it fall onto the desk. A single pearl fell off, bounced once, then rolled over the edge. "Another test, Julia? Shall I destroy it?" he asked, his voice harsh, grating. "Will that redeem me in your eyes?"

She shook her head. "The question doesn't arise. You now have what you've wanted all along." She jumped as Alex flattened his palm against the door, holding it closed.

Alex clamped his hands on her shoulders, turning her around to face him. "How in the hell would you know what I want? Have you ever asked? Did you ever listen?" His voice was low, raw, as he forced it out, giving his temper free rein. "All you ever did was decide what I wanted—like Pansy, the wrestling matches, making love in the front seat of your car. You gave and gave, Julia, without once giving yourself and your trust."

"Trust, Alex?" A choked laugh broke away from her. "You were so hung up on trust the other night in the car, so ready to take it personally even though the problem was mine, not yours—" Her voice caught on a sob, but she swallowed it down, took a deep breath, continued. "I never once lied to you, Alex. No matter how hard it was, I was always honest with you. I told you that I loved you. I trusted you enough that I believed you loved me back, even though you never said so."

Her statement hit him broadside like an armored tank, defeating him. She was right, of course. He cupped her chin, raised her head, forcing her to meet his gaze. "Is that the real issue, Julia? That I didn't say the words outright?"

"No, Alex, it isn't an issue at all," she whispered, jerking away from his hand. "I'd never questioned how you felt about me until I realized that neither you nor my father trusted *me*. You didn't believe in me enough to tell me the truth before I found out for myself. It's pretty obvious that you couldn't love me and expect so little of me at the same time."

"You're right." Alex lowered his arms, turned away from her to go to the desk. Bending over, he picked up the pearl, stared at the large, perfect teardrop as he rolled it between his fingers. "I knew that you expected me to betray you. Your father used that to convince me to keep his secret. He didn't have to twist my arm. The matter of the Veil had been settled between us. Neither one of us wanted you dragged into it, cheapened by it."

"I feel cheap, Alex, and small. I was so proud of myself for finally having the courage to grow beyond the past and take chances. I thought I was doing so well, yet the two people who meant the most to me couldn't see it. You both sold me short."

"Yes, we did, but not because of the Veil, Julia. Never that." He pocketed the pearl and walked toward her, his gaze burning into her. His hand shook as he smoothed her hair, twined a curl around his finger. "We were both afraid of losing you."

Julia blinked, pushing back sudden tears. He'd never played fair with her, always pushing her into feeling more than she was ready to handle, making her want more than she dared, teaching her how to dream again. Dreams were so unreasonable and persistent. One or two words of hope made them multiply like rabbits.

She groped behind her for the doorknob, twisted it. "Alex, don't do this to me . . . not now." She flinched at the sound of his fist hitting the door.

"Not now," he repeated flatly and backed off, too angry to be near anything breakable. "What in the hell does that mean, Julia? Am I to wait until you decide whether or not to forgive me for making an error in judgment?" He jammed his hands into his pockets. "I could swallow my pride and do that, but what about the next time something happens to make you doubt me." He paced away from her and back again. "At some point, I might not give you the right answer, do the right thing. I'd spend my life against the wall, praying the bullets would miss."

Each word hit Julia like a slap. "I wish I could say that you're wrong, Alex." She shrugged. "But I can't. I do have doubts and I could never subject either of us to that."

"Do you hear what you're saying?" Alex asked. "Your doubts have nothing to do with me or the Veil. It's you, Julia. You'll believe in anything but yourself."

"Yes," she whispered. "I was counting on you to teach me how—" A sob caught her suddenly and she sucked in her breath "—but it doesn't work that way. You can't teach me to believe in myself. It's something I have to work out on my own."

"Julia."

She steeled herself for another verbal blow.

"Love isn't blind, Julia. It is said that we love persons for their defects as well as their good qualities. I've been waiting a long time to discover the truth of that."

His hands clenched as Julia stepped into the hall and shut the door softly behind her, taking color and light with her.

Alone in the office, Alex stared at the Veil of Tears, then picked it up, spread it out, studying the workmanship, the detail. He was almost sorry that it was real. As a legend, its appeal had lasted for centuries. As a reality, the Veil would become a nine-day wonder, soon to be taken for granted, just another thing to be possessed, coveted, and perhaps stolen again.

Alex checked his watch and reached for the telephone. A minute later, his transatlantic connection was made. A soft voice with an Irish lilt came over the wire. "Hello, Miss Riley. Alex St. Ives here. Put Professor Connell on the line, please . . . yes, I'll wait."

He looked up as the door opened. Red silk swished around her as Julia marched stiffly across the office, and just as stiffly bent over to pick up a pair of red shoes lying in front of the chair. "Damn you, Alex," she said as she slipped one, then the other onto her feet. "Why can't you, just once, play fair?" Shooting him a glare that would have dropped Don Juan the Destroyer in his tracks, she marched out again.

Alex smiled. Julia was too much a fighter to simply give up, and if he didn't miss his guess, she had just shown him a rainbow in the dark.

Chapter Eighteen

"He just doesn't play fair, Dina," Julia said after telling Dina the unabridged story of her life since Alex had come on the scene. For over three weeks her emotions had been on a seesaw as she'd struggled to put it all in perspective. Earlier that afternoon, she'd broken down completely—tears, gibberish, the works. Dina's suggestion of a hen session had seemed to be a good idea. They'd retired to Julia's house with half a bakery, cocoa mix, marshmallows and a gallon of milk.

"Creep," Dina said around a mouthful of peanut-butter cookie.

"He's not a creep." Julia held out her cup for a refill. "He likes puppies and ladybugs and adolescent Hell's Angels."

"He's a creep. He had what he wanted. Why didn't he leave you alone after making his deal with your father? He didn't have to treat you as if you were the most perfect woman in the world."

I knew you then—a dreamer afraid to dream. Julia shook her head, trying to dislodge the memories that kept infiltrating her thoughts. "He didn't. He knew my faults."

"Even worse."

"Why?"

"Well, think about it, Julie. He is without exception the most gorgeous man I've ever seen. He's worth millions. He's cultured and sophisticated and has probably gone out with the most beautiful women in the world. What would he want with you?''

Friend. Companion. Support system. Lover. "I'm not so bad.''

"No, not bad. Especially since you highlighted your hair and had a make-over. The new clothes help.''

You're stunning. "Thanks.''

"Boy, did he lead you down the garden path. What I don't understand is how you fell for it.''

I'm a dreamer looking for a dream. "I tried not to.''

"It had to be his body. We're all fools for a body like his.''

He has shoulders broad enough to cry on. "If that were true, Dina, I'd have gone for Don Juan.''

"I'll bet Alex is a selfish lover.''

So what is this called, Julia? Uncontrollable lust? Self-indulgence? Charity? "He's not.''

"Well okay, so he has one redeeming virtue.''

See, I said please. "More than one.''

"For crying out loud, Julie, the man lied to you, used you—''

"Dina, do you use this method of psychology on your kids?''

"I have no idea what you're talking about.''

"I'm talking about you shoveling it on so thick I need to wear hip boots to wade through it.''

"Well, what about those?'' Dina pointed to the three small velvet boxes on the coffee table. "Don't tell me he isn't playing dirty pool. He's probably never been given the boot before and just wants you back so he can get even.''

Arrogance has its limits, Julia. "I could brain him for this.'' Julia fingered the pearls, perfect teardrops, ivory with the barest hint of pink and gold. One was dangling on a fine gold chain and the other two were set as earrings. Each piece had arrived separately, a week apart.

"Well it's the least you deserve after what he's done to you.''

I make mistakes, Julia. Bad ones. "It's driving me crazy to think he's dismantling the Veil. It's priceless, Dina.''

"So tell him you'd rather have it all in one piece.''

"I don't know where he is," Julia said with a note of anguish.

"A man like him doesn't do anything without a reason." Julia reread the note that had come with the last box:

I've only had two dreams—to find a woman I could love, and to find a priceless treasure that was totally unique. It didn't occur to me that they could be one and the same until I met you.

                                                    Alex

"I wish I knew," Julia said absently.

"Knew what?"

"Whatever he's up to. Why is he doing this? Where is he?"

"Do you care?"

If I hadn't already done so, I would have fallen in love with you tonight. "A lying, conniving, selfish, no-good creep like him? Why should I care?" Julia said tongue-in-cheek.

"Chloe called while you were at lunch."

"They're back from the honeymoon? If I'd known that I would have cried on her shoulder. She'd have talked some sense into me."

"I thought you wanted sympathy."

"Dina, I really feel sorry for your kids."

"Okay, if that's the way you feel, I'll let you wait and find out from Chloe."

"Find out what?"

"Where Alex is." Dina helped herself to a fresh bag of cookies. "He called Chloe this morning and gave her an itinerary of where he'd be and when. He must think that someone in San Francisco might give a flying fig."

Simon says, come here. Julia smiled.

THE NEXT TWO DAYS were an exercise in self-discipline and female vanity. She spent three hours at the hairdresser, four shopping for the right clothes, and a half hour at the car wash. Romance hadn't been this hard when she was a teen-ager.

She'd long since had all her ducks in a row. It had taken her less than a week to lick her wounds and decide what she wanted—really wanted—from life. Her ultimate goal boiled down to a four-letter word: Alex.

Finally, the day arrived when she knew Alex was right where she wanted him. With every form of modern feminine armament she could think of, Julia left her house with every ounce of courage she could muster. A misfit puppy wasn't going to do it this time.

The postman carrying a package with foreign postage met her on the front walk. "Package from overseas, Ms. Devlin."

"Thank you."

"Sign here, please."

Julia signed in a fast scrawl, handed him back his pen, grabbed the package, and hit the sidewalk at a trot.

"Ms. Devlin?"

Still on the move, she glanced at him over her shoulder. "I'm in a terrible hurry—"

"Yes, ma'am. I just wanted to tell you—" He paused and his face turned red. "You look real nice, Ms. Devlin."

She bumped into her car, and felt a smile spreading from the inside out. "Bless you," she called as she climbed into the car and tossed the package onto the seat.

The fastest route to the marina was bottlenecked for over a mile thanks to a multicar pileup. She wanted to cuss and honk and pace the highway with the rest of the trapped commuters, but things were getting a little too violent out there.

As she waited for the tow trucks to clear the road, the package drew her gaze and stimulated her curiosity. She reached for the box, frowning at the return address. Why would a museum in Ireland send her anything? Tearing the paper off, she read the cover letter several times, unable to believe what she was seeing. Her heart lurched like one of the crippled cars up ahead.

Enclosed were a photograph and bronze plaque. Her fingers traced the texture of the engraving on the plaque. She closed her eyes and laid her head back on the headrest, tears streaming down her face. *Darn you, Alex,* she thought. *I could start my own ocean with the tears I've shed because of you.*

She was a mess by the time she found Alex's boat. Her mascara was smeared, her makeup stripped and the corner of her shirttail was damp where she'd wiped her eyes for want of a tissue.

Curses and complaints were forgotten by the time Julia had repaired her makeup, fluffed her hair, and tied her emerald-green overshirt in a knot at her waist, tucking in the soggy corner. Her navy tank top and shorts were all that had survived without damage.

The *Dame Fortune* was last on the pier. Julia stopped on the dock, gripped by a full-scale anxiety attack. Determined not to give in to it, she walked the plank and stepped onto the boat.

Alex was bent over a compartment in the stern. His white shorts were wrinkled and his floral cotton shirt was loud enough to deafen a hard-rock band. "Nice buns," she commented with false bravado as she came to a halt a few feet behind him. "The legs aren't too shabby, either." Her gaze took a leisurely stroll over his body. Alex glanced up at her and straightened slowly. Unsmiling, he faced her with his hands on his hips, giving her a view of his tanned chest beneath the unbuttoned shirt.

"Dina is right. You have a great body."

Silence. Julia wanted to see that slow, lazy smile of his more than anything. "You could help me a little here," she said.

Nothing. The speech she'd rehearsed deserted her. All she could do was babble. "Okay, Alex. I shot first and dispensed with the questions altogether. I was really dumb. But I'm not going to take all the blame. I told you I needed a little time. All either one of us knows about love is what it shouldn't be." Her eyes narrowed as she watched him. His fists had clenched and his mouth was a tight, thin line. "Did it occur to you that our expectations might have been idealistic and impossible to live up to?'' She tossed her bag onto a chaise longue. ''Darn it! What do you expect, Alex? A perfect dream?''

No comment...until he spotted a corner of wood-framed bronze as it slipped out of her oversize purse. The entire Sixth Fleet would have been proud of his vivid expletives. ''I told Connell to wait a couple of weeks before sending you that.''

''A test, Alex?'' Julia taunted. ''Too bad Professor Connell jumped the gun. Now you'll never know whether I'm here because of what you've done or because I don't care about anything except that I love you.'' She smiled, feeling that surge of power at his frown. ''It's hell, isn't it—not knowing for sure?''

With a deliberate sway to her hips, she sauntered toward him, and planted her hands on her hips, mirroring his pose. ''But that's okay. Once you think about it for a while, you'll decide that you don't care about anything else, either, except that you love me.''

Alex stood very still, thinking how incredible Julia was—incredibly beautiful, incredibly welcome, incredibly saucy. There were a few signs of wear and tear, her lashes spiked by tears, the faded lip gloss, the corner of her shirt that was damp and wrinkled and limp. Yet she was facing him like a haughty queen, daring him to argue with her.

He leaned against the bulkhead and shoved his hands into his pockets. ''Are you sure about that?'' he asked.

Julia's eyebrows arched. ''That I love you? Of course I'm sure.''

Alex stared at her with an intensity that blinded her to all but the raw need in his eyes. ''That's not what I meant.''

Julia knew what he was asking and how important her answer was to him. Taking a deep breath, she held it to slow her galloping heartbeat. This was the moment of truth. A truth with risks and built-in responsibilities. She exhaled in a rush. ''Alex, I'm absolutely positive that you love me. No doubts and no suspicions.'' Her mouth curved somewhere between a smile and a grimace. "I will admit, however, to being a little scared."

Alex shifted slightly. "A little?"

Sighing, Julia threw up her hands. "Okay. A lot scared. Aren't you?"

"Terrified." He pointed at her purse. "What about that?"

"Oh, that? It was delivered by the mailman. He said I looked pretty."

"Julia—"

"You know, I was ready to brain you for taking the Veil apart. If I'd received one more pearl—" She tilted her head. "—did Professor Connell have anything to say about the missing pearls?"

"It's fitting that you have at least a part of the Veil." Alex shrugged. "I have a feeling that it was always meant for you."

Chills raced up her spine and she felt something move and come together inside herself, making her whole, as if what he'd said was true and the legend had come full circle. In a way, maybe it had. Alex had drawn parallels between her and that long-ago princess, parallels that had been right on target, except that unlike the legendary princess, she wasn't willing to give up—not anymore.

She bit her lip and looked at him uncertainly. "Alex ... I didn't know what to do until the pearls came, and I realized that you'd meant what you said about the Veil representing your dream. I wanted so badly to believe you then and there, but—" She shook her head, then spoke quickly, passionately. "But things have always come between me and the people I love. Da' robbed Nicholas because he believed that *things* could buy dreams and make them happen." Her voice lowered to a whisper. "I had to learn that things can't destroy. Only people have the power to ruin lives."

Alex shifted impatiently. She looked stricken and he wanted to end the conversation right now, communicate on a more basic level. But, uncertainty kept him rooted to the deck, waiting for confirmation that the last doubt was gone.

Doubts were contagious and he'd been plagued by his share in the last few weeks.

Julia stared down at her feet as a nervous laugh escaped her. "Well, so much for pretty speeches." And, so much for confession being good for the soul, she thought. At the moment, her soul felt miserable and lost.

Alex turned his back on her and gazed blindly at the bay. Frustration was like a spring wound too tightly inside him. "That 'pretty speech' is not what I need to hear, damn it!"

Need, not want. There was a world of difference in those two words, a difference that told Julia exactly how he felt. He needed the words—from her. He wasn't rejecting her or her convoluted apology. He was simply asking for the truth, whatever it might be, so that they could begin the future with honesty rather than lies.

"Alex," she called softly and waited for him to turn around. "The package from Professor Connell arrived when I was leaving the house to come here. If it hadn't been delivered until next week, I'd still be here today." She crossed her heart and held up her hand. "Honest."

"You've always been honest with me, Julia."

"True," she said solemnly. "But it should be said, shouldn't it?"

"Yes, it should be said." His voice was heavy with regret. "I'll remember that in the future."

"Alex, it might not have made a difference if you'd told me right away. I might have talked Da' into giving you the Veil and—"

"We'll never know, Julia." A corner of his mouth slashed upward in a wry grin. "But it doesn't matter. Your father told me that memories are only bad if they end that way. I don't think either one of us would have let that happen."

"We'll never know—thank God." Julia gave him a smile as shaky as her knees. "Alex? Isn't this where we should share a mad, passionate embrace?"

He reached her in one long stride and wrapped his arms around her, dipped her backward. "Like this?"

"Hmm." She turned on a mischievous grin that was pure Paddy Devlin. "You know, Alex, insecurity doesn't become you. You'll have to work on that."

"Later, we'll both work on it. Right now, I'm taking lessons in mad, passionate embraces."

"A kiss would be nice," she invited.

Alex straightened slowly as his expression turned from mildly lecherous to solemn. "Something else needs to be said, Julia." He raised his hand to stroke her cheek with his forefinger. His mouth quirked, humorless and bleak. "I've never had the occasion to use the words."

"A test run, Alex?" Julia's voice was soft, a little shaky.

Alex shook his head. "We're through with tests. This is for real, Julia. I love you. I always have."

Until this breathless, golden moment, Julia hadn't realized just how much she'd wanted to hear the words, hadn't really noticed their absence for all the special ways Alex had proven their truth to her. A brief flicker of anxiety crossed Alex's face, all arrogance and pride gone, and in its place she saw yearning, vulnerability. Her mouth curved in an impish smile. "Well heck, Alex, I knew that. Don't you think you haven't made it obvious? No one in the world knows how to say 'I love you' in as many ways as you do." She tightened her arms around him, stretched up on her tiptoes. "Now about that kiss..."

His mouth locked onto hers with three weeks' worth of need and hunger. It had been too long—a lifetime. Her body molded to his and her skin was warm, soft. She tasted like tears. He lifted his head, and opened his eyes, giving her his heart with a single look.

Her hand wrapped around the back of his neck, bringing him to her mouth as he slowly straightened, pulling her with him, one instead of two, drinking from the same cup of desire, tasting each other, sharing dreams, expressing love.

"Julia," Alex said against her mouth. "We're going below."

"Hmm. What for?" she asked teasingly.

With one arm still around her, Alex urged her toward the steps. He punctuated his plans with fleeting kisses on the tip of her nose, the corner of her mouth, her earlobe, her eyelids. "We're going to make dinner...make love...touch the stars...build dreams." His mouth found hers, breathing life into her. "And," he whispered roughly, "you can teach me how to see rainbows in the dark."

An animal with more skin than body wandered across the deck and sniffed at Julia's bag. The plaque slipped the rest of the way out and fell off the chaise, landing on the deck with a thud. The gold etching underlying the bronze gleamed in the sun:

VEIL OF TEARS
Returned to its rightful home.
Donated in memory of
Patrick Timothy Devlin

"You know, Alex," Julia said as she shut the cabin door, leaned against it, her eyes deep with promise. "Rainbows you can see in the dark are the best kind."

HARLEQUIN
American Romance®

RELIVE THE MEMORIES...

From New York's immigrant experience to the Great Quake of 1906. From the Western Front of World War I to the Roaring Twenties. From the indomitable spirit of the thirties to the home front of the Fabulous Forties. From the baby boom fifties to the Woodstock Nation sixties... **A CENTURY OF AMERICAN ROMANCE** takes you on a nostalgic journey through the twentieth century.

Revel in the romance of a time gone by... and sneak a peek at romance in a exciting future.

Watch for all the **A CENTURY OF AMERICAN ROMANCE** titles coming to you one per month over the next three months in Harlequin American Romance.

Don't miss February's **A CENTURY OF AMERICAN ROMANCE** title, #377—TILL THE END OF TIME by Elise Title.

A CENTURY OF
AMERICAN ROMANCE
1970s

The women... the men... the passions... the memories...